APPOINTMENT IN SAMARRA

APPOINTMENT IN SAMARRA

A NOVEL BY JOHN O'HARA

DEATH SPEAKS: There was a merchant in Bagdad who sent his servant to market to buy provisions and in a little while the servant came back, white and trembling, and said, Master, just now when I was in the market-place I was jostled by a woman in the crowd and when I turned I saw it was Death that jostled me. She looked at me and made a threatening gesture; now, lend me your horse, and I will ride away from this city and avoid my fate. I will go to Samarra and there Death will not find me. The merchant lent him his horse, and the servant mounted it, and he dug his spurs in its flanks and as fast as the horse could gallop he went. Then the merchant went down to the market-place and he saw me standing in the crowd and he came to me and said, Why did you make a threatening gesture to my servant when you saw him this morning? That was not a threatening gesture, I said, it was only a start of surprise. I was astonished to see him in Bagdad, for I had an appointment with him tonight in Samarra. —W. SOMERSET MAUGHAM

HARCOURT, BRACE AND COMPANY
NEW YORK

Typography by Robert Josephy
PRINTED IN THE UNITED STATES OF AMERICA
BY QUINN & BODEN COMPANY, INC., RAHWAY, N.J.

to

F. P. A.

APPOINTMENT IN SAMARRA

1

OUR STORY opens in the mind of Luther L. (L for LeRoy) Fliegler, who is lying in his bed, not thinking of anything, but just aware of sounds, conscious of his own breathing, and sensitive to his own heartbeats. Lying beside him is his wife, lying on her right side and enjoying her sleep. She has earned her sleep, for it is Christmas morning, strictly speaking, and all the day before she has worked like a dog, cleaning the turkey and baking things, and, until a few hours ago, trimming the tree. The awful proximity of his heartbeats makes Luther Fliegler begin to want his wife a little, but Irma can say no when she is tired. It is too much trouble, she says when she is tired, and she won't take any chances. Three children is enough; three children in ten years. So Luther Fliegler does not reach out for her. It is Christmas morning, and he will do her the favor of letting her enjoy her sleep; a favor which she will never know he did for her. And it is a favor, all right, because Irma likes Christmas too, and on this one morning she might not mind the trouble, might be willing to take a chance. Luther Fliegler more actively stifled the little temptation and thought the hell with it, and then turned and put his hands around his

3

wife's waist and caressed the little rubber tire of flesh across her diaphragm. She began to stir and then she opened her eyes and said: "My God, Lute, what are you doing?"

"Merry Christmas," he said.

"Don't, will you please?" she said, but she smiled happily and put her arms around his big back. "God, you're crazy," she said. "Oh, but I love you." And for a little while Gibbsville knew no happier people than Luther Fliegler and his wife, Irma. Then Luther went to sleep, and Irma got up and then came back to the bedroom, stopping to look out the window before she got into bed again.

Lantenengo Street had a sort of cottony silence to it. The snow was piled high in the gutters, and the street was open only to the width of two cars. It was too dark for the street to look cottony, and there was an illusion even about the silence. Irma thought she could yell her loudest and not be heard, so puffily silent did it look, but she also knew that if she wanted to (which she didn't) she could carry on a conversation with Mrs. Bromberg across the way, without either of them raising her voice. Irma chided herself for thinking this way about Mrs. Bromberg on Christmas morning, but immediately she defended herself: Jews do not observe Christmas, except to make more money out of Christians, so you do not have to treat Jews any different on Christmas than on any other day of the year. Besides, having the Brombergs on Lantenengo Street hurt real estate values. Everybody said so. The Brombergs, Lute had it on good authority, had paid thirty thousand for the Price property, which was twelve thousand five

4

hundred more than Will Price had been asking; but if the Brombergs wanted to live on Lantenengo Street, they could pay for it. Irma wondered if it was true that Sylvia Bromberg's sister and brother-in-law were dickering for the McAdams property next door. She wouldn't be surprised. Pretty soon there would be a whole colony of Jews in the neighborhood, and the Fliegler children and all the other nice children in the neighborhood would grow up with Jewish accents.

Irma Fliegler had hated Sylvia Bromberg since the summer before, when Sylvia was having a baby and screamed all through a summer evening. She could have gone to the Catholic hospital; she knew she was having a baby, and it was awful to have those screams and have to make up stories to tell the nice children why Mrs. Bromberg was screaming. It was disgusting.

Irma turned away from the window and went back to bed, praying that she would not get caught, and hating the Brombergs for moving into the neighborhood. Lute was sleeping peacefully and Irma was glad of the warmth of his big body and the heavy smell of him. She reached over and rubbed her fingers across his shoulder, where there were four navel-like scars, shrapnel scars. Lute belonged on Lantenengo Street, and she as his wife belonged on Lantenengo Street. And not only as his wife. Her family had been in Gibbsville a lot longer than the great majority of the people who lived on Lantenengo Street. She was a Doane, and Grandfather Doane had been a drummer boy in the Mexican War and had a Congres-

5

sional Medal of Honor from the Civil War. Grandfather
Doane had been a member of the School Board for close
to thirty years, before he died, and he was the only man
in this part of the State who had the Congressional Medal
of Honor. Lute had the French Croix de Guerre with
palm for something he said he did when he was drunk,
and there were a couple of men who got Distinguished
Service Crosses and Distinguished Service Medals during
the War, but Grandfather Doane had the only Congressional Medal of Honor. Irma still thought she was en-
titled to the medal, because she had been Grandfather
Doane's favorite; everyone knew that. But her brother
Willard and his wife, they got it because Willard was
carrying on the name. Well, they could have it. It was
Christmas, and Irma did not begrudge it to them as long
as they took care of it and appreciated it.

Irma lay there, fully awake, and heard a sound: cack,
thock, cack, thock, cack, thock. A car with a loose cross-
chain banging against the fender, coming slowly up or
down Lantenengo Street, she could not make out which.
Then it came a little faster and the sound changed to cack,
cack, cack, cack-cack-cack-cack. It passed her house and she
could tell it was an open car, because she heard the flapping
of the side curtains. It probably was a company car, a
Dodge. Probably an accident at one of the mines and one of
the bosses was being called out in the middle of the night,
the night before Christmas, to take charge of the accident.
Awful. She was glad Lute did not work for the Coal &
Iron Company. You had to be a college graduate, Penn

6

State or Lehigh, which Lute was not, to get any kind of a decent job with the Coal & Iron, and when you did get a job you had to wait for someone to die before you got a decent promotion. And called out at all hours of the day and night, like a doctor, when the pumps didn't work or something else happened. And even your ordinary work on the engineering corps, you came home dirty, looking like an ordinary miner in short rubber boots and cap and lunch can. A college graduate, and you had to undress in the cellar when you came home. Lute was right: he figured if you sell two Cadillacs a month, you make expenses, and anything over that is so much gravy, and meanwhile you look like a decent human being and you're not taking chances of being crushed to death under a fall of top rock, or blown to hell in an explosion of black damp. Inside the mines was no place for a married man, Lute always said; not if he gave a damn about his wife and children.

And Lute was a real family man. Irma shifted in bed until her back was against Lute's back. She held her hand in back of her, gently clasping Lute's forearm. Next year, according to Hoover, things would be much better all around, and they would be able to do a lot of things they had planned to do, but had had to postpone because of this slump. Irma heard the sound of another loose cross-chain, fast when she first heard it, and then slow and finally stopping. The car was getting a new start, in low gear. Irma recognized it: Dr. Newton's Buick coach. Newton, the dentist, and his wife Lillian who had the house two doors below. They would be getting home from the

7

dance at the country club. Ted Newton was probably a little plastered, and Lillian was probably having her hands full with him, because she had to get home early on account of being pregnant. Three months gone, or a little over. Irma wondered what time it was. She reached out and found Lute's watch. Only twenty after three. Good Lord, she thought it was much later than that.

Twenty after three. The country club dance would just be getting good, Irma supposed. The kids home from boarding school and college, and the younger marrieds, most of whom she knew by their first names, and then the older crowd. Next year she and Lute would be going to those dances and having fun. She could have gone to the one tonight, but she and Lute agreed that even though you knew the people by their first names, it wasn't right to go down to the club unless you were a member. Every time you went, whoever you were the guest of had to pay a dollar, and even at that you were not supposed to go under any circumstances more than twice in any quarter of the year. That was the rule. Next year she and Lute would be members, and it would be a good thing, because Lute would be able to make better contacts and sell more Cadillacs to club members. But as Lute said: "We'll join when we can afford it. I don't believe in that idea of mixing your social life with your business life too much. You get signing checks for prospects down at the country club, and you wind up behind the eight-ball. We'll join when we can afford it." Lute was all right. Dependable and honest as the day is long, and never looked at another woman, even

8

in fun. That was one reason why she was content to wait until they could really afford to join the club. If she had married, say, Julian English, she would be a member of the club, but she wouldn't trade her life for Caroline English's, not if you paid her. She wondered if Julian and Caroline were having another one of their battle royals.

I I

The smoking room of the Lantenengo Country Club was so crowded it did not seem as though another person could get in, but people moved in and out somehow. The smoking room had become co-educational; originally, when the club was built in 1920, it had been for men only, but during many wedding receptions women had broken the rule against their entering; wedding receptions were private parties, and club rules could be broken when the whole club was taken over by one party. So the feminine members had muscled in on the smoking room, and now there were as many females as males in the room. It was only a little after three o'clock, but the party had been going on forever, and hardly anyone wondered when it would end. Anyone who wanted it to end could go home. He would not be missed. The people who stayed were the people who belonged on the party in the first place. Any member of the club could come to the dance, but not everyone who came to the dance was really welcome in the smoking room. The smoking room crowd always started out with a small number, always the same people. The Whit Hofmans, the Julian Englishes, the Froggy Ogdens

9

and so on. They were the spenders and drinkers and socially secure, who could thumb their noses and not have to answer to anyone except their own families. There were about twenty persons in this group, and your standing in the younger set of Gibbsville could be judged by the assurance with which you joined the nucleus of the smoking room crowd. By three o'clock everyone who wanted to had been in the smoking room; the figurative bars were let down at about one-thirty, which time coincided with the time at which the Hofmans and Englishes and so on had got drunk enough to welcome anyone, the less eligible the better.

So far nothing terrible had occurred. Young Johnny Dibble had been caught stealing liquor from someone's locker and was kicked in the behind. Elinor Holloway's shoulder strap had slipped or been pulled down, momentarily revealing her left breast, which most of the young men present had seen and touched at one time or another. Frank Gorman, Georgetown, and Dwight Ross, Yale, had fought, cried, and kissed after an argument about what the team Gorman had not made would have done to the team Ross was substitute halfback on. During one of those inexplicable silences, Ted Newton was heard to say to his wife: "I'll drink as much as I God damn please." Elizabeth Gorman, the fat niece of Harry Reilly, whose social-climbing was a sight to behold, had embarrassed her uncle by belching loud and unashamed. Lorimer Gould III, of New York, who was visiting someone or other, had been told nine times that Gibbsville was dull as dishwater the year 'round, but everyone from out of town thought it was the peppiest place in the country at Christmas. Bobbie Hermann, who was posted for non-payment of dues and restaurant charges, was present in a business suit, gloriously drunk and persona grata at the inner sanctum (he was famous for having said, on seeing the golf course without a person playing on it: "The course is rather delinquent today"), and explaining to the wives and fiancées of his friends that he would like to dance with them, but could not because he was posted. Everyone was drinking, or had just finished a drink, or was just about to take one. The drinks were rye and ginger ale, practically unanimously, except for a few highballs of applejack and White Rock or apple and ginger ale, or gin and ginger ale. Only a few of the inner sanctum members were drinking Scotch. The liquor, that is, the rye, was all about the same: most people bought drug store rye on prescriptions (the physicians who were club members saved "scrips" for their patients), and cut it with alcohol and colored water. It was not poisonous, and it got you tight, which was all that was required of it and all that could be said for it.

The vibrations of the orchestra (Tommy Lake's Royal Collegians, a Gibbsville band) reached the smoking room, and the youngest people in the room began to hum Something To Remember You By. The young men addressed the girls: "Dance?" and the girls said: "Love to," or "Sa-well," or "Uh-huh." Slowly the room became less crowded. A few remained around one fairly large table in a corner, which by common consent or eminent domain or something was conceded to be the Whit Hofman-crowd's table. Harry Reilly was telling a dirty story in an Irish brogue, which was made slightly more realistic or funny by the fact that his bridgework, done before the Reillys came into the big money, did not fit too well, and Harry as a result always whistled faintly when he spoke. Reilly had a big, jovial white face, gray hair and a big mouth with thin lips. His eyes were shrewd and small, and he was beginning to get fat. He was in tails, and his white tie was daintily soiled from his habit of touching it between gestures of the story. His clothes were good, but he had been born in a tiny coal-mining village, or "patch," as these villages are called; and Reilly himself was the first to say: "You can take the boy out of the patch, but you can't take the patch out of the boy."

Reilly told stories in paragraphs. While he was speaking he would lean forward with an arm on his knee, like a picture you have seen of a cowboy. When he came to the end of the paragraph he would look quickly over his shoulder, as though he expected to be arrested before finishing the story; he would finger his tie and close his mouth tight, and then he would turn back to his audience and go into the next paragraph: ". . . So Pat said . . ." It was funny to watch people listening to Harry telling a story. If they took a sip of a drink in the middle of a paragraph, they did it slowly, as though concealing it. And they always knew when to laugh, even when it was a Catholic joke, because Reilly signaled the pay-off line by slapping his leg just before it was delivered. When everyone had laughed (Reilly would look at each person to see that he or she was getting it), he would follow with a short history of the story, where he had heard it and under what circumstances; and the history would lead to another story. Everyone else usually said: "Harry, I don't see how you remember them. I hear a lot of stories, but I never can think of them." Harry had a great reputation as a wit —a witty Irishman.

Julian English sat there watching him, through eyes that he permitted to appear sleepier than they felt. Why, he wondered, did he hate Harry Reilly? Why couldn't he stand him? What was there about Reilly that caused him to say to himself: "If he starts one more of those moth-eaten stories I'll throw this drink in his face." But he knew he would not throw this drink or any other drink in Harry Reilly's face. Still, it was fun to think about it. (That was the pay-off line of the story: Old maid goes to confession, tells priest she has committed a sin of immorality. Priest wants to know how many times. Old maid says once, thirty years ago—"but Faa-thurr, I like to think aboat it.") Yes, it would be fun to watch. The whole drink, including the three round-cornered lumps of ice. At least one lump would hit Reilly in the eye, and the liquid would splash all over his shirt, slowly wilting it as the Scotch and soda trickled down the bosom to the crevice at the waistcoat. The other people would stand up in amazed confusion. "Why, Ju!" they would say. Caroline would say, "Julian!" Froggy Ogden would be alarmed, but he would burst out laughing. So would Elizabeth Gorman,

13

laughing her loud haw-haw-haw, not because she enjoyed seeing her uncle being insulted, nor because she wanted to be on Julian's side; but because it would mean a situation, something to have been in on.

"Didn't you ever hear that one?" Reilly was saying. "Mother of God, that's one of the oldest Catholic stories there is. I heard a priest tell me that one, oh, it must of been fifteen twenty years ago. Old Father Burke, used to be pastor out at Saint Mary Star of the Sea, out in Collieryville. Yess, I heard that one a long while ago. He was a good-natured old codger. I remember . . ."

The liquid, Julian reflected, would trickle down inside the waistcoat and down, down into Reilly's trousers, so that even if the ice did not hurt his eye, the spots on his fly would be so embarrassing he would leave. And there was one thing Reilly could not stand; he could not stand being embarrassed. That was why it would be so good. He could just see Reilly, not knowing what to do the second after the drink hit him. Reilly had gone pretty far in his social climbing, by being a "good fellow" and "being himself," and by sheer force of the money which everyone knew the Reillys had. Reilly was on the greens committee and the entertainment committee, because as a golfer he got things done; he paid for entire new greens out of his own pocket, and he could keep a dance going till six o'clock by giving the orchestra a big tip. But he was not yet an officer in the Gibbsville Assembly. He was a member of the Assembly, but not a member of the governors and not eligible to hold office or serve on the important committees. So he was not unreservedly sure of his social standing, and damn well Julian knew it. So when the drink hit him he most likely would control himself sufficiently to remember who threw it, and he therefore would not say the things he would like to say. The yellow son of a bitch probably would pull out his handkerchief and try to laugh it off, or if he saw that no one else thought there was anything funny about it, he would give an imitation of a coldly indignant gentleman, and say: "That was a hell of a thing to do. What was the idea that?"

"And I would like to say," Julian said to himself, "that I thought it was about time someone shut him up."

But he knew he would not throw this drink, now almost gone, or the fresh drink which he was about to mix. Not at Harry Reilly. It was not through physical fear of Reilly; Reilly was more than forty, and though a good golfer he was short-winded and fat, and unquestionably would do anything in the world to avoid a fist fight. For one thing, Harry Reilly now practically owned the Gibbs-ville-Cadillac Motor Car Company, of which Julian was president. For another thing, if he should throw a drink at Harry Reilly, people would say he was sore because Reilly always danced a lot with and was elaborately at-tentive to Caroline English.

His thoughts were interrupted by Ted Newton, the dentist, who stopped at the table for a quick straight drink. Ted was wearing a raccoon coat, the first season for it if not actually the very first time he had had it on. "Going?"

said Julian. That was all he felt like giving to Newton, and more than he would have given him if Newton had not been a Cadillac prospect. Had a Buick now.

"Yeah. Lillian's tired and her folks are coming tomorrow from Harrisburg. They're driving over and they'll be here around one, one-fifteen."

Never mind their schedule, thought Julian. "Really?" he said aloud. "Well, Merry Christmas."

"Thanks, Ju," said Newton. "Merry Christmas to you. See you at the Bachelors'?"

"Right," said Julian, and added in an undertone, while the others said good-night to Newton: "And don't call me Ju."

The orchestra was playing Body and Soul, working very hard at the middle passage of the chorus. The musicians were very serious and frowning, except the drummer, who was showing his teeth to all the dancers and slapping the wire brushes on the snare drum. Wilhelmina Hall, six years out of Westover, was still the best dancer in the club, and was getting the best rush. She would get twice around the dance floor with the same partner, then someone would step out of the stag line and cut in. Everyone cut in on her, because she was such a good dancer, and because everyone said she was not in love, unless it was with Jimmy Malloy, and she certainly wasn't in love with him. At least that's what everybody said. The males who cut in on her were of all ages, whereas Kay Verner, now at Westover, and much the prettiest girl, got her rush almost exclusively from the prep school-college crowd. And she was in love with Henry Lewis. At least that's what everyone said. Constance Walker, the little fool, was not wearing her glasses again, as if everyone in the club didn't know she couldn't see across the table without them. She was known on the stag line as a girl who would *give you a dance;* she was at Smith, and was a good student. She had a lovely figure, especially her breasts, and she was a passionate little thing who wasn't homely but was plain and, if she only knew it, didn't look well without her glasses. She was so eager to please that when a young man would cut in on her, he got the full benefit of her breasts and the rest of her body. The young men were fond of saying, before leaving to cut in on Constance: "Guess I'll go get a work-out." The curious thing about her was that four of the young men had had work-outs with her off the dance floor, and as a result Constance was not a virgin; yet the young men felt so ashamed of themselves for yielding to a lure that they could not understand, in a girl who was accepted as not attractive, that they never exchanged information as to Constance Walker's sex life, and she was reputed to be chaste. The worst thing that was said about her was: "Yeah, you may think she isn't attractive, and I agree with you. But did you ever see her in a bathing suit? Hot-cha!"

The band was playing Something To Remember You By.

The stag line was scattered over the floor by the time the band was working on the second chorus of the tune, and when Johnny Dibble suddenly appeared, breathless,

17

at the place where his cronies customarily stood, there were only two young men for him to address. "Jeez," he said. "Jeezozz H. Kee-rist. You hear about what just happened?"

"No. No," they said.

"You didn't? About Julian English?".

"No. No. What was it?"

"Julian English. He just threw a highball in Harry Reilly's face. Jeest!"

III

Al Grecco knew the road from Philadelphia to Gibbsville pretty much as an engineman knows the right-of-way. On a regularly scheduled run, an experienced engineman can look at his watch and tell you that in four-and-one-half minutes his train will be passing a schoolhouse to the right of the tracks. Or, he can look out at a haystack or a barn or other landmark, and tell you to the half-minute what time it is. Al Grecco could do almost the same thing. He knew the 94½ miles from Philadelphia to Gibbsville—he knew it cold. And it certainly was cold tonight. The gasps of wind told him that. It was warm in the car, with the heater on. He was driving a V-61 Cadillac coach, and he had lowered the window in the door at his right about three inches from the top. He was an expert driver. He had made the trip to Philadelphia several times under two hours, leaving Gibbsville in the early morning; and tonight he automatically checked his time as he was passing the gate posts which marked the entrance

18

to the Lantenengo Country Club: two hours and a little over forty-five minutes from his hotel in Philadelphia. Not bad, considering the snowdrifts and the condition of the roads down on the lower entrance to Reading, where cars were scattered all along both sides of the road. He was going as fast as he could with safety. It was a business trip.

Although he never had seen anything but the roof of it, Al knew that the country club was built on a plateau. The clubhouse was scarcely visible from the state highway. Cars leaving the club did not come into view from the highway until they were a third of the way down the long drive, which opened upon the highway at the gate posts. Al Grecco noticed as he was passing that another Cadillac, a big sedan job, was just coming into sight on the drive. The moment he saw the car he recognized it. He more or less made it his business to be able to recognize important cars, and this sedan looked important. It was a demonstrator, and would be driven by Julian English, the Cadillac distributor.

"The louse," said Al. But he was not angry with Julian. It was because of an order from Julian that he had had to go to Philadelphia. It looked like Julian was going to have a good party some time between Christmas and New Year's, because he had asked Ed Charney, the big shot, if he could get him a case of champagne, good champagne, and deliver it the day after Christmas. Ed, of course, said he'd be only too glad to get some good champagne, and he had attended to the matter himself. Ed had phoned

Philadelphia and made sure that it was good champagne. Ed liked Julian English. Julian English belonged to the Lantenengo Street crowd and he was the kind of a guy that was a high class guy and would be a high class guy in any crowd. You could tell by looking at him he was a high class guy. And he always spoke to the boys on the street. He wasn't like some of them (mostly the older guys), who would do business with Ed, say business at the bank or insurance or something on that order, but they wouldn't even see Ed when they met him on the street. Or even guys who didn't know Ed, they would call up and say this was So-and-so, president of such and such a company, and could Ed do them a favor and get a case of genuine Scotch at a good price. In the early days Ed would try to put himself out for the respectable people, the ones that thought they were high class. But Ed saw it didn't pay; they didn't appreciate it when he did them a favor, and they didn't even say hello to him the next time he saw one of them on the street. So there were only a few of the Lantenengo Street crowd who could get a favor out of Ed without paying cash on the line for it. But Julian English certainly was one of them. And it wasn't only because he spoke to you; it was the way he did it. He spoke to you like a human being, and now and then he even sat down for a cup of coffee with Ed. "That English, he's my boy," Ed once said, and that was enough. "For my money," Ed said, "I will take that English. He's a right guy." That was plenty. In Ed's position you had to be a good judge of what a man was like, and the English was copacetic.

And Al agreed with Ed. Not that it would have made any difference if he didn't agree with Ed. You either agreed with Ed, between Reading and Wilkes-Barre, or you got a job in the mines. That was the *least* that could happen to you if you didn't agree with Ed: you just weren't in the mob any more. The worst could happen to you was you would get held by a couple of the boys while a couple others kicked you till they got tired kicking you, and then they would put a couple of slugs in you and that was that. But Ed very seldom had occasion to do that kind of thing. In the beginning, yes. There were several cases that the state police were still bothering about that Al knew more about than he wished he knew. That was when Ed was beginning to organize booze and the girls and the numbers racket. He had to put the screws on a few people here and there, or they would have become pests. You had to be tough in this business, or you weren't anything. You didn't get anywhere. Just the same, you had to be regular, you had to be on the up-and-up with those that treated you right. Al Grecco turned up his coat collar. He had felt a chill, and even though there was no one else in the car he felt a little ashamed, because he recognized that the chill was kid stuff; the way you feel when you have done something very good for somebody, or the way you feel about your mother. That was the way he felt about Ed Charney. He felt loyal.

Recognizing this he wanted to do something to show how loyal he could be, and the nearest thing at hand that gave him any chance to do something for Ed was the champagne. He turned to see that the champagne was still covered with blankets and secure against bumps. Ed would want that goods delivered in the best possible shape. Then he remembered the sedan, with English in it. He reduced his speed to thirty miles an hour and allowed the sedan to overtake him.

In a short time the sedan did overtake him, and Al Grecco could see by the way English was driving that he was sore about something. As a rule English was an artistic driver, as good to a car as men used to be to horses. And this particular job that English was driving was a demonstrator, which he kept tuned up all the time. But now English shot the car up over a rut and pushed through a six-foot drift in passing Grecco. Not that there wasn't plenty of room, and not that Al Grecco wouldn't have moved over or stopped if English had blown his horn. English didn't blow his horn, though. He just tramped on the gas and gave the sedan hell. The sedan hit the drift with a hard wallop, swaying from side to side, and almost as soon as he hit the drift and punched a hole in it, English swung the steering wheel and got back on the cleared part of the road. If you could call it cleared.

Stew stuff, Al Grecco decided.

In the few seconds that it took English to pass him Al Grecco noticed that English had his hat on the back of his head, which wasn't like English. English wasn't what you would call a snappy dresser, but he was always neat. Al also noticed that there was a woman in the car, slumped low in the front seat, low and as far away from English as

22

she could get. That would be Mrs. English. It never occurred to Al Grecco that it could be anyone else, because
Al never had heard anything about English and other
women—and if English had been a chaser Al would have
heard about it. Around Gibbsville if you were a chaser it
meant you had to go to the roadhouses, and Al made it
his business to know who went to the roadhouses. A lot
of wise guys in Gibbsville thought they were getting away
with murder by taking their girl friends to the country
hotels in the Pennsylvania Dutch part of the county. The
wise guys thought they were pretty smart, going to those
places instead of showing at the Stage Coach, which was
the big roadhouse, where the drinks were six bits apiece
and there was dancing and a hat-check-girl and waiters in
uniform and all that front. But if the chasers only knew
how wrong they were! Al made it his business to know
about the chasers, because you never could tell when it
would come in handy to know that So-and-so was cheating, especially if So-and-so happened to be some local big
shot that could be useful to Ed up at the courthouse or in
politics or even at a bank. Al remembered one time such
information had come in handy. There was a councilman
who was not on the take. Ed for some reason hadn't been
able to get to him with a dime, not a dime. One night Ed
got the tip that this councilman was going to shoot off his
mouth about a couple of speakeasies which Ed was interested in. This councilman was making a big play to get
the Republican nomination for mayor. So Al happened to

23

be there when Ed got the tip, and Al said: "Who did you say's going to do that?"

"Hagemann," said Ed.

"Oh, no he isn't," Al said, and told Ed why Hagemann wasn't going to shoot off his mouth. And was Ed pleased! He went to Hagemann's office and he said to him something like this: Mr. Hagemann, you're a great Church man and you represent the good element in this town and all that, so if it gets around that you've been going places with a certain lady about thirty years old that wears glasses. . . . And Ed didn't have to say any more. Hagemann just got up and shut the door and when Ed left they were the best of friends and still were. Ed even arranged it that Hagemann could get away with cheating on the one with glasses. Oh, in this business you had to look for all the angles.

Al Grecco stepped on it to keep up with English, who now had the accelerator down to the floor, and was keeping it there. You could tell that that was what he was doing, because when the wheels of the sedan got out of the tracks the car would leap up to the side of the road, slapping the long pile of snow. Al noticed that Mrs. English, who had her fur collar turned up higher than her ears, did not turn on English. That meant she was mad. Any woman ordinarily would be sitting up on the seat and bawling her husband out. But if he was any judge, Al was sure she was not saying a word. He began to wonder about this English dame.

He just had a feeling, that was all, but he went back in

24

his memory and tried to recollect something, anything at all, that fitted in with the idea he was beginning to get about her. The idea he was beginning to get about her was that she might be a cheater herself. But he could not remember anything. He knew she never had been to any of the country hotels. She got loud once in a while at the Stage Coach, but no worse than a lot of others, and English was always there when she was. No, it was just one of those things. You got an idea about some person and you didn't have any reason for it; but Al Grecco in his twenty-six years had learned one thing, namely, that if you had a hunch about a person, a real hunch that kept bothering you, something usually happened to prove that your hunch was either dead wrong or dead right.

It was seven miles and just a little over from the country club to the Gibbsville Bank & Trust Building, and practically all of the last three miles was a new and nearly straight stretch of road, which had been easier to clear; it was protected from winds by a railroad embankment on one side. Al Grecco had to step on it some more when English hit the stretch, because English was letting it out for all the sedan would take. Al kept his mind on the driving now. He did not want to get too close to English, and make English sore; but he did not want to lose him; he wanted to be close by if English got into trouble. But English was all right. One of those guys that can drive when they're drunk or sober, the only difference being that when they're drunk they have no consideration for what they might be doing to the car.

When the two cars reached Gibbsville Al Grecco made up his mind that he would best please Ed Charney by following English all the way home, so he turned up Lantenengo Street after the sedan. He followed about a block behind the sedan, all the way out Lantenengo Street to Twentieth Street. The Englishes had their house on Twin Oaks Road, but you could see all of Twin Oaks Road from Twentieth and Lantenengo. Al stopped. English had shifted into second for the uphill grade and the snow of Twentieth Street. He made the turn all right, and in a few seconds he stopped in front of the house. The lights of the car went out, and then the porch light went on, and Al could see Mrs. English on the porch, opening the door, the light on in one of the rooms of the downstairs floor. Then English himself on the porch, the downstairs light snapped out just as a light was turned on in a bedroom upstairs. English was leaving the car out all night. He must be cockeyed. Well, that was his business.

Al Grecco put his car in reverse and backed into Twentieth Street and then turned the car and drove down Lantenengo Street. He would go right to the Apollo, the all-night restaurant where you usually looked for Ed Charney. But suddenly he realized he wouldn't find Ed there. This was the one night of the year you wouldn't find Ed there. "Jesus Christ," said Al Grecco. "Me forgetting it was Christmas." He lowered the window of the car and addressed the darkened Lantenengo Street homes that he was passing: "Merry Christmas, you stuck-up bastards! Merry Christmas from Al Grecco!"

2

JULIAN ENGLISH snapped awake, and knew that he had beaten the arrival of Mary, the maid, by one step. He was correct: Mary appeared in the doorway and said: "Mrs. English says it's eleven o'clock, Mr. English." In a lower key she said: "Merry Christmas, Mr. English."

"Merry Christmas, Mary. Did you get your envelope?"

"Yes, sir. Mrs. English give it to me. Thank you very kindly, and my mother says to tell you she made a novena for you and Mrs. English. Shill I close the windows?"

"Yes, will you please?" He lay back until Mary left the room. Such a pretty day. Bright; and there were icicles, actually icicles, hanging in the middle of the windows. With the holly wreath and the curtains they made you think of a Christmas card. It was quiet outside. Gibbsville, the whole world, was resting after the snow. He heard a sound that could mean only one thing; one of the Harley kids next door had a new Flexible Flyer for Christmas, and was trying it out belly-bumpers down the Harley driveway, which was separated from the English driveway only by a two-foot hedge. It would not take long for the room to get warm, so he decided to lie in bed for a few minutes.

There ought to be more days like this, he thought. Slowly, without turning his head, he pulled himself up to a half sitting position and reached out for the package of Lucky Strikes on the table between his bed and Caroline's bed. Then he remembered to know better than to look in the direction of Caroline's bed—and looked. He was right again: Caroline had not slept in her bed. Everything returned to him then, as though in a terrible, vibrating sound; like standing too near a big bell and having it suddenly struck without warning. His fingers and his mouth lit a cigarette; they knew how. He was not thinking of a cigarette, for with the ringing of that bell came the hangover feeling and the remorse. It took him a little while, but eventually he remembered the worst thing he had done, and it was plenty bad. He remembered throwing a drink at Harry Reilly, throwing it in his fat, cheap, gross Irish face. So now it was Christmas and peace on earth.

He got out of bed, not caring to wait for warmth and luxury. His feet hit the cold hardwood floor and he stuck his toes in bedroom slippers and made for the bathroom. He had felt physically worse many times, but this was a pretty good hangover. It is a pretty good hangover when you look at yourself in the mirror and can see nothing above the bridge of your nose. You do not see your eyes, nor the condition of your hair. You see your beard, almost hair by hair; and the hair on your chest and the bones that stick up at the base of your neck. You see your pajamas and the lines in your neck, and the stuff on your lower lip that looks as though it might be blood but never is. You first brush your teeth, which is an improvement but leaves something to be desired. Then you try Lavoris and then an Eno's. By the time you get out of the bathroom you are ready for another cigarette and in urgent need of coffee or a drink, and you wish to God you could afford to have a valet to tie your shoes. You have a hard time getting your feet into your trousers, but you finally make it, having taken just any pair of trousers, the first your hands touched in the closet. But you consider a long, long time before selecting a tie. You stare at the ties; stare and stare at them, and you look down at your thighs to see what color suit you are going to be wearing. Dark gray. Practically any tie will go with dark gray suit.

Julian finally chose a Spitalsfield, tiny black and white figure, because he was going to wear a starched collar. He was going to wear a starched collar because it was Christmas and he was going to have Christmas dinner with his father and mother at their house. He finally finished dressing and when he saw himself in a full length glass he still could not quite look himself in the eye, but he knew he looked well otherwise. His black waxed-calf shoes gleamed like patent leather. He put the right things in the right pockets: wallet, watch and chain and gold miniature basketball and Kappa Beta Phi key, two dollars in silver coins, fountain pen, handkerchiefs, cigarette case, leather key purse. He looked at himself again, and wished to God he could go back to bed, but if he should go back to bed he would only think, and he refused to think until after he had had some coffee. He went downstairs, holding on to the banister on the way down.

As he passed the living-room he saw a piled row of packages, obviously gifts, on the table in the middle of the room. But Caroline was not in the room, so he did not stop. He went back to the dining-room and pushed open the swinging-door to the butler's pantry. "Just some orange juice and coffee, Mary, please," he said.

"The orange juice is on the table, Mr. English," she said.

He drank it. It had ice, glorious ice, in it. Mary brought in the coffee and when she had gone he inhaled the steam of it. It was as good as drinking it. He drank some of it black, without sugar, first. He put one lump of sugar in it and drank some more. He put some cream in it and lit a cigarette. "I'd be all right if I could stay here," he thought. "If I could just stay here for the rest of my life and never see another soul. Except Caroline. I'd have to have Caroline."

He finished his coffee, took a sip of ice water, and left the dining-room. He was standing in front of the table, with its pile of gifts, when he heard someone stamping on the porch, and almost immediately the door opened and it was Caroline.

"Hello," she said.

"Hello," he said. "Merry Christmas."

"Yeah," she said.

"I'm sorry," he said. "Where've you been?"

"Took some things to the Harley kids," she said. She hung up her camel's hair coat in the closet under the stairs. "Bubbie said to wish you a Merry Christmas and he told me to ask you if you wanted to ride on his new Flexie. I told him I didn't think you would, this morning." She sat down and began to unbuckle her arctics. She had beautiful legs that not even the heavy woolen plaid stockings could distort. "Look," she said.

"I'm looking," he said.

"Don't be funny," she said, and pulled her skirt down. "I want you to listen. This is what I want to say: I think you'd better take that bracelet back to Caldwell's."

"Why? Don't you like it?"

"I like it all right. It's one of the most beautiful things I've ever seen, but you can't afford it. I know how much it cost."

"So what?" he said.

"Well, just this. I think we'll probably need every cent we can save from now on."

"Why?"

She lit a cigarette. "Well, you fixed it last night. No point in going into *why* you threw that drink at Harry, but I just want to tell you this much, you've made an enemy for life."

"Oh, no. Naturally he's sore, but I'll be able to fix it. I can handle that."

"That's what you think. I'll tell you something. Have you any idea how news travels in this town? Maybe you think you have, but listen to me. I just came from the Harleys', the only people I've seen except Mary since last night, and almost the first thing Herbert Harley said when I got in the house was, 'Well, I'm glad somebody put Harry Reilly in his place at last.' Of course I tried to laugh it off as if it were just a joke between you and Harry, but do you realize what that means, Herbert Harley's knowing about it so soon? It means the story's got all over town already. Somebody must have told the Harleys over the phone, because I know Herbert hasn't had his car out. There aren't any tracks in their driveway."

"Well, what of it?"

"What *of* it? You stand there and ask me what of it? Don't you realize what that means, or are you still drunk? It just means that the whole town knows what you did, and when Harry realizes that, he'll do anything short of murder to get even with you. And I don't have to tell you that he won't have to commit murder to get even with you." She stood up and smoothed her skirt. "So—I think you'd better take the bracelet back to Caldwell's."

"But I want you to have it. I paid for it."

"They'll take it back. They know you."

"I can afford it," he said.

"No, you can't," she said. "Besides, I don't want it."

"You mean you don't want to take it from me?"

She hesitated a moment, and bit her lip and nodded. "Yes. I guess that's what I mean."

He went to her and put his hands on her arms. She did not move except to turn her head away from him.

"What's the matter?" he said. "Reilly doesn't mean anything to you, for God's sake, does he?"

"No. Not a thing. But you'd never believe that."

"Oh, ridiculous," he said. "I never thought you were
having an affair with him."

"Didn't you? Are you sure you didn't?" she freed herself. "Maybe you didn't actually think I was having an
affair with him, but part of the time you wondered
whether I was. That's just as bad. And that's the real
reason why you threw the drink in his face."

"I might have thought you kissed him, but I never
thought you were having an affair with him. And the only
real reason why I threw a drink in his face was I just
happen to dislike him. I can't stand his stupid Irish face,
that's all. And those stories."

"His face looked pretty good last summer when you
needed money, and by the way, here's something you'd
better not overlook. Perhaps you think people are going
to be on your side if it comes to the point where people
take sides in this. Perhaps you think all your friends will
stick by you, and maybe you think that's going to frighten
him because he wants to run the Assembly. Well, just
don't count too much on that, because practically every
single one of your best freinds, with one or two exceptions,
all owe Harry Reilly money."

"How do you know?"

"He told me," she said. "Maybe Jack and Carter and
Bob and the rest would like to be on your side, and maybe
in any other year they would stick by you, but I don't

33

have to tell you there's a depression in this country, and Harry Reilly's practically the only man around here with any money."

"I'll bet he comes to our party," said Julian.

"If he does you can thank me. I'll do my best, but my heart won't be in the work." She looked at him. "Oh, God, Ju, why did you do it? Why do you do things like that?" She began to cry, but when he went to her she held him away. "It's all so awful and I used to love you so."

"I love you. You know that."

"It's too easy. The things you called me on the way home—whore and bitch and a lot worse—they weren't anything compared with the public humiliation." She accepted his handkerchief. "I've got to change," she said.

"Do you think Mother and Dad know about it?"

"No, I doubt it. Your father'd be over here if he knew. Oh, how should I know?" She walked out and then came back. "My present is at the bottom of the pile," she said.

That made him feel worse. Under all the other packages was something she had bought days, maybe weeks, before, when things were not so bad as they now appeared to be. When she bought that she was concentrating on him and what he would like; rejecting this idea and that idea, and deciding on one thing because it was something *he* wanted or something *he* would want. Caroline was one person who really did put a lot of thought into a gift; she knew when to choose the obvious thing. One time she had given him handkerchiefs for Christmas; no one else had given him handkerchiefs, and they were what he

34

wanted. And whatever was in that package, she had bought with him alone in mind. He could not guess from the size of the box what was inside it. He opened it. It was two gifts: a pigskin stud box, big enough to hold two sets of studs, with plenty of room inside for assorted collar buttons, collar pins, tie clasps—and Caroline had put in a dozen or so front and back collar buttons. The other gift was of pigskin, too; a handkerchief case that collapsed like an accordion. Both things had J. McH. E. stamped in small gilt letters on the top cover, and that in itself showed thought. She knew, and no one else in the world knew, that he liked things stamped J. McH. E., and not just J. E., or J. M. E. Maybe she even knew why he liked it that way; he wasn't sure himself.

He stood at the table, looking down at the handkerchief case and stud box, and was afraid. Upstairs was a girl who was a person. That he loved her seemed unimportant compared to what she was. He only loved her, which really made him a lot less than a friend or an acquaintance. Other people saw her and talked to her when she was herself, her great, important self. It was wrong, this idea that you know someone better because you have shared a bed and a bathroom with her. He knew, and not another human being knew, that she cried "I" or "high" in moments of great ecstasy. He knew, he alone knew her when she let herself go, when she herself was not sure whether she was wildly gay or wildly sad, but one and the other. But that did not mean that he knew her. Far from it. It only meant that he was closer to her when he was close, but (and this was the first time the thought had come to him) maybe farther away than anyone else when he was not close. It certainly looked that way now. "Oh, I'm a son of a bitch," he said.

II

In the middle of the front page of the *Gibbsville Sun,* the morning paper, there was a two-column box, decorated with Santa Claus and holly doo-dads, and in the center of the box was a long poem. "Well, Mervyn Schwartz finally got it."

"What?" said Irma.

"Shot in a whorehouse last night," said her husband.

"What!" exclaimed Irma. "What are you talking about?"

"Here it is," said her husband. "Right here on the front page. Mervyn Schwartz, thirty-five, of Gibbsville, was shot and killed at the Dew Drop—"

"Let me see," said Irma. She took the paper out of her husband's hands. "Where? . . . Oh, *you,*" she said, and threw the paper back at him. He was laughing at her with a high, soft giggle.

"Think you're funny," she said. "You oughtn't to say things like that where the children might hear you."

He continued to laugh and picked up the paper and began to read Mervyn Schwartz's Christmas poem. Mervyn Schwartz formerly had contributed his holiday poems (Christmas, Washington's Birthday, Easter, Memorial Day, July 4, Armistice Day) to the *Standard,* the afternoon paper; but the *Standard* had not run his Armistice

Day poem on the front page, so now he was in the *Sun*. Lute Fliegler read the first verse aloud, very sing-song and effeminate.

"What time do you want dinner?" said Irma.

"Whenever it's ready," said Lute.

"Well, you only had breakfast an hour ago. You don't want dinner too early. I thought around two o'clock."

"Okay by me," he said. "I'm not very hungry."

"You oughtn't to be," she said. "The breakfast you ate. I was thinking I'd make the beds now and Mrs. Lynch could put the turkey on so we could eat around two or ha' past."

"Okay by me."

"The kids won't be very hungry. Even Curly was stuffing himself with candy a while ago till I hid the box."

"Let him eat it," said her husband. "Christmas comes but once a year."

"Thank heaven. All right. I'll give them the candy, on one condition. That is, if you take care of them when they have stomach ache in the middle of the night."

"I'll be only too glad. Go ahead, give them all the candy they want, and give Teddy and Betty a couple highballs." He frowned and rubbed his chin in mock thoughtfulness. "I don't know about Curly, though. He's a little young, but I guess it'd be all right. Or else maybe he'll take a cigar."

"Oh, you," she said.

"Yes-s-s, I think we better just give Curly a cigar. By

the way, I'm going to take Teddy out and get him laid tonight. I—"

"Lute! Stop talking like that. How do you know one of them didn't come downstairs without you hearing them? They'll be finding things out soon enough. Remember what Betty said last summer."

"That's nothing. How old is Teddy? Six—"

"Six and a half," she said.

"Well, when I was Teddy's age I had four girls knocked up."

"Now stop, Lute. You stop talking that way. You don't have any idea how they pick things up, a word here and there. And children are smarter than you give them credit for. You don't have to go anywhere today, do you?"

"Nope. Why?" He lit a Camel, taking it out of the package in the lower right pocket of his vest.

"Well, no reason. Last Christmas remember you had to drive to Reading."

"That was *last* Christmas. Damn few Caddies being given for Christmas presents this year. I remember that trip. That was a sport job. A LaSalle, it was, not a Caddy. That Polish undertaker up the mountain, Paul Davinis. He wanted it delivered Christmas and he didn't want his kid to see it so we asked to keep it in Reading. And then when we did deliver it the kid knew he was going to get it all along. His mother told him beforehand. He smashed it up New Year's Eve."

"You never told me that," said Irma.

"You never asked me, as the snake charmer said to her

husband. By the way, did Mrs. Lynch say she'd mind the kids tonight?"

"Uh-huh."

"Well, then I better phone Willard and tell him we'll go along. I'll get that Studebaker sedan. We can get six in it comfortably. It's a seven-passenger job, but we can sit three in the front and three in the back and we won't have to use the extra seats. How many are going?"

"I think twelve. Ten or twelve. It depends. If Emily's father and mother come down from Shamokin she and Harvey won't be able to come along, but it won't make any difference. They were going in Walter's car, so if they don't go, that makes two less in that car."

"I better call the garage and make sure about the Studebaker." He went to the telephone. "Hello, this is Lute Fliegler. Merry Christmas. Listen, that Studebaker sedan, the black one. The one we took on a trade-in from Doc Lurie. Yeah. Doc Lurie's old car. Well, listen. Don't let anybody take it out, see? I asked the boss if I could use it tonight and he said okay, see? So I just wanted to make sure none of you thieves took it out. If you want to go any place you can use my Rolls. Seriously, Joe, you want to do me a favor, you can put the chains on the Studie. Okay? Swell." He hung up, and addressed Irma. "Well, that's settled."

"You can call Willard later," she said. "I told him we'd call if we couldn't go, so he'll take it for granted we're going."

"What about liquor?" said Lute.

"Well, it's Willard's party. I should think he'd supply the liquor."

"Oh, yeah? Do you know how much liquor costs at the Stage Coach? Seventy-five cents a drink, baby, and they won't sell it to everybody. I don't think Willard intends to supply the liquor, not at six bits a shot. I think I better make some gin and take a quart along, just in case. It wouldn't be right to expect Willard to buy all the liquor and everything else for a party of twelve people."

"Maybe there'll only be ten."

"All right. What if there *is* only ten? They have a cover charge of a dollar and a half or two dollars, and there goes twenty bucks already, not including ginger ale and White Rock, and sandwiches! You know what they charge for a plain ordinary chicken sandwich at the Stage Coach? A *buck*. If Willard gets away under forty bucks he's lucky, without buying a single drink. No, I better make some gin. Or on second thought, there's that quart of rye the boss gave me. I was going to save it, but we might as well use it tonight."

"Oh, the gin's good enough. You make good gin. Everybody says so."

"I know I do, but gin's gin. I think I'll turn square for once in my life and take the rye. Maybe the others will bring their own, so we won't have to get rid of the whole quart."

"I don't want you to drink much if you're going to drive," said Irma.

"Don't worry. Not over those roads. I know. I'll put

the quart into pint bottles and keep one pint in my over-coat pocket when we get to the Stage Coach. Then the others will think I only have a pint and they'll go easy. But I imagine everybody will bring their own, if they have any sense."

"I imagine," she said. "I'm going upstairs now and make the beds. I'll see if the pants of your Tux need pressing."

"Oh, God. That's right. Do I have to wear that?"

"Now, now, don't try and bluff me. You look nice in it and you know it. You like to wear it and don't pretend you don't."

"Oh, I don't mind wearing it," he said. "I was just thinking about you. You'll be so jealous when all the other girls see me in my Tux and start trying to take me outside. I just didn't want to spoil your evening, that's all."

"Applesauce," said Irma.

"Why don't you say what you mean? You don't mean applesauce."

"Never mind, now, Mister Dirty Mouth." She left.

What a girl, he thought, and resumed reading his paper; Hoover was receiving the newsboys for Christmas. . . .

I I I

It was about two o'clock, U. S. Naval Observatory Hourly By Western Union time, when Al Grecco appeared in the doorway of the Apollo Restaurant. The Apollo was a hotel and restaurant. There had been a hotel on the site of the Apollo for close to a century, but the

41

Pennsylvania Dutch family who had the restaurant before George Poppas took it over had not kept the hotel part open. Then when George Poppas, who actually was wearing those white Greek kilts when he arrived in Gibbsville, began to make money on the restaurant, someone mentioned that the building had been a hotel for nearly a hundred years, and George spent a lot of money on making the place a hotel again. The rooms were small and had a fireproof look about them, with steel beds and other furniture. The hotel was clean, the rooms were small and cheap, and the Apollo got a big play from salesmen who had their swindle sheets to think of. The John Gibb Hotel, Gibbsville's big inn, was expensive.

Al Grecco was one of the few permanent guests of the Apollo. He had a room there, for which he paid nothing. Ed Charney had some kind of arrangement with George Poppas, in which no money changed hands. Ed wanted Al to be at the Apollo to receive messages and so on. Whenever there were strangers from other mobs in town on business, or friends who just happened to be passing through Gibbsville, they always looked up Ed Charney at the Apollo. And if Ed was not there, he wanted someone to be on hand, and that someone usually was Al Grecco.

Al had his hat on but was carrying his dark blue overcoat. There was not a customer in the place. Smitty, who was a taxi driver and two-bit pimp, was sitting at the marble counter, drinking a cup of coffee, but Smitty was always at the counter drinking coffee. George Poppas was standing behind the cigar counter. He looked as though he were sitting down, but Al knew better. George leaned with his fat hands folded, supporting himself on the cigar counter, and appearing to be in great pain. George always appeared to be in great pain, as though he had eaten, an hour ago, all the things that can give you indigestion. Al once had seen him in a crap game make fifteen straight passes and win over twelve thousand dollars, but he still appeared to be in great pain.

Loving Cup was behind the counter, and seemed to be the only waiter in the place. Loving Cup was about twenty, perhaps less; slight, with a bad complexion and a terrible breath. The boys were always kidding Loving Cup about his ears, from which he got his name. They were at least a third as long as his whole head, and stuck out. Also, the boys often had kidded Loving Cup about his lonely sex life, until one night for a gag they took him to the Dew Drop and paid for his entertainment. But when he came downstairs Mimi said to them: "Well, you wise guys, this kid got more than any of you. Howdia like that? He's the only man in the crowd." And Loving Cup listened delightedly, his eyes bright and gleaming and wicked and small. From that night on the boys made no cracks about Loving Cup and his lonely sex life. They still referred to him as Loving Cup, and called him Bertha, but they had some respect for him.

Al did not speak to George Poppas. They had a mutual contempt for each other; George for Al, because Al was a minor member of the mob; and Al for George because George did not belong to the mob at all. They never spoke, except in crap games, when they confined their remarks to "You're faded" and the other language of the game. Al placed his coat on a hanger and removed his hat, using both hands in taking off the hat so as not to disturb his hair.

He took the *Philadelphia Public Ledger*, which was lying on the counter in front of George. He sat down at the mob's table, which was in the very front of the restaurant, in a corner just back of the front window, where various crustaceans were squirming about in a pool. Al looked at the front page and saw that that Hoover was going to entertain some newsboys for Christmas. He turned over to the sport pages.

"Hyuh," said a voice. It was Loving Cup.

"Oh, hyuh, Loving Cup," said Al.

"Two over? Bacon well done? Coffee?" said Loving Cup.

"No," said Al. "Gimme the bill of fare."

"What for?" said Loving Cup. "You can read the paper."

"God damn it! Get me the bill of fare before I cut your heart out."

"All right, all right," said Loving Cup, running away. He came back with a menu and laid it beside Al's right arm. "There."

"What are you, a Jew or something? Didn't they tell you it's Christmas, or don't they have Christmas where you come from? Say, where *did* you come from, anyway, sweetheart?"

"That's my business," said Loving Cup. "The turkey is all right. You want some of that? I thought you was having breakfast."

"It's Christmas, you lug," said Al.

"Yeah, I know," said Loving Cup. "What are you gonna have, or do I have to wait here all day while you spell out the words?"

"Crack wise, Bertha," said Al. "I'll have that a dollar and a half dinner."

"What kind of soup you want?"

"I don't want any soup," said Al.

"It goes with the dinner, so you don't have to pay extra. I'll bring you the cream of tomato. I just seen the chef spit in it." He jumped away as Al reached out for him. He went laughing to the kitchen.

Al read his paper. There was always some stumble bum from Fargo fighting in Indianapolis. Every time you picked up the paper and looked under Fight Results there was somebody from Fargo doing a waltz somewhere. Either they were all would-be fighters in that town, or else they just used the name of the town and didn't come from there at all, like the Gibbsville Miners, the pro football team. Practically every man on the team was an All American, but they never heard of Gibbsville before they came there to play football. They all talked like Snake Eyes O'Neill, who came from Jersey City and was one of the mob. Snake Eyes never said r. Dollah. Fawd. Hoit. Boint. Thoid. Likka. Never said r. Al wondered where Fargo was. It was past Chicago. He knew that.

They had one good boy from that town. Petrolle. Billy Petrolle, the Fargo Express. But the rest of them! God, what a gang of tankers they were. He wondered just what was the angle on there being so many fighters from Fargo. Maybe Ed would know. Ed could usually tell him when something puzzled him.

Ed had said he wouldn't be down till around four o'clock. He had to spend Christmas with the wife and kid, God knows why. Al did not like to think of Annie Charney. The kid was swell; six years old and fat and healthy-looking. He wasn't like Ed, but for the present more like Annie. She was fat and healthy-looking and blonde, like most Polacks. Ed didn't care for her any more. Al knew that. Ed cared for Helene Holman, who was a torch singer like Libby Holman and sang at the Stage Coach. Ed really cared for Helene. He played around a little, but Al knew Helene was the only one he really cared for, and Helene really cared for him. With her it was slightly different, because nobody else would even look cockeyed at Helene as long as Ed cared for her, but even taking that into consideration Al knew Helene really cared for Ed. And she was good for him. You could tell when Ed and Helene were getting along. Ed was easier to get along with then. Tonight, or this after', when Ed showed up at the Apollo, he probably would be in a bad humor. That was the way Annie affected him. Whereas if he had spent the day with Helene he would have been in a good humor. But Al knew that Ed wouldn't think of spending Christmas with Helene. Ed was a family man, first and

last, and that was the one day in the year he would spend
with the kid, at home.

"Here," said Loving Cup.

Al looked at the blue plate. "For a buck fifty I don't
call that much turkey," he said.

"What's the matter, Mr. Grecco? Is it too small?" said
Loving Cup.

"Small? For Christ's sakes. And wuddia say, how about
giving me some white meat? If I'm gonna pay a buck
fifty for turkey I wanna get some white meat, not this
God damn dark meat."

"Shall I take it back?"

"Sure, take it back," said Al. "No, wait a minute. The
hell with it, and the hell with you. You'll take a couple
hours."

"That's right, Mr. Grecco. It's Christmas. You said so
yourself just a minute ago."

"Screw, bum," said Al. Loving Cup pretended to pay
no attention to him and dusted off the table cloth, but out
of the corner of his eye he was watching Al, and when Al
made a grab for his wrist Loving Cup leapt away. Then
he snickered and went back to the counter.

Al usually had breakfast at this time, if he was up. He
ate eggs and bacon for breakfast, had a small steak or
something like that at seven in the evening, and then after
midnight he usually ate what he called his big meal: a
thick steak with boiled potatoes, piece of pie, and many
cups of coffee. He was about five feet six with his high
heels, and weighed about 130 pounds with his suit on. He

had been with Ed Charney and eating regularly for four years, but he still did not gain much weight. Stayed about the same. His bones were small, and he was a thin little man in every part of him. He was born in Gibbsville, the son of Italian parents. His father worked on a navvy gang and supported six children, of whom Al was the third. Al's name was not Al, and it was not Grecco. His real name was Anthony Joseph Murascho, or Tony Murascho, until he was eighteen. He had been kicked out of the parochial school for striking a nun when he was fourteen; carried newspapers, stole, was house-man in a pool room, served a year in prison for burgling the poorbox in one of the Irish Catholic churches, and was arrested several other times: once when a false alarm was turned in (he had an honest alibi); once for attempted rape (the girl could not positively identify more than two of the six suspects); once for breaking the seals on a freight car (the railroad detectives listened to his father's plea, and they had a good case against four other boys, so out of kindness to the old man they did not prosecute Tony); once for stabbing a colleague in a poolroom argument (no one, not even the victim, could swear Tony had done it; and anyway it was only a slight wound).

It was when he was eighteen, the same year of his life that he went to the county jail, that he got the name of Al Grecco. At that time he decided to be a prizefighter, and though he had a lingering touch of gonorrhea, he went into training and studied the sweet science under Packy McGovern, Gibbsville's leading and only fight promoter. Packy told him he was a born fighter, had the real fighting heart, and that the clap was no worse than a bad cold. He made Tony lay off women, alcohol, and cigarettes, and do a lot of bag-punching. He showed Tony how to hold his elbows and how to keep his right foot in position so he could move his body backward without taking a backward step; that was footwork. He taught Tony how to scrape an opponent's eyes with the palm of the glove, and also how to use his thumb, and also how to butt. He of course instructed Tony never to enter a ring without first knocking a few dents into the aluminum-cup supporter which is supposed to be a protection against foul blows. You never know when you can claim foul and get away with it, and if the cup is not dented no club physician would dare allow the claim. Tony Murascho, who up to that time had been known only as a tough little guinny, was matched to fight a preliminary bout at McGovern's Hall.

As it happened, Lydia Faunce Browne was assigned to write a feature story about that fight card. Lydia Faunce Browne was not a Gibbsville girl originally. She came from Columbus, Ohio, and had been in Gibbsville five years when her husband deserted her. He was younger than Mrs. Browne, who at the time of the desertion was forty-nine, and he left behind, besides Lydia, a large bill at the Lantenengo Country Club, another big bill at the Gibbsville Club, and several other bills. For a time Mrs. Browne eked out a living and paid a little on the bills by teaching auction bridge to the wives of the Jewish storekeepers, but she finally flattered Bob Hooker, editor of the *Standard*, into giving her a job on the staff of the *Standard*. She told him he was a real man for his editorial on his dead dog. She became the pest of the *Standard* office on her own hook, and was being built up big by Bob Hooker, who regarded himself as the William Allen White-Ed Howe-Joseph Pulitzer of Gibbsville. He began to regard Lydia as the local Sophie Irene Loeb, and paid her $35 a week, with three exceptions the highest journalistic salary in the town.

Lydia was always being sent down in the mines, much against the wishes of the miners, who think it is unlucky for a woman to enter a mine; or riding in locomotive cabs, or spending a night in prison, or interviewing visiting celebrities, such as George Luks (who later wanted to know where in the name of God they dug her up) and Rabbi Stephen S. Wise and Gifford Pinchot (five times). Lydia's secret favorite adjective for herself was keen; and she went around looking keen during all her waking hours. She felt sorry for prostitutes on all occasions; she thought milk for babies ought to be pure; she thought Germany was not altogether responsible for the World War; she did not believe in Prohibition ("It does not prohibit," she often said). She smoked cigarettes one right after the other, and did not care who knew it; and she never was more than five minutes out of the office before she was talking in newspaper argot, not all of it quite accurate. She had a hell of a time with the spelling of names.

She went out to cover the prizefights with Doug Campbell, sports editor of the *Standard*. No nice women ever went to prizefights in Gibbsville, no matter what they did in New York, and Lydia's story the next day began:

I went to the boxing match last night.

I went to the boxing match, and to be completely frank and honest, I enjoyed myself. What is this taboo that man-made convention has placed upon women going to boxing matches? Can it be that men are just a little selfish, depriving women of the fun and beauty of the boxing match? And I use the word beauty advisedly, after long and careful consideration. For there was beauty in Mc-Govern's Hall last night. Let me tell you about it.

To you women who cannot attend boxing matches because of the aforementioned masculine taboo that has been placed on attendance at the "fights" by women, permit me a few words of explanation. The principal contest of the evening, like all good things, is called the "wind-up" and it comes last. It follows the introductory "bouts" which are known as "preliminaries" or "prelims" I believe they were called by my friend Mr. Doug Campbell, popular sports editor of the *Standard*, who escorted me to Mc-Govern's Hall and showed me the "ropes." In the "pre-lims" one sees the lesser known lights of the boxing fra-ternity, and it is considered a kind of obscurity to be rele-gated to the "prelims." But it was in a "prelim" that I saw real beauty.

A mere strip of a lad, hardly more than a boy he was, and his name is Tony Morascho. Doug Campbell informed me that it was the début of Tony Morascho but I sincerely trust it will not be Tony's last, for there was beauty personified, grace in every ripple of his lithe young frame, symmetry and rhythm and the speed of a cobra as it strikes the helpless rabbit. Beauty! Do you know El Grecco, the celebrated Spanish artist? Surely you do. Well, there was El Grecco, to the life. . . .

That was how Al Grecco got his name.

He could not live the name down. The gang at the poolroom and at the gym called him El Grecco, and for a gag Packy McGovern billed him as Al Grecco on the next card. The name followed him into prison—was, in fact, waiting for him there; Lantenengo County Prison was ruled by a warden who, though no deep student of penology, believed in permitting his wards to have newspapers, cigarettes, whiskey, assignations, cards—anything, so long as they paid for it. And so when Al Grecco was sent up on the poorbox burglary matter he was not altogether unknown at the Stoney Lonesome, as the prison was called.

When Al had served his time he came out with some idea of turning square. He wanted to turn square, because he had seen so many ex-convicts in the movies who came out with one of two plans: either you turned square, or you got even with the person who got you sent up. He could not get even with Father Burns, the curate who had caught him burgling the poorbox, because it was a sacrilege to hit a priest, and anyhow Father Burns had been transferred to another parish. And so Al decided to turn square. First, though, there were two things he wanted to do. There was no one to give him money while he was in prison, and he felt he had been deprived of the two most important things you can have. He had about ten dollars, his earnings in prison, but that was not enough for a big night. He wanted twenty. So he got in a game of pool, to get his eye and his stroke back, and surprised himself by being pretty good. That gave him confidence, and he asked if he could take a cue in a money game. He lost all his money in the game and Joe Steinmetz, the crippled man who owned the place, would not stake him. Steinmetz would give him a job, he said, but no money to shoot pool with. So Al walked out of the place, wishing he had insulted Joe. Outside the poolroom, which was the next building to the Apollo hotel and restaurant, Al saw Ed Charney, sitting in his Cadillac sedan. Ed was smoking a cigar, and seemed to be waiting for someone. Al waved his hand and said, "Hyuh, Ed." All the poolroom gang spoke to Ed, although Ed did not always answer. Now he beckoned to Al. Al made the distance to the car in three jumps.

"Hello, Ed," he said.

"When'd you get out? Somebody spring you?" said Ed. He took his cigar out of his mouth and smiled benevolently at Al. Al was surprised and pleased that Ed Charney should know so much about him.

"No, I did my time," he said. "I got out today." He

leaned with one arm on the rear door of the sedan. "I didn't know you knew me."

"I make it my business to know a *lot* of people," said Ed. "How'd you like to make a sawbuck?"

"Who do you want knocked off?" said Al.

Ed glared and put the cigar back in his teeth, but then took it out again. "Don't talk tough, kid. That don't get you any place. That don't get you any place except up in that jail house or else—" he snapped his fingers. "Nobody has to knock anybody off, and the sooner you get them ideas out of your head the better off you are."

"You're right, Ed," said Al.

"I know I'm right. I make it my business to be right. Now if you want to make that sawbuck, all I want you to do—can you drive a car?"

"Yeah. What kind? This one?"

"This one," said Ed. "Take it out the Gibbsville Motors or whatever you call it. English's garage. Tell them I sent you out to have it washed and wait till they're done with it and then bring it back here." He reached in his pocket and took a ten-dollar bill from a roll. "Here."

"A sawbuck for that? Do you want me to pay for washin' it?"

"No. Charge it. I give you the sawbuck because you just got outa the can. Keep your nose clean." Ed Charney got out of the car. "Keys in the car," he said. He walked toward the Apollo, but turned after a few steps. "Say," he said. "Who the hell ever told you you was a prizefighter?"

Al laughed. There was a guy for you: Ed Charney, the

big shot from here to Reading and here to Wilkes-Barre. Maybe the whole State. What a guy! Democratic. Gave a guy ten bucks for doing nothing at all, nothing at all. Knew all about you. Made it his business to know all about you. That night Al Grecco did not get quite so drunk as he had planned; he waited until the next night, when he had thirty dollars from a crap game. *That* night he got good and drunk, and was thrown out of a house for beating up one of the girls. The day after that he took a job with Joe Steinmetz.

For three years he worked for Joe Steinmetz, more or less regularly. No one could beat him shooting straight pool, and he had great skill and luck in Nine Ball, Ouch, Harrigan, One Ball in the Side and other gambling pool games. He saw Ed Charney a couple of times a week, and Ed called him Al. Ed seldom played pool, because there were only six tables in the place, and though he could have had any table by asking for it or even hinting that he wanted to play, he did not take advantage of his power. When he played he played with Snake Eyes O'Neill, the wisecracking, happy-go-lucky guy from Jersey City, who was always with Ed and, everybody said, was Ed's bodyguard. Snake Eyes, or Snake, as Ed called him, carried a revolver unlike any Al ever had seen. It was like any ordinary revolver except that it had hardly any barrel to it. Snake was always singing or humming. He never knew the words of a song until after it was old, and he used to make sounds, "Neeyaa, ta ta ta tata, tee ta tee, laddie deetle," instead of singing the words. He was not called

Snake Eyes because he had eyes like a Snake. Far from it. The name was a crapshooting term. He had big brown eyes that were always smiling. O'Neill was tall and skinny and in Al's opinion was the snappiest dresser he ever had seen. Al counted up one time and he figured O'Neill had at least fourteen suits of clothes, all the latest cut from Broadway, New York City. Ed Charney was not a very snappy dresser. Ed had quite a few suits, but he did not change them much. His pants often needed pressing, and he often put his hat on so that the bow on the band was on the wrong side of his head. There were always cigar ashes on the lapels of his coat. But Al knew one thing: Ed wore silk underwear. He'd seen it.

In the last year before he got a job with Ed, Al frequently sat at Ed's table in the Apollo. By that time Al was shooting such good pool that Joe cut him in on the weekly take of the poolroom, and Al had permission to use house money when he wanted to play pool for money. He was only twenty-one and thinking of buying a half interest in the place. He spent plenty, but he made plenty; anywhere from fifty to two hundred bucks a week. He had a car—a Chevvy coop. He bought a Tuxedo. He went to Philadelphia when there was a musical comedy and he knew a girl there that worked in night clubs and shows, who would sleep with him if he let her know he was coming to town. He liked the name Al Grecco, and never thought of himself as Tony Murascho. The boys who sat at Ed Charney's table would not have known who was meant if the name Tony Murascho had been mentioned.

But they knew Al Grecco for a good kid that Ed liked well enough to ask him to eat with him once in a while. Al Grecco was no pest, and did not sit at the table unless he was asked. He never asked any favors. He was the only one who ever sat at the table who had nothing to do with the stock market, and that was a big relief. All the others, from Ed Charney down, were in the market or only temporarily out of it.

Al lived then at Gorney's Hotel, which was not quite the worst hotel in Gibbsville. He never went near his home and did not go out of his way to speak to any of his brothers or sisters if he saw them on the street. They did not try to persuade him to come home, either. When they needed money badly they would send one of the younger kids to the poolroom, and Al would give the kid a five or a ten, but Al did not like this. It put him off his game. After giving away a five or a ten he would get over-anxious in trying to make it up, and the result would be he would lose. He wished the old man would support his family himself. And what about Angelo and Joe and Tom; they were all older than Tony—Al. And Marie, she was old enough to get married and the other kids didn't have to go to school all their life. *He* didn't. The old man ought to be glad he didn't have to work in the mines. Al knew that the old man would have worked in the mines, and glad to get the bigger wages, but all he could do was navvy gang work. Even so, the old man ought to be glad he had outdoor work instead of mucking in a drift or robbing pillars or being on a rock gang in

57

tunnel work. That kind of work was hard work. Or at least Al thought so. He never had been in the mines himself—and never would, if he could help it.

One afternoon Joe Steinmetz didn't come to work and he didn't come to work. Joe did not like the telephone, because it interfered with a man's privacy, and the next day when he again did not show up, Al took the Chevvy up to Point Mountain, where Joe lived with his wife. There was a crêpe on the door. Al hated to go in, but he thought he ought to. . . . It was Joe, all right. Mrs. Steinmetz was alone and hadn't been able to leave the house except to have a neighbor get a doctor. Joe had died of heart disease and was good and dead by the time the doctor had sent the undertaker.

Joe left everything to his wife. She wanted Al to work for her, keep the poolroom going, and at first he thought it would be a good idea. But a few days of taking the day's receipts all the way out to her house showed him he didn't want to work for her. She offered to sell the good will and fixtures for five thousand dollars, but Al never had had that much money all at once in his life and there were only two ways he could borrow it; from the banks or from Ed Charney. He didn't like banks or the people who worked in them, and he didn't want to ask Ed. He didn't think he knew Ed well enough to ask him for money. Anyhow, not that kind of money; five grand. So the poolroom went to Mike Minas, a Greek friend of George Poppas's, and Al went to work for Ed Charney. He just went up to Ed and said: "Yiz have any kind of a job for me, Ed?" and Ed said yes, come to think of it, he had been thinking of offering him a job for a long time. They agreed on a fifty-dollar-a-week salary, and Al went to work. At first he merely drove Ed around on business and pleasure trips; then he was given a job of some importance, that of convoy to the booze trucks. He would follow two or three Reo Speedwagons, in which the stuff was transported. If a state policeman or a Federal dick stopped the trucks, it was Al's business to stop too. It was an important job, because he took a chance of being sent to prison. When he stopped, it was his job to try to bribe the cops. It was an important job, because he carried up to ten thousand dollars cash of Ed's money in the Nash roadster which he used on these trips. It was up to him to use his head about bribing the cops; one or two of them wouldn't be bribed, but most of them would listen to reason unless they had been sent out to pinch a truck or two to make a showing. He had to be smooth in his bribery offers to some of them. Some of them would take anything from a gold tooth to ten thousand dollars, but hated to be approached in the wrong way. On the few occasions when the cops refused to be bribed, it was Al's job to get to the nearest telephone, tell Ed, and get Jerome M. Montgomery, Ed's lawyer, working on the case. Al never was arrested for attempted bribery. In fact he was so successful generally that Ed took him off the convoy job and made him a collector. Ed trusted him and liked him, and made a lot of money for him, or gave him a lot of money. Sitting there at breakfast on this Christmas morning Al Grecco could write a check for more than four thousand dollars, and he had thirty-two one-thousand-dollar bills in his safety deposit box. For a kid of twenty-six he was doing all right.

Now Loving Cup suddenly was standing at his table. "On the phone, you," said Loving Cup.

"Who is it? Some dame?" said Al.

"Don't try and bluff me," said Loving Cup. "I know you're queer. No, it's a party I think they said the name was Jarney or Charney. That was it. Charney."

"Wise guy," said Al, getting up. "I'll cut your ears off. Is it Ed?"

"Yeah," said Loving Cup, "and he don't sound like Christmas to me."

"Sore, eh?" Al hurried to the telephone. "Merry Christmas, boss," he said.

"Yeah. Same to you," said Ed, in a dull voice. "Listen, Al, my kid got his arm broke—"

"Jesus, tough! How'd he do that?"

"Oh, he fell off some God damn wagon I bought him. So anyhow I'm staying here till he gets the arm set and all, and I won't be down till I don't know when. Annie is all hysterical and yelling her head off—shut up, for Christ's sake, can't you see I'm phoning. So I'm staying here. Now listen, Al. Do you have a date for tonight?"

"Nothing I can't break," said Al, who had no date. "I had a sort of a date, but it can wait if you want me to do anything."

"Well, I hate to ask you, but this is what I want you should do. Drive up to the Stage Coach and stay there

60

till they close up and keep an eye on things, see what I mean? And tell Helene I'll be there if I can make it, but you stay there anyhow, will you kid? There's fifty bucks in it for you on account of lousing up your date. Okay?"

"Kay," said Al. "Only too glad, Ed."

"Okay," said Ed. "Just stick around and keep an eye on everything." He hung up.

Al knew what he meant. Helene was not a teetotaler by any means. In fact Ed encouraged her to drink. She was more fun when she drank. But she was liable to get drunk tonight, because it was Christmas, and Ed didn't want her to become reckless with the spirit of giving.

3

ANYONE in Gibbsville who had any important money made it in coal; anthracite. Gibbsville people, when they went away, always had trouble explaining where they lived. They would say: "I live in the coal regions," and people would say, "Oh, yes, near Pittsburgh." Then Gibbsvillians would have to go into detail. People outside of Pennsylvania do not know that there is all the difference in the world between the two kinds of coal, and in the conditions under which anthracite and bituminous are mined. The anthracite region lies roughly between Scranton on the north and Gibbsville on the south. In fact Point Mountain, upon which Gibbsville's earliest settlement was made, is the delight of geologists, who come from as far away as Germany to examine Gibbsville Conglomerate, a stone formation found nowhere else in the world. When that geological squeeze, or whatever it was that produced veins of coal, occurred, it did not go south of Point Mountain, and coal is found on the north slope of Point Mountain, but not on the south side, and at the eastern face of Point Mountain is found Gibbsville Conglomerate. The richest veins of anthracite in the world are within a thirty-mile sector from Gibbsville, and when those veins are being worked, Gibbsville prospers. When the mines are idle, Gibbsville puts on a long face and begins to think in terms of soup kitchens.

The anthracite region, unlike the bituminous, is a stronghold of union labor. The United Mine Workers of America is the strongest single force in the anthracite region, and under it the anthracite miner lives a civilized life compared with that of the miner in the soft coal regions about Pittsburgh, West Virginia, and the western states. The "coal and iron" police in the anthracite region have been so unimportant since the unionization of the mines that they seldom are mentioned. A candidate for governor of Pennsylvania cannot be elected without the support of the U.M.W.A., and the Pennsylvania State Police never are called "black cossacks" in the anthracite region. A candidate for any political office in the anthracite counties would not think of having anything printed without getting the typesetters' union label on his cards and billboards. The union is responsible for the Pennsylvania mining laws, which are the best in the world (although not yet the best there could be), and labor conditions, so far as labor strife was concerned, were all right in 1930, and had been all right since the disastrous strike of 1925. At that time the union called a strike which lasted 110 days, the longest strike in anthracite history. There was no violence beyond the small squabble, and there was no starvation among the miners. But anthracite markets disappeared. Domestic sales were hurt permanently; the oil burner was installed in thousands of homes. Anthracite is practically smokeless, and was satisfactory to home owners, but they could not get anthracite during the strike, and when the oil burner was installed there was no point in going back to coal. And so, as a result of the 1925 strike, the anthracite industry went back to work without nearly the demand for the product that there had been when the strike was called 110 days before. There had been another long strike in 1922, and the two strikes taught consumers that the industry was not dependable. The feeling was that any time the union felt like it, it would call a strike, shutting off the supply of anthracite.

Thus what were boom times for the rest of the country were something less for Gibbsville. The year of Our Lord 1929 saw many of the mines near Gibbsville working on a three-day a week basis. The blasts of the giant whistles at the collieries, more powerful than those of any steamship, were not heard rolling down the valleys as they had been before the 1925 strike, every morning at five and six o'clock. The anthracite industry was just about licked.

Still there were a great many people in Gibbsville who had money in 1930. The very rich, who always had money, still had a lot of money. And the merchants and bankers, doctors and lawyers and dentists who had money to play the market continued to spend their principal. Mr. Hoover was an engineer, and in a mining country engineers are respected. Gibbsville men and women who were in the market trusted that cold fat pinched face as they had trusted the cold thin pinched face of Mr. Coolidge, and in 1930 the good day's work of October 29, 1929, continued to be known as a strong technical reaction.

II

William Dilworth English (B.S., Lafayette College; M.D., University of Pennsylvania), father of Julian McHenry English, had a salary of $12,000 a year as chief of staff of the Gibbsville Hospital. He lived within that salary, almost to the dollar. His income from private practice was about $10,000, and this totaled up to more than he could spend in a year, without being foolish. In addition to that his wife, Elizabeth McHenry English, had an income which in 1930 was about $6,000. In other years it had been more than that, but Dr. English, in investing his wife's money, had been no wiser than a lot of other men whose wives had money to invest.

Dr. English came from one of the oldest families in Gibbsville. He was of Revolutionary stock. He wore a ring with an indistinguishable crest (he took it off when he operated). Adam English, one of his ancestors, had come to Gibbsville in 1804, two years after Gibbsville was re-founded (Gibbsville was founded by Swedes in 1750, as nearly anyone could make out; the Swedes had been massacred by the Leni Lenape Indians, and the Swedish name of the original settlement has been lost). Old Adam English, as Dr. English called him, who certainly would have been old if he had lived till 1930, was a Philadelphian. It was not old Adam's father, but *his* father who had fought in the Revolution.

65

The Englishes were not exactly coal people. They were more in the railroad, the Philadelphia & Reading. But of course the railroad and the coal and iron once had been all one company. It was much better in those days, Dr. English said, because you could get passes on the railroad if someone in your family happened to be connected with either the railroad or the coal company. But Dr. English did not desire a return to those days, the days when he was in college and at The University (whenever a Gibbsvillian speaks of The University he means Pennsylvania and nowhere else). He rarely spoke of those days, for, as he said, a dark and bitter cloud had been drawn over what should have been remembered as the happiest days of his life. He referred, of course, to the fact that the summer after he got his M.D., his father, George English, stuck a shotgun in his mouth and blew his head all over the hayloft of the English stable. Dr. English thought of his father as a coward. Two or three times in their married life the doctor had said to his wife: "If George English had been anything but a coward he would have gone to the directors like a man and said, 'Gentlemen, I have been using the bank's funds for my own uses. I am willing to work hard and make it up.' And I know the directors would have admired that stand, and they would have given him a chance to make good. But . . ." And his wife would sympathize with him and try to comfort him, although she knew that her father, for one, would have tried to send George English to jail. As it was, he opposed her marriage to Billy English. Her father had said: "He may be all right. I don't know. But his education was paid for out of stolen money. That's enough for me." But how was Billy to know that? she argued. "He knows it now," said her father. Yes, he knew it, she went on, and he was anxious to start private practice so he could make good every penny. And he had. Within ten years of his graduation Billy English had paid off the money his father had taken from the bank. It had been a struggle, in a way; what with young Julian's arrival in the world. Still, Julian had not been deprived of anything, thanks to her own income. Despite the dark, bitter cloud that hung over Dr. English's college days, Julian, who wanted to go to Yale, was sent to Lafayette. And, probably out of spite, Julian did not accept the invitation to join Phi Delta Theta, his father's fraternity, but had joined Delta Kappa Epsilon. By that time his father had given up hope that Julian would study medicine. He had pointed out to Julian that "when I die, you'll have this practice that I've been years building up. I don't understand it. Plenty of boys in this town would give their right arm for just this chance." Poor Dr. English, people would say; starting out that way, with that handicap, and then his only son not taking advantage of that wonderful opportunity. No wonder the doctor was such a stern-looking man. He'd had his troubles.

He represented the best things in the community. He was a member of the County Medical Society, the Medical Club of Philadelphia, the Gibbsville Chamber of Commerce, the Gibbsville Community Chest (director), the

Children's Home Association (life subscriber), the Y.M. C.A. (director), Lantenengo County Historical Society, the Gibbsville Club (board of governors), the Lantenengo Country Club (board of governors), the Gibbsville Assembly (membership committee), the Union League of Philadelphia, the Ancient and Arabic Order-Nobles of the Mystic Shrine, the Scottish Rite Masons (32°), and the Liberty (formerly Germania) Hook & Ladder Company Number 1 (honorary). He also was a director of the Gibbsville National Bank & Trust Company, the Gibbsville Building & Loan Company, the Gibbsville-Cadillac Motor Car Company, the Lantenengo Lumber Company, and the Gibbsville Tap & Reamer Company. Episcopalian. Republican. Hobbies: golf, trapshooting. All that in addition to his work at the hospital and his private practice. Of course he didn't do nearly the private practice he used to. He was more or less giving that up and specializing on surgery. He left the little stuff to the younger men that were just starting out—childbirth and tonsils and ordinary sickness.

If there was one thing he loved, outside of his wife and son, it was surgery. He had been doing surgery for years, in the days when the ambulances from the mines were high black wagons, open at the rear, drawn by two black mules. It was almost a day's drive from some of the mines to the hospital, in the mule-drawn-ambulance days. Sometimes the patient or patients would bleed to death on the way, in spite of the best of care on the part of the first aid crews. Sometimes a simple fracture would

68

be joggled into a gangrenous condition by the time the ambulance got off the terrible roads. But when that occurred Dr. English would amputate. Even when it didn't look like gangrene Dr. English would amputate. He wanted to be sure. If the case was a skull fracture and Dr. English knew about it in time, he would say to the one man in the world he hated most: "Say, Doctor Malloy, I've ordered the operating room for five o'clock. Man brought in from Collieryville with a compound fracture of the skull. I think it's going to be very interesting, and I'd like you to come up and see it if you have time." And Mike Malloy, in the old mule-ambulance days, would be polite and tell Dr. English he would be very glad to. Dr. Malloy would get into his gown and follow Dr. English to the operating room, and by saying "I think this, Doctor English" and "I think that, Doctor English," Dr. Malloy would direct Dr. English in trephining the man on the table. But that was in the old days, before Dr. English overheard one of the surgical nurses saying: "Trephine this afternoon. I hope to God Malloy's around if English is going to try it." The nurse later was dismissed for being caught undressed in an interne's room, a crime of which she had been guilty many times, but which had been overlooked because she knew at least as much medicine as half of the men on the staff, and more surgery than several of the surgeons. But even without her assistance Dr. English continued to do surgery, year after year, and several of the men he trephined lived. The dismissal of that nurse had one effect: Dr. Malloy

69

never again spoke to Dr. English. "Need I say more?" Dr. English said, in telling his wife of Malloy's strange behavior.

I I I

One look at his father told Julian that the old man had not heard anything about the scene in the smoking-room of the country club. The old man greeted him about as usual, with Merry Christmas thrown in, but Julian expected that. He knew there was nothing wrong when he saw the old man's mustache flatten back and the crow's feet behind his shell-rim spectacles wrinkle up in the smile that he saved for Caroline. "Well, Caroline," said the doctor. He took Caroline's right hand in his own and put his left hand on her shoulder. "Help you with your coat?"

"Thanks, Father English," she said. She put her packages down on the hall table and was helped out of her mink coat. The old man took it to the closet under the stairs and put it on a hanger. "Haven't seen you in I guess it must be two weeks," he said.

"No. Christmas preparations—"

"Yes, I know. Well, we didn't do very much in the way of shopping. I thought it over and I told Mrs. English, I said I think checks would be more acceptable this year, wherever we can—"

"Doc-tor!" came a voice.

"Oh, there she is now," said the doctor.

"Merry Christmas!" Caroline called out.

"Merry Christmas, Mother," shouted Julian.

"Oh, you're here," she replied, and appeared at the top of the steps. "I was just about to say we ought to call you up. It must have been a good party at the club." Julian saw his father's expression change. Mrs. English came downstairs and kissed Caroline, and then Julian.

"Now let's all have a nice cocktail," said Mrs. English, "and then we can tell Ursula to start serving while everything's still hot. You two are so late. What kept you? Did you really get in so late last night? How was the dance?"

"I couldn't get the car started," said Julian. "Cold."

"What?" said the old man. "Couldn't get it started? I thought that apparatus you put in your garage, I thought—"

"It wasn't in the garage. I left it out all night," said Julian.

"Our driveway was blocked," said Caroline. "*We're* out in real *country*. It was drifted as high as the roof."

"Was it?" said the doctor. "I never knew it to drift that high out where you are. Remarkable. Well, I s'pose a Martini. Martini, Caroline?"

"Fine for me," said Caroline. "What about you, Julian?"

"Now, Caroline," said the doctor. "He'll drink anything, and you know it."

"See our tree?" said Julian's mother. "Such a skimpy little thing, but they're so much trouble. I like a spruce, but they're so much trouble I don't think it's worth it when there aren't any children in the house."

"We have a small tree, too," said Caroline.

"When Julian was a boy, do you remember those trees? You must have been here during the holidays when we had a tree, weren't you, Caroline?"

"No, I don't think I ever was. Julian used to hate me then, remember?"

"Funny, isn't it?" said Julian's mother. "Tsih, when I look back. You're right. He didn't like to play with you, but my gracious, I don't think he disliked you. He was in awe of you. But we all were. Still are." Caroline gave her mother-in-law a hug.

"Oh, now, Mother," she said. "Julian did hate me. Probably because I was older."

"Well, you wouldn't think it now," said the older woman. "I mean that both ways. You wouldn't think he ever hated you, and you certainly wouldn't think you were older. Julian, why don't you go to the 'Y' or something? Let me look. Turn your face over that way. . . . You are. You're getting a double chin. Julian, really."

"Very busy man," said Julian.

"Here we are," said the doctor. "Drink this one, Caroline, and you and I can have another before we sit down."

"We can all have another one," said his wife, "but we'll have to take it in to the table with us. I don't want to keep the girls any later than necessary. But that doesn't mean you're to bolt your food. Bad for the digestion."

"It is if you don't masticate—" said the doctor.

"Doctor, please don't say that," said his wife. "Chew your food is just as good a word. Well, shall we have a toast?"

72

"Yes, I think so," said the doctor. He raised the glass. " 'God bless us, everyone,' " he said; and all momentarily serious and self-conscious, they drank their drinks.

Caroline and Julian, in the car, waved to Dr. and Mrs. English, and then Julian slowly took his foot off the clutch and the car pulled away. The clock on the dashboard said 4:35.

Julian reached in his pocket and took out the Christmassy envelope, which had been on his plate, exactly like the envelope that had been on Caroline's plate. He laid it in Caroline's lap. "See how much it's for," he said.

She opened the envelope and looked at the check. "Two hundred and fifty," she said.

"How much was yours?" he said.

She opened her envelope. "Same thing," she said. "Two hundred and fifty. Really, that's too much. They're sweet." She stopped herself and he looked at her without turning.

"What is it?" he inquired.

"Oh," she said. "It's just that they're so swell. Your mother is such a darling. I don't see how you—if she finds out about last night, your performance, do you realize how ashamed she'll be?"

"She's my mother," he said.

"Yes, she is. It's pretty hard to believe sometimes."

"Am I going to be bawled out the rest of the way home?" he said.

73

"No," she said. "What's the use? What are you planning to do about Harry?"

"Harry? I don't know. I could call him up," he said.

"No, that's not enough. I think the best thing is for you to take me home and then go to his house and apologize in person."

"Fat chance," said Julian.

"All right. But if you don't, I go to no more parties with you. That means I'll stay home from everything that we've accepted, and another thing, *our* party is *off*. If you think I'm going to make a spectacle of myself for people to talk about, going around to parties and having people feel sorry for me because of your behavior—I just won't do it, Ju, I won't do it, and that's that."

"If there's anything I hate, it's that's that," he said. "All right. I'll go to his house. He's probably forgotten about it, and my going there will bugger things up proper."

"Please promise me you *won't* bugger things up. You can handle him, Ju, if you're just careful. I didn't mean it when I said you couldn't. You can. Turn on some of that English charm and he'll fall for it. But please make it right so there won't be a situation for the rest of the holidays. Will you, darling?" Her tone had changed completely, and her earnestness thrilled him. She was not quite so handsome when she was being earnest, but she so seldom wanted anything enough to be earnest about it that she became a new and rare Caroline.

"One condition," he said.

"What?"

"Will you do it?" he said.

"I won't promise till I know what it is. What's the condition?"

"That you be in bed when I get home," he said.

"Now? In the afternoon?"

"You always used to love to in the daylight." He reached over and put his hand high on the inside of her leg.

She nodded slowly.

"Ah, you're my sweet girl," he said, already grateful. "I love you more than tongue can tell."

She spoke no more the rest of the way home, not even goodbye when she got out of the car, but he knew. It was always that way when they were away from their home, and made a date to go to bed when they got home. When they made a date like that she thought of nothing else until they got home. She wanted nothing else, and no one else could take anything of her, not even the energy that goes into gregarious gayety. Always she seemed then to crouch a little, although she didn't actually crouch. But whenever they did that, from the moment she agreed, to the ultimate thing, she began to submit. And driving away he knew again, as he had known again and again, that with Caroline that was the only part of their love that was submission. She was as passionate and as curious, as experimental and joyful as ever he was. After four years she was still the only woman he wanted to wake up with, to lie glowing with—yes, and even to have intercourse

75

with. The things that she said, the words he had taught her, and the divining queries that they put to each other —they were his and hers. They were the things that made her fidelity so important, he believed; and when he thought of how important those things were, the words and the rest, he sometimes could understand that the physical act in unfaithfulness can be unimportant. But he doubted that infidelity is ever unimportant.

He stopped the car at Harry Reilly's house, where Reilly lived with his widowed sister and her two sons and daughter. It was a low stone and brick house, with a vast porch around three sides. He pushed the bellbutton, and Mrs. Gorman, Reilly's sister, came to the door. She was a stout woman with black hair, with a dignity that had nothing to do with her sloppy clothes. She was near-sighted, wore glasses, but she recognized Julian. "Oh, Julian English. Come on in," she said, and left the door open for him to close. She did not bother to be polite. "I guess you want to see Harry," she said.

"Yes, is he here?" he said.

"He's here," she said. "Go on in the living-room and I'll go up and tell him. He's in bed."

"Oh, don't disturb him," said Julian, "if he's still asleep."

She made no answer. She went upstairs. She was gone less than five minutes.

"He can't see you," she said.

He stood and looked at her, and she returned his look without a word and her expression said, "It's up to you."

"Mrs. Gorman, you mean he won't see me?" said Julian.

"Well, he said to tell you he can't see you. It's the same difference."

"I came here to apologize for last night," said Julian.

" I know you did," she said. "I told him he was a fool to raise a stink about it, but you can't change him. He has a right to stay sore if he wants to."

"Yes, I know."

"I told him what he should of done was give you a puck in the mouth when you threw the drink at him, but he said there were other ways of fixing you." She was completely ruthless and honest, but Julian had a suspicion that she was a little on his side.

"You don't think it would do any good if I went upstairs?"

"Only make matters worse, if you want my opinion. He has a black eye."

"Black eye?"

"Yes. It isn't much of a one, but it's there. The ice from the drink. You must of slung it pretty hard. No, I guess the best thing you can do is go. You won't get anywhere hanging around here now, and he's upstairs waiting till you go so he can curse you out once you get outside."

Julian smiled. "Do you think if I leave and he curses me out, it'd be all right if I came back then?"

Her face became a little angry. "Listen, Mr. English, I don't wan't to stick my two cents in this one way or the other. It's none of my affair. But I want to tell you this much. Harry Reilly is a sore pup, and there isn't anything funny about it when he gets sore."

"Okay. Well, thank you."

"All right," she said. She did not go to the door with him.

He did not look back, but he knew as well as he could know anything that Harry Reilly was watching him from an upstairs window, and probably Mrs. Gorman was watching with him.

He drove home, parking the car in front of his house, and went inside. He took as long as he could with his hat and coat, scarf and arctics. He walked slowly up the stairs, letting each step have its own full value in sound. It was the only way he knew of preparing Caroline for the news of Reilly's refusal to see him, and he felt he owed her that. It would not be fair to her to come dashing in the house, to tell her by his footsteps that everything was all right and Reilly was not sore, only to let her down.

He sensed that she had understood the slow steps. She was in bed, the dazzling light coming in the windows from the west, and she was reading a magazine. It was *The New Yorker*, and not the newest one. He recognized the cover. It was a Ralph Barton drawing; a lot of shoppers, all with horribly angry or stern faces, hating each other and themselves and their packages, and above the figures of the shoppers was a wreath and the legend: Merry Xmas. Caroline had her knees up under the bed-clothes, with the magazine propped against her legs, but

78

she was holding the cover and half of the magazine with her right hand.

She slowly closed the magazine and laid it on the floor. "Did you have a fight with him?" she said.

"He wouldn't see me." Julian lit a cigarette and walked over to the window. They were together and he knew it, but he felt like hell. She was wearing a black lace negligée that he and she called her whoring gown. Suddenly she was standing beside him, and as always he thought how much smaller she was in her bare feet. She put her arm inside his arm, and her hand gripped the muscle of the arm.

"It's all right," she said.

"No," he said, gently. "No, it isn't."

"No, it isn't," she said. "But let's not think of it now." She moved her arm so that it went around his back under the shoulder blades, and her hand moved slowly down his back, along his ribs, his hips and buttocks. He looked at her, doing all the things he wanted her to do. Her reddish brown hair was still fixed for the day. She was not by any means a small girl; her nose rubbed under his chin, and he was six feet tall. She let her eyes get tender in a way she had, starting a smile and then seeming to postpone it. She stood in front of him and kissed him. Without taking her mouth away she pulled his tie out of his vest and unbuttoned his vest, and then she let him go. "Come on!" she said, and lay with her face down in the pillow, shutting out everything else until he was with her. It was the greatest single act of their married life. He knew it, and she knew it. It was the time she did not fail him.

v

It was dark when Al Grecco bundled up, preparatory to starting his lonely drive to the Stage Coach. He bought cigarettes and chewing gum. He regretted that there was no one to see him getting into Ed Charney's "coop." He liked doing that, driving away alone, in that car, before the muggs who hung around the Apollo. It showed them how he stood with Ed, compared to them.

It was an eighteen-mile drive, with a dozen tiny coal-mining patches to break up the stretches of lighted highway. The road was pretty good, but Al told himself that if he was any judge, it would be drifted again before he got home. In the patches the snow was piled high on each side of the streets. He counted only six persons in all the patches between Gibbsville and Taqua, the next fairly big town, fourteen miles from Gibbsville. That showed how cold it was. In all the houses in the patches the curtains were down, and the hunkeys, the schwackies, the roundheaders, the broleys—regional names for non-Latin foreigners—probably were inside getting drunk on boilo. Boilo is hot moonshine, and Ed did not approve of it, because if the schwackies once stopped drinking boilo, they would drink his stuff. Still, there was nothing to do about it. But it was cheating, in a way, for the schwackies to be celebrating Christmas; they celebrated Christmas all over again on January 6, Little Christmas. In each patch there

80

was one exception to the curtained windows of the houses; that was in the doctor's house. There was a doctor in each town, living in a well-built house, with a Buick or a Franklin in front of the house. More than once Al had found it a good thing to know, that the doctors usually kept one car in front of the house—either the Buick or Franklin, or the Ford or Chevvy. More than once Al had drained gasoline from the doctors' cars, and never once had been caught.

He tore along the highway, clipping off the fourteen miles to Taqua in twenty-one minutes. His best time was twelve minutes, but that was in the summer, with a load of "white"—alcohol. Twenty-one minutes tonight wasn't bad. But he gave up trying to make time from Taqua to the Stage Coach. Too many turns in that road, and all uphill. You come to a fairly steep hill on that stretch, you climb the hill and think you're set, but then you find it's only the beginning of the real hill. Once you get on top of the hill it is only a few hundred yards to the crossroads, which is where the Stage Coach is built. If you want to you can go on and climb some more hills, because the Stage Coach is built on a plateau, one of the coldest places in Pennsylvania. There has been an inn on the site of the Stage Coach as long as there has been a road. It was one of those things that had to be. Anyone who climbed that hill in the old days had to rest his horses—and get a toddy for himself. And motorists liked to pause there for the same reason. It was a natural place to stop traveling.

A wrought-iron coach-and-four. six feet long over all,

hung from a post in front of the inn. The Stage Coach was only two years old, still new as Gibbsville things went, and Ed was making improvements all the time. A business acquaintance of Ed's in New York had sent Ed a fat, rosy-cheeked young man to do the decorating. The young man had been driven once back to New York by the practical jokes of the boys, but Ed gave out the word to leave him alone, so the pansy came back and did a very good job of the Stage Coach. People from the cities often commented on the Stage Coach, how surprising it was to see such a really nice place in all that coal-region squalor.

Ed, of course, owned the place, but it was run by Foxie Lebrix, who had been headwaiter in one of the big New York hotels—which one he never would say. Foxie was a strong, bulky Frenchman, about fifty-five years old, with white hair and a black mustache. He could tear a deck of cards in half, or break a man's jaw with a single punch. He also could cook stuff that only a few of the Lantenengo Street crowd ever had heard of, and just as few could pronounce. He was thought to be a killer, but nobody knew that for sure. Al Grecco treated him with respect.

"Hello, Fox," said Al, in Lebrix's office.

"Hello," said Lebrix.

"The big boy tell you I was coming?" said Al.

"He dit," said Lebrix. He was dipping a cigar in brandy, using his left hand, and giving the impression of not letting his right hand know what the left hand was doing. He saved the right hand for his little gestures. "Thee lady is resting," he tossed his head back to indicate up-

82

stairs. "She was a little onder the wather wan Ed phoned."

"She know I'm coming?"

"She will. If you want the truth, she was cockeye dronk."

"Oh, yeah? She's liable to—"

"She wawnt leave the room. I have Marie to watch her." Marie was Lebrix's common law wife. Anyhow, that's what she said. "You want to see her? She started to drink when she got op, without eating breakfast. She can't do dat. She can't drink at all. But no. 'It's Christmas. I have to drink. I have to get dronk. It's Christmas.' God damn son of a bitch a bastard. I wish Ed would take her some other place. She is more trobble than she is worth."

"Oh, well," said Al.

"Aw, well. Sure. Aw, well. If I had a woman do like that you bet she would not do it twice."

"Oh, well, you know how it is, Fox," said Al.

Lebrix nodded. "Oh, pardon," he said. "You have your dinner? Have a drink?

"No, just a cuppa coffee."

"Café Royale?"

"No, thanks, Fox. Just coffee. No drinks for me tonight."

"Too bad. I'll order coffee." He pushed a button under the top of the desk and told a waiter to serve Al's coffee. "Lots of reservations tonight. Several parties from Gibbsville, and a big dinner from Taqua. Jews. And that politician, Donovan, he has the nerve to reserve a table for ten for tonight. Cheap bastard son of a bitch."

83

"He'll pay," said Al.

"Sure he'll pay. He'll hand me a century, like a big heavy spender, and I'm soppose to thank him politely, but then I give him his change and it's ten sawbucks. The waiters are lucky if they get a tip. That's the way he is, the cheap bastard son of a bitch. I'd like to give him a Mickey Finn. I never gave one of those in my life, but if I do, he will be the first."

"You can't do that."

"*I* know. You want to sit with Helene tonight?"

"I guess that's the best way."

"Yes, I think so. Some of our guests, they get some of this so-called champagne in their bellies, and Miss Holman will begin to think she is Mistinguett."

"What?"

"French entertainer. Yes, if your job is to keep an eye on her, you better be where she can see you so she will not forget herself. It's Christmas, my friend. She may give something away."

"Huh. That's exactly what I was thinking."

"So?" said Lebrix.

4

THEY were driving south on the way to the club, down South Main Street. Caroline was smoking a cigarette and holding Julian's hand. He took the hand away to do *shave-and-a-haircut* on the horn button, signaling to the Cadillac just ahead of their own.

"Who's that?" said Caroline.

"A good prospect," said Julian. "Young Al Grecco."

"Who's he? I know him by name. Who is he?"

"He's a sort of a yes man for Ed Charney," said Julian. The coupé in front turned off to the left, to the Lincoln Street bridge, and apparently Al Grecco did not hear the signal. He did not turn his head or answer with *bay-rum* on the horn of the coupé.

"Oh, he's the one that went to Philadelphia for the champagne. Did he get it?" said Caroline.

"If Mr. Charney wants champagne, whoever is told to get it, gets it."

"Oh, I don't believe it. Why are people so afraid of him?"

"I'm afraid of him," said Julian.

"You are not. You're not afraid of anyone. My big strong man. My mate."

"Nuts to you, sister," he said.

"Don't call me sister, and don't say nuts."

"Say masticate," said Julian. "God, did you ever hear anyone like Mother? Did you hear her telling the old gent not to say masticate? You know she hasn't the remotest idea why she doesn't like the word."

"I'll bet she has. Women aren't that dumb."

"I say she hasn't the remotest idea why she doesn't like the word. Somewhere in the back of her mind the sound of the word has a dirty connotation, but what it is she isn't sure. So she thinks she prefers simple language. Did you ever masticate?"

"None of your business."

"Did you?"

"I'm getting a little tired of this," said Caroline.

"So am I," said Julian. They rode for a while, and then he said: "When are we going to have a kid?"

"I don't know. When *are* we?" she said.

"No, seriously, *when* are we?"

"You know. The five years will be up soon."

"The Five Year Plan," he said slowly. "Well, maybe you're right."

"I know I'm right. Look at these kids, Jeanie and Chuck. Married less than two years, hardly more than a year, and Jeanie may have to have false teeth. Mind you, false teeth, and do you remember her teeth? She had the loveliest strong white teeth I ever saw—"

"Except yours."

"Well, except mine. But hers were beautiful and just

86

right. Smallish and nice and really sparkling. Mine are bigger, and they don't sparkle."

"They dazzle me," he said. He snapped off the headlights. "We'll use your sparkling teeth for headlights."

"Put the lights on, you fool," she said. "No kidding, it's awful. She's only twenty-one. Just twenty-one, and she's absolutely a married woman. A married woman with a child. And—"

"And a husband. And what a husband."

"Exactly!" said Caroline. "Chuck. That little twirp. Jeanie. Why, he isn't good enough to . . ."

"To what. Finish it."

"No, I'm not fooling. Chuck running around with that girl from Kresge's and the other day at bridge club Barbara Schultz spoke up and said, 'Well, I think someone ought to defend poor Chuck.' Poor Chuck! She said, 'If Jeanie had taken the trouble to keep herself attractive, Chuck wouldn't chase after other girls.' Golly it made me mad. She must have read that somewhere. I didn't say anything, and neither did anyone else, but you could see what everybody was thinking. Barbara's such a fool for letting herself in for that. Why, she did everything but handcuff Chuck to make him marry her."

"She did? I didn't know that. I knew they had dates, but I never thought—"

"No? Well, here's something else you didn't know. Mrs. Schultz was so sure Barbara was going to get Chuck that she made reservations for two for a trip around the world—"

"Well, she and old Stinker went around the world."

"Yes, but Mother told me that she was in Mr. Schultz's office when—"

"God damn it to hell!" said Julian. He stopped the car. "Cross-link broke. I might as well fix it now while I'm sober." He got out of the car and fixed the link. They did not speak to each other during the five-minute wait. Cars drove by and one or two stopped, recognizing Julian and the car, asking if they could help, but he sent them on.

He started the car again. "Hyuh, baby," he said. "What were we talking about? Had we finished with Chuck?"

"Mm."

"What's the mattah, honey sugah lamb pie, what's the mattah you all?"

"Listen, Ju. Listen to me, will you?"

"Listen to you? Why, Mrs. English, one of the most attractive features of the Cadillac is the minimum of noise in the motor. Just let me show—"

"No. Don't be funny."

"What's the matter? Did I do something wrong? Did I say something? Christ, I thought we were getting along fine."

"We were, but something you said worried me. See, you don't even remember saying it."

"Well, come on. Out with it, dearie. What did I say?"

"When you stopped the car. When you got out to fix the chain, you said something about you were going to fix it now, while you were sober."

"Oh," he said.

"As if—"

"I get it. You don't have to draw a map."

"Now you're annoyed. Aren't you?"

"No. Yes, slightly. I don't know. What the hell. I don't blame you."

"I'm sorry, darling. I don't want to be a wet towel or anything, but I couldn't go through another half hour like that last night—I'd rather die."

"I know. I'm terribly sorry, Callie. I won't get drunk."

"Please don't," she said. "Please. And I'll do anything. Let's get through these holidays without any more mess or jam or anything. I don't want to give you a pep talk—"

"I know you don't. I don't blame you."

"You're my sweet Ju and I love you. I don't mean don't drink. You know."

"Uh-huh. I promise."

"No, don't promise. Just don't. You don't have to. Lots of times you go to parties and don't get crazy. So be like that tonight. I'll do anything, any of the things you like. Anything. Do you know what I'll do?"

"What?"

"I'll come out in the car with you at intermission and stay with you, the way we used to."

"I know, but—that's what I'd love. It *would* be fun."

"We haven't done that since we've been married."

"Yes we did. At Lake Placid."

"Yes, but we haven't here, at home, and I want to, don't you?"

"Yes, but what about, you know, business?" he said. She hated to name the contraceptive devices.

"I won't bother. We can start having a baby."

"Do you mean it?" he said.

"I never meant anything so much in my life," she said. "And there's one way to prove it."

"Yes, that's true. Just by being here. Just by coming out here." They had arrived at the club parking grounds. "Uh-huh."

"Oh, my sweet lovely Caroline," he said.

"Not now," she said. "I said intermission."

They got out of the car. Ordinarily Julian would have stopped the car at the steps near the vestibule, where the women got out of chauffeur-driven and husband-driven and beau-driven cars, but tonight they had not thought of it. Julian drove the car in and out of lanes, twisting and maneuvering until he had got as close to the verandah as he could, to make as short as possible the walk through the snow. Arm in arm he and Caroline, their arctics flopping, went up to the verandah and around to the vestibule. Caroline said she would be right down, and Julian went out again to the verandah and all the way around the clubhouse to the men's locker room.

It was a grand night for a party. It was cold, and the snow-covered golf course seemed not to be separate from the farmlands that bounded the course on the second, fourth, and seventh holes. In the summer the golf course was so neatly shaved that it made him think of a farmer in his Sunday suit surrounded by other farmers in overalls and straw hats. But now in the night there was no way of telling, if you did not know, where club property ended and real farmland began. As far as you could see the world was white and blue and purple and cold. You learn by living with your mother and father and people that it is bad to lie in the snow for a long time, but when all the world is covered with snow and moonlight it doesn't look as if it would do you any harm. But it was just a picture now, so it doesn't do you any harm. Julian took in a deep breath and felt very much like a healthy, clean-living person for so doing. "I ought to get more of that," he said, and went in to the locker room.

Many men said hello and hyuh to him, and he said hyuh and hello back at them six or seven times. He didn't have an enemy in the place. Then he heard someone say, "Hello, Socker." He looked to see who it was, although he knew who it was. It was Bobby Herrmann.

"Hello, Rum Dumb," he said.

"Yeah, Rum Dumb," said Bobby in his slow difficult way of speaking. "Jesus Christ. You have a nerve calling me Rum Dumb, I'll say."

"Nuts," said Julian. He was taking off his coat and hat and putting them in his locker.

Everyone seemed to think that the job of kidding Julian was being taken over by Bobby. "Jesus Christ," said Bobby. "I've done a whole lot of things in my life, but by Jesus if I ever sunk so low that I had to throw ice in a man's face and give him a black eye. My God."

Julian sat down at the table. "Cocktail. Straight liquor.

Highball. What'll you have, Ju?" said Whit Hofman.

"Cocktail, I guess."

"Martinis in this shaker," said Hofman.

"Fine," said Ju.

"Trying to ignore me," said Bobby. "Trying to give me the old high hat. The old absent treatment. Well, all right. Go ahead. Ignore me. Give me the old high hat. I don't care. But the least you can do, English, the least you can do is go in there and pay for an extra subscription to the dance."

"Huh?" said Julian.

"You heard me. You're responsible for there being one less man here tonight and the club needs the money, so don't forget, you sock out an extra five bucks when you pay your subscription."

"Who is this man?" said Julian to Whit. Whit smiled. "Did he come here with a member?"

"That's all right," said Bobby. "Don't worry about me."

"Depression or no depression, I think the membership committee ought to draw the line somewhere," said Julian. "I don't mind Jews or Negroes, or even a few people with leprosy. They have souls, the same as you or I. But when a man goes to his club he likes to think he's going to associate with human beings, and not some form of reptile life. Or is it insect? Turn around, Herrmann, till I decide just what you are. Have you got wings?"

"Don't worry about me. I'll get by."

"That's just the trouble," said Julian. "We ought to

have state cops stationed at the club entrance, just to keep people like you away."

"It's a good thing we didn't have state cops here last night. As it was it's a wonder somebody didn't send for them. Or the God damn marines or something."

"There you go, talking about the war again," said Julian. "You never got over that God damn war. That's your trouble. You don't hear Whit, or Froggy—"

"That's all right," said Bobby. "When there was a war, I was in it. I wore a uniform. I wasn't one of these God damn slackers playing sojer boy at some college. Lafayette or Lehigh or wherever it was. S.A.T.C. Saturday Afternoon Tea Club. Yes, sir. When old Uncle Sam needed me, I heeded the call and made the world safe for democracy, and when the war was over I stopped fighting. I didn't do like some people that put on a uniform back in 1917 and then did their fighting by throwing drinks around in the presence of respectable people at a country club, thirteen or fourteen years after the war was over. Nineteen-thirty. That's what some people are. Veterans of 1930. The Battle of the Lantenengo Country Club Smoking Room. Surprise attack."

The others were laughing, and Julian knew he was coming off a very bad second best. He finished his drink and rose to go.

"Not driving you away, are we?" said Bobby.

Julian looked at Whit, deliberately turning his back on Bobby. "Something wrong with the can, Whit? Or don't you smell it?"

93

Whit gave a neutral smile. "Going in?" he said.

"Let him go, Whit," said Bobby. "You know how he is when he has a drink in his hand. Of course you're safer when it's a cocktail. There aren't any lumps of ice in a cocktail to give you a black—"

"Well, bye bye," said Julian. He walked out of the locker room, but as he left he heard Bobby say in a very loud voice, loud enough not to be missed by Julian: "Say, Whit, I hear Harry Reilly's thinking of buying a new Lincoln. He doesn't like that Cadillac he bought last summer." The locker-room loved it.

Julian walked on, through the smoking-room, through the dining alcoves, out to the dance floor, through to the foyer at the foot of the stairs. That was where you waited for your lady. Julian said hello and good evening to a great many people, and waved especially gayly to Mildred Ammermann, who was giving tonight's dinner. She was a tall, toothy girl, captain of the women's golf team. Her father was a drunken roué, quite rich in real estate, and nominally a cigar manufacturer. He never came to the club except on nights like this, when Mr. and Mrs. Ammermann would entertain a few of their—her—friends at a smaller table. Mildred, towering above Losch, the club steward, and pointing, daintily for her, with one finger as she held a small stack of place-cards in her left hand, apparently was one woman who had not heard about the business of the night before. It was axiomatic in Gibbsville that you could tell Mill Ammermann anything and be sure it wouldn't be repeated; because Mill probably was thinking of the mashie-niblick approach over the trees to the second green. Julian derived some courage from her smile. He always had liked Mill anyway. He was fragmentarily glad over again that Mill did not live in New York, for in New York she would have been marked Lesbian on sight. But in Gibbsville she was just a healthy girl. Good old Mill.

"What are you thinking?" said Caroline, suddenly standing beside him.

"I like Mill," he said.

"I do too," said Caroline. "Why, did she do something or say something?"

"No. I just like her," he said. "I've been learning how to take it."

"How?"

"Mr. Robert Herrmann is in his best form, ribbing me about last night—"

"Oh, Lord, where? In the locker room? Were there a lot of people there?"

"Yes. Whit and Froggy and the usual crowd. He told me I ought to sock out five bucks to cover Harry's subscription to the dance. And then he started kidding me about the war being over or something. How I waited till 1930 before I did my fighting, and a lot of stuff about calling out the state police."

"Mm. I suppose we can expect an evening of that."

"Why? Has anyone said anything to you?"

"No, not exactly. Kitty Hofman came in the johnny while I—"

"God, you women, going to the can together! Why do you always—"

"Do you want to hear what she had to say? Or are you going to go into all that again?"

"I'm sorry."

"Well, Kitty, you know how she is. Comes right out with it. She said she heard Harry had a black eye, and I said yes, I knew he had. And she said Whit is worried. Did he say anything to you?"

"No. He didn't get much chance, with Bobby holding forth. I didn't wait to talk to Whit."

"Well, apparently Whit knows Harry has money in the garage."

"Sure he knows. It's no secret. As a matter of fact I think I told Whit myself. Yes, I did. I had to tell him, because when Whit heard about it last summer he wanted to know why I hadn't come to him, and I told him everybody came to him. Didn't I tell you that?"

"No, you didn't. But anyhow, Kitty said Whit's worried, because Harry is a bad man to have as an enemy. I told you that."

"I know you did. Well, we can't go on standing here like this. There's Jean and Froggy. Let's go over there."

They went over there. Jean was Caroline's best friend, and Froggy was one of the group whom Julian regarded as his best friends. He had no single best friend, had had none since college. His best friend in college was with the Standard Oil in China, and he never heard from him except about once a year. With these people Julian felt safe and at ease. Froggy, thirty-four, was not quite five years older than Julian. Froggy had lost an arm in the war, and probably because of that Julian felt less close to him than to the other men of the same age who had been in France. Julian's war record had been made in college, as a member of the S.A.T.C., and he still had the feeling that he should have enlisted to fight and not to go to college. Year by year the feeling grew less strong, and he believed he did not care any more, but he still did. He always did when he saw Froggy for the first time on any day; Froggy, who had been a beautiful swimmer and tennis player. With Jean, Julian had complete ease. Everything that they ever could have been to each other, Jean and Julian had been. They had been passionately in love all one summer long ago; a demi-vierge affair that left them, when it did leave them finally, with a feeling toward each other which was far more innocent than that of two children, and made them ready really to love someone else. Julian knew, because Jean had told him, that she had "gone the limit" with Froggy the very first night she had a date alone with him, and Julian honestly believed he was glad for her.

Now they talked about people who were visiting the So-and-sos; whether the Reading crowd was coming up for the dance; how swell or how perfectly terrible some of the girls looked; whether Julian had had a flat tire, as they had seen his car stopped on the road to the club; wasn't it wonderful, or wasn't it? the way the highway department got the roads clear so quickly; such a lovely corsage; oh, smoke a Camel, you can't tell the difference; Mill's father looks worse than ever; there was one thing about the Ammermanns, and that was when they gave a party they didn't spare the pennies. Then Mill and her mother and father were seen to take their places, standing just inside the ballroom (living-room when the furniture was not cleared away), and forming a little reception line. In less than three minutes there was a milling crowd in the foyer, all waiting to say good evening a bit stiffly to Mr. and Mrs. Ammermann, and very friendly hello to Mill. The orchestra, Ben Riskin and his Royal Canadians, from Harrisburg, took their places and with two thumps of the bass drum burst forth into (boom boom) Oh, Give Me Something To Remember You By. "Now please don't drink too much," said Caroline, and went to find her place at the festive board.

11

The festive board now groaned under the Baked Alaska. The Ammermann dinner party was just about over. Until one o'clock the men, young and old, would see to it that Mill was not left standing without a partner; after that whatever dances she got she would have got without giving the dinner. Tomorrow's papers would carry the list of guests, and then the dinner would be history. Next Christmas the big dinner at the club Christmas dance would be given by someone else. Whatever she did, Mill Ammermann must not give another large dress-up party for at least a year.

Tonight's dinner, as almost every guest was able to tell at a glance, was the club's two-fifty dinner. This was a club dinner dance, and all members were invited. At a dinner such as the Ammermann's, the hostess could arrange with the steward for the dollar-fifty (roast chicken), the two-dollar (roast turkey), or the two-fifty (filet mignon), and this had been the filet mignon dinner. The Ammermanns had just that much money, and their position in Gibbsville was just that certain and insecure, that they had to give the best of everything. Conforming to custom, the Ammermanns did not supply drinks, nor did they pay the dance subscriptions. A man on accepting an invitation to the dinner was paired off with a woman or girl. The custom for unmarried, unengaged men was to accept the dinner invitation with his card, and then to telephone the hostess and ask if she wanted him to escort someone to the dinner. All this was arranged beforehand, much more subtly than might be supposed. There were certain sad birds among the girls who had to be invited to many dinners, and it was understood by the hostess that certain men would make themselves available to take these sad birds to the dinner. But it was also understood by every hostess that a popular, attractive young man should not be designated the escort of any but popular attractive girls. Then there was another group of girls, to which Mill Ammermann herself belonged, who got to the dance somehow, usually with a married couple who were friends of hers, or as extra girl on a party of four or six. Mill, and girls like her, could tell almost to the foot how far they would dance, and if they danced more than that distance they could inquire of themselves what was wrong. Usually the answer, to girls like Mill, was that some young husband was sore at his wife and wanted to tell Mill all about it because Mill was such a pal. So understanding. And didn't misunderstand when you gave her what amounted to a rush. Sometimes, of course, Mill and the girls like her would get a real rush—by a man who had drunk more than usual. Whatever was cruel about the system, there were some things to be said for it; for one thing, by the time a girl was twenty-five she usually was prepared, knew precisely what to expect, of every dance that she went to. Only a very few girls of Mill's type went to a dance with sadly foolish hopes that this dance would be different from any other. And there was one other unwritten, unspoken agreement among the dancing men: if a Gibbsville girl of doubtful popularity inveigled an out-of-town man to come to a club dance, the Gibbsville men did go a little bit out of their way to see that she made a good showing. They danced with her twice instead of once in a night; with the result that all but the saddest of the sad birds married themselves off to out-of-town men. Of course when they once married their ugly duckling days were forgiven and forgotten; such girls took their places with the most popular girls. But it had to be marriage, not merely an engagement, but the man could be the worst heel, stupid, badly dressed—anything, so long as he was not a Jew. Not that any Gibbsville girl of the country club-Lantenengo Street set ever married a Jew. She wouldn't have dared.

By the time a man reached junior year in college he knew how he was situated in the country club social life. Julian, for instance, had known for years that what had happened tonight would always happen: that he would sit at table between one attractive girl and one sad bird. Always the attractive men, or those who were accepted as attractive in Gibbsville, were given a sad bird as a duty and an attractive girl as a reward. The attractive girls far outnumbered the sad birds. On Julian's right sat Jean Ogden; on his left was Constance Walker, who danced as though her sex life depended on it. Constance was a distant cousin of Caroline's.

All during dinner Julian's thoughts kept returning to Caroline. Constance, prolonging what had long since ceased to be a slightly amusing tradition, always called Julian, Cousin Julian, or plain Cousin. He danced once with Constance between courses, and he found himself incredulous all over again at her physical resemblance to Caroline. The two girls were almost exactly the same height and weight, and there was no denying that Constance had a lovely figure. Yes, she had it a little on Caroline, or at least he thought she had; she was fresher than Caroline—to him. He knew that under a bright light the small of Caroline's back showed an unmistakable patch of down. He knew where the cicatrix of Caroline's vaccination stood out on her left thigh; but though he had seen Constance many times in a bathing suit, he wasn't sure that she had been vaccinated at all. He was thinking of this as he danced with Constance, and he was on the verge of asking her whether she was vaccinated when he became aware that he was holding her tight and she was holding him just as tight, and for good reason. He felt ashamed of himself and sorry for Constance. It was a dirty trick to get this kid excited. It was a low trick to be excited himself. He slowly relaxed his hold.

But the process of comparing the girl he was dancing with, eating with, with the girl he had married, who was her cousin, gave him something to enjoy in secret. Whenever he was on a party and did not drink too much he needed a secret game to play or a mental task to perform the while he apparently was observing the amenities. Caroline was thirty-one and Constance was still in college and probably about ten years younger than Caroline. The cousins were pretty good types of their respective colleges: Caroline had gone to Bryn Mawr, Constance was at Smith —the plain girl who goes to Smith and competes with the smart Jewesses for Phi Beta Kappa, as distinguished from the pretty girls who go to Smith and write to Yale. Caroline was the perfect small-town girl at Bryn Mawr; from private school in her home town, to a good prep school, to Bryn Mawr and the Bryn Mawr manner, which means quick maturity and an everlasting tendency to enthusiasms. Constance knew everything, but Caroline still was finding things out—the capital of South Dakota, the identity of Mike Pingatore, the location of Dalhousie, the handicap system in polo, the ingredients of a Side Car. He wondered why he put so much stress on the education of the two girls, and then he stumbled upon a truth: that Caroline was an educated girl whose education was behind her and for all time would be part of her background, whereas with Constance and girls like her—oh, what difference did it make? Constance was an unimportant little girl. But he was glad he discovered that about Caroline and her education. It was worth remembering, and as happened so often when he made a discovery about her, he wanted to tell Caroline about it, to try it out on her and see if she agreed with it. He knew what she would say. She would say—and it would be the truth—that she had been telling him practically that for years.

The dinner guests stood up and he looked for Caroline. He saw she was too far away to have it worth making a point of going to her. That turned out to be an error in judgment.

When the Ammermann dinner party rose, that did not mean all the people eating in the dining room rose too. The Ammermann party was the largest and therefore the most important, but there were many smaller parties of varying size and degrees of importance. One of these was a squat little dinner given by Mrs. Gorman, Harry Reilly's sister. There were eight at her table: two Irish Catholic doctors and their wives; Monsignor Creedon, pastor of the Church of SS. Peter & Paul; and Mr. and Mrs. J. Frank Kirkpatrick, the Philadelphia criminal lawyer and his wife. They were having the two-fifty dinner, and champagne from a bucket under the table, in more or less open defiance of Sec. 7, Rule XI, House Rules & Regulations, Lantenengo Country Club. Mrs. Gorman always went to the big dances at the club, and always she was the hostess at a small dinner, like tonight's. Her guests all took each other for granted after the first awkward politeness. They ate in silence and at the coffee, which was served at the table, the men would sit back and burn their cigars, and the men and women would watch, completely un-self-consciously, the gay folk at the largest dinner party. They would watch without staring—except Monsignor Creedon, who would sit with his hands folded somewhat ecclesiastically on the table in front of him, sometimes folding the tinfoil of his cigar, sometimes telling a story in a softly musical voice and a beautifully modulated brogue. He knew everyone in Gibbsville, and he was a member of the club; but he belonged to the club for the golf, and in the dining-room he never spoke to anyone unless he was first spoken to. It was a spurious display of dignity, but it had the right effect on his non-Catholic acquaintances, as well as on his parishioners. He had been made old and philosophical before his time, because Church politics had deprived him, his parish, and Gibbsville of the bishopric they all had been trying for years to get. The Cardinal hated his guts, everyone said, and fought against making SS. Peter & Paul's a cathedral and Father Creedon a bishop. Instead he was elevated to the monsignori, made rural dean and irremovable rector of SS. Peter & Paul's—and thereby tacitly informed that he was to discontinue all activity tending to make a cathedral out of SS. Peter & Paul's. It was a sad blow for him as well as for the rich laymen of his parish, who loved Creedon, and for the more powerful Masons in the Coal & Iron Company, who respected this man whom they never could understand. "I'm a strong Presbyterian," they would say, "but let me tell you, nobody says anything against Father Creedon in my hearing and gets away with it, Catholic or no Catholic."

There were those among his parishioners who secretly resented Monsignor Creedon's serving on non-sectarian committees in community activities, but this sort of criticism could be traced to disgruntled Knights of Columbus. The Coal & Iron was ruled by the Masons, who admired Monsignor Creedon, and who tolerated the Knights of Columbus. The latter felt that their pastor ought to use his influence more frequently in advancing "Knights." He never did. He used his influence in coaxing better company houses for the miners' families out of the directorate; or in wangling contributions for poorer parishes than his own. The U.M.W.A. organizers and field workers hated Monsignor Creedon because he was so close to the bigwigs of the company.

On the other hand, he did sometimes use his influence to help a Protestant. He got them bail, helped them get jobs. He had bought a Cadillac from Julian, instead of a Lincoln from the Ford dealer, who was a Catholic. He bought three Fords for his curates to atone for patronizing Julian's business. Three years ago he had driven his car, a Buick, to Julian's garage and went in Julian's office and said: "Good morning, son. Do you have any nice black Cadillac sedans today?" He bought a car right off the floor and paid cash for it. His curates' cars went to the

Ford dealer for repairs and service, but he always bought his tires and other needs at Julian's garage.

Julian wanted to go to the bathroom after the dinner party stood up, and on his way to the men's locker room he had to pass Mrs. Gorman's table. He looked at Mrs. Gorman and she did not speak to him, but that was not unusual. But he felt the chill that passed between him and the men at the table. Kirkpatrick nodded politically and showed his teeth, but the doctors frankly snubbed him, and Monsignor Creedon, whose round, bluish face usually smiled sadly above that purple thing he wore under his Roman collar, nodded just once and did not smile. It took Julian a few seconds to figure it out, because in his dealings with Catholics he so often forgot to consider the Catholic point of view. But by the time he was alone in the men's room he had it figured out: they all regarded his insulting Harry Reilly as an insult to themselves. There was no other reason why he should throw a drink at Reilly, so it must be because he was an unattractive Irish Catholic whom he could insult freely. He did not believe they were quite right. But one thing he knew; if the Catholics had declared war on him, he was in a tough spot. In the Smith-Hoover campaign two men, one a jeweler and the other a lime and cement dealer, had let it be known that they were members of the Ku Klux Klan and were outspokenly against Smith because he was a Catholic. Those two were the only Gibbsville business men who had come out in the open. And now both of them were bankrupt.

Drying his hands Julian thought it might be a good idea

to sound out Monsignor Creedon, and he sat down to wait for the priest to come back to the locker-room. He pushed the button and told William, the locker-room waiter, to get a bottle of Scotch out of his locker and put it with two glasses and ice and clubsoda on a small table near the locker. He poured himself a mild drink and lit a cigarette.

Men and boys wandered in, making cracks about his being exclusive. Bobby Herrmann came in and before he could say anything Julian told him to keep his trap shut. One or two of the younger kids showed by the expression of their faces when they saw the extra empty glass and the bottle of Scotch that they thought Julian was being ignored. It was pretty funny. They wanted to be nice, he could see, and they wanted to have a drink, but their wanting to be nice and their wanting a drink were not enough to make them associate with an outcast. What the hell had he done? he wondered. He had thrown a drink in a man's face. An especially terrible guy who should have had a drink thrown in his face a long while ago. It wasn't as if Harry Reilly were a popularity contest winner or something. If most people told the truth they would agree that Reilly was a terrible person, a climber, a nouveau riche even in Gibbsville where fifty thousand dollars was a sizable fortune. Julian thought back over some other terrible things, really terrible things, that people had done in the club without being made to feel they had committed sacrilege. There was the time Bobby Herrmann or Whit Hofman or Froggy Ogden—no one knew which—wanted to test a carboy of alcohol which Whit had bought. One of the three (they all were very drunk at the time) touched a match to the alcohol to see if it was genuine, and a table, chairs, a bench, and part of a row of lockers were ruined or destroyed before the fire was extinguished. There was the time a member of a visiting golf team was swinging a mashie in the locker-room and Joe Schermerhorn walked into the swing and got a broken jaw, lost his beautiful teeth and went a little bit nuts so that two years later, when his car went off the Lincoln Street bridge, people said it was suicide. Did they hold that against the visiting golfer? Hardly. He still visited the club and got drunk with the boys. There was the time Ed Klitsch wandered stark naked upstairs to the steward's living quarters and presented himself, ready for action, to the steward's wife. That was remembered as a good joke. There were innumerable vomitings, more or less disastrous. There was the hair-pulling, face-scratching episode between Kitty Hofman and Mary Lou Diefenderfer, after Kitty heard that Mary Lou had said Kitty ought to be suppressed by the vice squad. There was the time Elinor Holloway— heroine of many an interesting event in club history— shinnied half way up the flagpole while five young gentlemen, standing at the foot of the pole, verified the suspicion that Elinor, who had not always lived in Gibbsville, was not naturally, or at least not entirely, a blonde. There was the time, the morning after a small, informal party for a visiting women's golf team, when a Mrs. Goldorf and a Mrs. Smith, and Tom Wilk, the Reverend

Mr. Wilk's son, and Sam Campbell, the caddymaster, all had to have the stomach pump. That was complicated by the fact that they were all together, in bed or on the floor, in Sam's room upstairs in the caddyhouse. There was the time Whit Hofman and Carter Davis got so sore at a New York orchestra that wanted too much money to play overtime, that they broke all the instruments and pushed the bass drum all the way down the club hill to the state highway. The result of that was a nice suit, some Philadelphia publicity, and a temporary blacklisting of the club by the musicians' union. There were numerous physical combats between husbands and wives, and not always the husbands that matched the wives. Kitty Hofman, for instance, had been given a black eye by Carter Davis when she kicked him in the groin for dunking her head in a punch bowl for calling him a son of a bitch for telling her she looked like something the cat dragged in. And so on. Julian had another drink and a fresh cigarette.

And then there were people. Terrible people, who didn't have to do anything to make them terrible, but were just terrible people. Of course they usually did do something, but they didn't have to. There was (Mrs.) Emily Shawse, widow of the late Marc A. Shawse, former mayor of Gibbsville, and one-time real estate agent, who had developed the West Park section of Gibbsville. Mrs. Shawse did not participate in club activities, but she was a member. She came down to the club summer afternoons and sat alone on the porch, at one end of the porch, watching the golfers and tennis players and the people in the pool. She would have a fruit lemonade on the porch, and have one sent out to Walter, her Negro chauffeur. She would stay an hour and leave, and go for a drive in the country, presumably. But if she wasn't having an affair with Walter, Gibbsville missed its guess. No one ever had seen her speak with Walter, not even good-morning-Walter, good-morning-Mrs.-Shawse; but it certainly looked fishy. Walter had the car, a Studebaker sedan, at all hours of the day and night. He always had money to bet on the races, and he was a good customer at the Dew Drop Inn, where the Polish and Lithuanian girls had not been brought up to draw the color line. Julian prided himself on the fact that he had blocked the sale of a Cadillac to Mrs. Shawse. She had wanted one, or at least was ready to buy one in exchange for a little attention, in a nice way, from Julian. She had put him in a tough spot for a while. He couldn't just say he didn't want to sell her a car. He eventually solved the problem by telling her he would give her only a hundred and fifty in a trade involving the Studebaker, which then was worth, trade-in value, about six times that much, and when she still was not rebuffed he sent Louis, the pimply, bowlegged carwasher, with the demonstrator, instead of going himself. Mrs. Shawse kept the Studebaker. There was Harry Reilly's own nephew, Frank Gorman, a squirt if ever there was one. Frank got drunk at every last party the minute his mother went home. It was because of him that she came to the club dances. He was at Georgetown, having been kicked out of Fordham and Villanova, not to mention Lawrenceville, New York Military Academy, Allentown Prep and Gibbsville High School. Frank was a spindle-shanked young man who wore the most collegiate clothes, the kind that almost justify the newspaper editorials. He had a Chrysler roadster, a raccoon coat, adenoids, and some ability as a basketball player. He was a loud-mouth and a good one-punch fighter, who accepted invitations of the younger set as though they were his due. He was the kind of young man who knows his rights. His uncle secretly hated him, but always referred to him, with what was mistaken for bashful pride, as that crazy kid. There was the Reverend Mr. Wilk, who had had the club raided under the Volstead Act. There was Dave Hartmann, who wiped his shoes on clean towels and in seven years had not been known to violate the club rule against tipping servants and caddies, and who belonged to the club himself but would not let his wife and two daughters become members. Dave manufactured shoes, and he needed the club in his business, he said. Besides, what would Ivy and the girls get out of the club, when the Hartmann home was in Taqua? It'd be different, he said, if he had his home in Gibbsville. Julian had another Scotch and soda.

He wanted to go on thinking about the terrible people, all members of this club, and the people who were not terrible people but who had done terrible things, awful things. But now he got nothing out of it; it made him feel no better, no surer of himself. It had in the beginning, for there were many things he had thought of that were worse things than he had done. What Ed Klitsch had done, for instance. A thing that could have a terrible effect on a decent woman like Mrs. Losch; or it might have made Losch think that his wife invited Klitsch's little attention. And so on. But the trouble with making yourself feel better by thinking of bad things that other people have done is that you are the only one who is rounding up the stray bad things. No one but yourself bothers to make a collection of disasters. For the time being you are the hero or the villain of the thing that is uppermost in the minds of your friends and acquaintances. You can't even say, "But look at Ed Klitsch. What about Carter and Kitty? What about Kitty and Mary Lou? Aren't I better than Mrs. Shawse?" The trouble with that is that Ed Klitsch and Carter and Kitty and Mary Lou and Mrs. Shawse have nothing to do with the case. Two more kids looked at Julian and said hyuh, but they did not hover thirstily and wait for him to offer them a drink. He wondered about that again, and as it had many times in the last year and a half, Age Thirty stood before him. Age Thirty. And those kids were nineteen, twenty-one, eighteen, twenty. And he was thirty. "To them," he said to himself, "I am thirty. I am too old to be going to their house parties, and if I dance with their girls they do not cut in right away, the way they would on someone their own age. They think I am old." He had to say this to himself, not believing it for a moment. What he did believe was that he was precisely as young as they, but more of a person because he was equipped with experience and a permanent face. When he was twenty, who was thirty? Well, when he was twenty the men he would have looked up to were now forty. No, that wasn't quite right. He had another drink, telling himself that this would be his last. Let's see; where was he? Oh, yes. When I was forty. Oh, nuts. He wished Monsignor Creedon would heed the call of nature. He got up and went out to the verandah.

It was a fine night. (Fine had been a romantic word in his vocabulary ever since he read *A Farewell to Arms,* but this was one time when he felt justified in using it.) The fine snow was still there, covering almost everything as far as the eye could see. The fine snow had been there all the time he had been inside, having dinner, dancing with Constance and Jean, and sitting by himself, drinking highballs too fast. He took a deep breath, but not too deep as experience had warned him against that. This was real, this weather. The snow and what it did to the landscape. The farmlands that once, only a little more than a century ago, and less than that in some cases, had been wild country, infested with honest-to-God Indians and panther and wildcat. It still was not too effete. Down under that snow rattlesnakes were sleeping, rattlers and copperheads. A high-powered rifle shot away, or maybe a little more, there were deer, and there were Pennsylvania Dutch families that never spoke English. He remembered during the war, during the draft, when someone had told him about families near the Berks County line, but still in this county. They not only couldn't understand about the war; many of them never had been to Gibbsville. That alone was enough to make a story when he first heard it. Now he wished he had heard more. He resolved to go into it further, find out more about the peculiarities of his native heath. Who did Kentucky think it was that it could claim exclusive rights on hill-billys? "I guess I love this place," he said.

"Good evening, son," said a voice.

He turned. It was Father Creedon. "Oh, Father. Good evening. Cigarette?"

"No, thank you. Cigar for me." The priest took a cigar from a worn, black leather case. He amputated the end of the cigar with a silver cutter. "How are things with you?"

"Fine," said Julian. "Huh. As a matter of fact, anything but fine. I suppose you heard about my performance last night with a friend of yours."

"Yes. I did. You mean Harry Reilly?"

"Uh-huh."

"Well, it's none of my affair," said Monsignor Creedon. "But I wouldn't let it worry you if I were you. I don't imagine Harry Reilly likes to be missing the dancing and all that, but he's a reasonable kind of a fellow. Go to him and tell him you're sorry, and make him think you mean it. He'll listen to reason."

"I did go. Didn't Mrs. Gorman tell you? I went to see him this afternoon and he wouldn't see me."

"Oh, he wouldn't, eh? Well, the next time you see him tell him to go to hell." He chuckled. "No. Don't. I wouldn't want to have that on my conscience. A priest of

God stirring up animosities and so forth and so on. I don't know. You didn't ask me for my advice anyways. But if you can forget for a minute that I'm a priest, and just between you and me, I think Harry Reilly is a horse's ass."

The old man and the young man laughed. "You do?" said Julian.

"I do. If you ever tell that I'll fix your feet, young man. But that's what I think."

"So do I," said Julian.

"We're both right, son," said Monsignor Creedon. "Harry is ambitious. Well, Cæsar was ambitious. A lot of people are ambitious. I was ambitious myself, once, and I got a nice kick in the teeth for it. Ambition's all right, if you know when to stop. As F. P. A. would say, I can take my ambition or leave it alone. Oh, yes, ambition is all right, just as long as you don't get too ambitious."

"Do you read F. P. A.?"

"My God, yes. I get the *World* every day. Of course I'm a Republican, but I have the *World* delivered with the *Ledger*. I miss Broun, though, since he isn't with the *World* any more. Do you read the *World?* I didn't know Cadillac dealers could read. I thought all they had to do was make an X mark on the back of a check."

"I never was meant to be a Cadillac dealer or any other kind of dealer, Father," said Julian.

"That sounded to me as though—you're not a frustrated literary man, by any chance are you? God forbid."

"Oh, no," said Julian. "I'm not anything. I guess I should have been a doctor."

115

"Well—" the priest stopped himself, but his tone made Julian curious.

"What, Father?"

"You won't think this sounds awful? No, of course you won't. You're a Protestant. Well, I'll tell you. I've had my moments of wishing I'd taken some other life work. That doesn't sound bad to you, because you weren't brought up to believe in the true vocation. Well, I guess I better go inside. I keep forgetting I'm an old man."

"How about a drink?" said Julian.

"I will if it isn't too late. I'm fasting." He looked at his big silver watch. "All right. I've time. I'll have one with you."

Surprisingly, no one had taken the bottle of Scotch off the table in Julian's absence. The thieves, which was to say everyone, probably thought the owner of the bottle was in the toilet and was apt to surprise them in the act of stealing the liquor, a heinous offense.

"Oh, Scotch. Fine," said the priest. "Do you like Irish whiskey?"

"I certainly do," said Julian.

"I'll send you a bottle of Bushmill's. It isn't the best Irish whiskey, but it's good. And this stuff is real. Ed Charney sent me a case of it for a Christmas present, heaven only knows why. I'll never do anything for that one. Well, your very good health and a happy New Year. Let's see. Tomorrow's St. Stephen's Day. He was the first martyr. No, I guess we better stick to happy New Year."

"Cheerio," said Julian.

The old priest—Julian wondered exactly how old he was—drank his highball almost bottoms up. "Good whiskey," he said.

"That came from Ed Charney, too," said Julian.

"He has his uses," said the priest. "Thank you, and good-by. I'll send you that Bushmill's tomorrow or next day. 'Bye." He left, a little stoop-shouldered but strong-looking and well-tailored. The talk had given Julian a lift, and the air had sobered him up. The tails hanging over his buttocks, the sleeves of his coat, the legs of his trousers were still cold, covered with cold, from his stand on the verandah, but he felt fine. He hurried out to dance with Caroline and others.

The orchestra was playing Three Little Words. He spotted Caroline, dancing with—it would be—Frank Gorman. Julian cut in, being no more polite about it than he had to.

"Have we met?" said Caroline.

"Ouimet. The name of a golfer. Francis Ouimet," said Julian. "How did you ever remember the name?"

"Where have you been? I looked around for you after I came down from the johnny, but were you anywhere to be seen? Did you greet me at the foot of the stairs? Did you come dashing forth to claim the first dance? Did you? No. You did not. Then an hour passes. And so on."

"I was having a very nice chat with Father Creedon."

"Father Creedon? You were not. Not for long. He's been sitting with Mrs. Gorman and her party most of the evening. You were getting drunk and you just happened to give him one drink so you could truthfully say you'd been with him. I know you, English."

"You're wrong as hell. He was with me for a long time. And I learned something."

"What?"

"He thinks Harry Reilly is a horse's ass," said Julian. She did not reply.

"What's the matter with that? I think so too. I see eye to eye with Rome on that."

"How did he happen to say that? What did you say that made him say that?"

"I didn't say anything to make him say that. All I said was . . . I don't remember how it started. Oh, yes. He asked me how I felt and I said fine, and then I said no, anything but fine. I was standing outside on the verandah, and he came out for a breath of air, and so we got to talking and I said I supposed he'd heard about my altercation with Harry and I told him I'd been around to apologize, and I said Harry had refused to see me, and then Creedon said he thought Harry was a horse's ass."

"That doesn't sound much like him."

"That's what I thought, but he explained it beforehand. He said he wasn't talking as a priest, but just as man to man. After all, darling, there's no law that says he has to dearly love all the people who go to his church, is there?"

"No. Well, I'm just sorry you talked to him about it. Even if he doesn't go right back and tell—"

"Oh, for God's sake. You were never so wrong in your whole life. Father Creedon's a swell guy."

"Yes, but he's a Catholic, and they stick together."

"Oh, nuts. You're trying to build this up into a world catastrophe."

"Oh, yeah? And what are you doing? You're trying to pass it off as though it were the least important thing in the world, just a little exchange of pleasantries. Well, you're wrong, Julian."

"Aw-haw. Now we're getting to the Julian stage. I get it."

"Will you listen? This thing isn't going to blow over and be forgotten, and I wish you'd stop thinking it is. I've tried to tell you what you should have known yourself, that Harry Reilly is a bad enemy."

"How do *you* know? How do you know so much about Harry Reilly's characteristics or avenging moods or what-have-you? If you don't mind my saying so, you give me a pain in the ass."

"Okay," said Caroline.

"Oh, I'm sorry. Believe me? I'm sorry. Please forgive me." He held her closer. "Have we still got a date for midnight?"

"I don't know."

"You don't know? Just because I said that?"

"Oh, I think you're unfair. I think it's a dirty trick, and you always do it. You make me very angry about something and then you refuse to go on with the discussion, but instead you blithely talk about love and going to bed. It's a dirty trick, because if I refuse to talk about loving you,

you become the injured party and so on. It's a lousy trick and you do it all the time."

The music stopped but almost immediately resumed with Can This Be Love? The orchestra was not doing so well with the back-time, and that disturbed Julian, whose ear for jazz was superb.

"See?" said Caroline.

"What?"

"I was right. You're sulking."

"For God's sweet sake, I'm not sulking. Do you want to know what I was thinking?"

"Go ahead."

"Well, this'll make you mad, I have no doubt, but I was thinking what a lousy band this is. Does that make you sore?"

"In a way, yes," said Caroline.

"I was thinking what a foolish economy it is to save money on an orchestra. After all, the most important thing at a dance is the music, isn't it?"

"Must I talk about that?"

"Without the music there would be no dance. It's like playing golf with cheap clubs, or playing tennis with a dollar racket, or bad food. It's like anything cheap." He drew his head back, away from her so he could observe the effect of his words. "Now you take a Cadillac—"

"Oh, cut it out, Ju. Please."

"Why?"

"Because I want you to. Because you ought to."

"What's the matter? My God, you're sourball tonight. You ask me not to drink, and I don't drink. You—"

"Oh, yeah?"

"Well, you asked me not to get tight, and I'm not a bit tight. You said I could drink. Let's go outside. I want to talk to you."

"No. I don't want to go out."

"Why not?"

"It's too cold, for one thing. And I don't feel like it."

"Well, that's the best reason. Does that mean you're not going to keep our date at intermission?"

"I don't know. I'm not sure." She spoke slowly.

He said nothing. Then presently she spoke. "All right," she said. "I'll go out with you."

They danced to the foyer, broke, and ran to the anonymous sedan nearest the verandah. They got in and she sat with her arms drawn close to her ribs. He lit a cigarette for her.

"What is the matter, darling?" he said.

"God, I'm cold."

"Do you want to talk, or are you going to just say how cold you are?"

"What do you want to talk about?" she said.

"About you. Your attitude. I want to try to find out what's eating you. There isn't a single thing I've done tonight that you can find fault with."

"Except calling me a horse's ass."

"You're crazy! I didn't call you that. That was what

old What's Iss called Harry Reilly. I said you gave me a pain in the ass, which isn't quite the same."

"All right."

"And I said I was sorry, and I am sorry. But that's not the point. We're just quibbling—"

"You mean I am."

"Yes, frankly. I do mean that. Oh, Christ! What the hell is it? Please say something. Tell me what's the matter. Bawl me out or do anything you like, but don't sit there freezing like a martyr. Like some kind of a St. Stephen."

"What?"

"St. Stephen was the first martyr. Father Creedon told me that."

"My, you kept the talk on a high plane, didn't you?"

"Will you for the last time, will you tell me why you have a fig—what's the matter?"

"I'm freezing, Julian. I've got to go in. I shouldn't have come out without a coat."

"I'll look around in the other cars and borrow a robe, if you'll stay."

"No, I don't think we'd better," she said. "I'm going in. This was a mistake, coming out here."

"You had no intention of talking when you came out."

"No. I don't suppose I did, but I didn't want to have a scene on the dance floor."

"Have a scene on the dance floor! All right. You can go. I won't keep you. Just one question. *Is* there something I've done? Any one thing that you're sore about?"

"No. Not exactly. No. There isn't."

"One more question. Maybe I'd better not ask it."

"Go ahead," she said, with her hand on the door of the sedan.

"All right: Is there something you've done? Have you done anything? Have you fallen in love with someone else?"

"Or necked someone else?" she said. "Or laid someone else while you were sneaking your drinks in the locker room? No. My attitude, as you call it, comes from something much more subtle than that, Julian, but we won't go into it now."

He took her in his arms. "Oh, I love you so much. I always will. I always have and I always will. Don't do this." She held up her chin while he kissed her neck and rubbed his mouth and nose against her breast, but when he cupped his left hand over her right breast she said, "No. No. I don't want you to do that. Let me go, please."

"Have you got the curse?"

"Please don't talk that way, say things like that. You know perfectly well I haven't."

"That's right. I do. I thought you might have got it suddenly."

"You think that's the only possible explanation for the way I feel?"

"At least there is some explanation, or there ought to be. You won't tell me what it is?"

"It'd take too long. And now I *am* going. It isn't like

123

you to keep me waiting out here with the temperature near zero."

"Mm. Giving me a break. Okay. Let's go." He got out of the car and made one last effort to take her in his arms by carrying her to the verandah, but she was on the steps without even seeming to spurn his gesture. She went inside and immediately went up the stairs to the ladies' quarters. He knew she did not expect him to be waiting when she came down, so he went out and joined the stag line. He saw Mill Ammermann and he was waiting for her to dance or be danced close enough to the stag line and he was going to cut in on her, when suddenly something happened that was like migraine: he did not see anyone in the room nor anything, yet the people and the lights and the things hurt his eyes. And the reason for it was that in one and the same instant he remembered that he had not asked Caroline to say yes or no about the date at intermission—and he realized that he did not need to ask her.

He recovered a sense which may not have been sight, but whatever it was it enabled him to find his way back to the locker-room, where there was enough liquor for anyone in the world to get drunk.

5

WHEN Caroline Walker fell in love with Julian English she was a little tired of him. That was in the summer of 1926, one of the most unimportant years in the history of the United States, and the year in which Caroline Walker was sure her life had reached a pinnacle of uselessness. She was four years out of college then, and she was twenty-seven years old, which is as old as anyone ever gets, or at least she thought so at the time. She found herself thinking more and more and less and less of men. That is the way she put it, and she knew it to be sure and right, but she did not bother to expand the -ism. "I think of them oftener, and I think of them less often." She had attained varying degrees of love, requited and unrequited—but seldom the latter. Men, and damn good men, fell in love with her with comforting regularity, and she had enough trouble with them, in one way or another, to make it impossible for her to tell herself honestly that she was unattractive. She was sorry she was not beautiful—until a nice old gentleman, a Philadelphian who painted society women's portraits, told her that he never had seen a beautiful woman.

That summer she thought of her life after college in

three ways: she thought of it as unicellular, but a life that reversed the amoeba's performance. The days got together and formed one life, losing their separate identities. Again, she thought of those four years as calendar years, broken formally by the Assembly (New Year's Eve), the July 3 Assembly, Easter, Hallowe'en, Labor Day. Put together they made four years, the length of time she had passed at Bryn Mawr, and like the years of college in that they seemed so long a time and so short a time, but also not at all like the college years, because she felt she had got something out of college. These four years had not had the compactness of college, and they seemed wasted.

They were wasted. She took her turn teaching the Italian and Negro children at the Gibbsville Mission, which is what passes for the Junior League in Gibbsville. But she didn't like it. She had no poise or assurance with those children, or any group of children, and she knew she was not a teacher. She almost loved two or three of the children, but somewhere in the back of her mind she recognized the reason: the Mission children that she liked best were the ones who were least like the other Mission children and more like Lantenengo Street children, the children of her friends. There was one exception: a red-headed Irish brat who she was certain had let the air out of her tires and hid her hat. He never called her Miss Walker or Miss Car'line, as the other little sycophants did. He was about eleven years old—the limit of Mission children was twelve years of age—and he had a face that it would take him at least twenty more years to grow up to. She liked

him but she hated him; she was afraid of him and the way
he sometimes would stare at her when he wasn't making
trouble. At home when she thought of him she would tell
herself that he was a child whose great energy could and
ought to be directed into useful channels. He was just a
mischievous kid, and he could be "saved." . . . Thus
practically her entire sociological knowledge at the time.
She was to learn a little more.

The Gibbsville Mission was an old, three-story brick
house in the very dingiest part of Gibbsville, and was supported by Lantenengo Street contributions. Babies were
brought there to be cared for through the day by girls
like Caroline, and a professional nurse. Then in the afternoon, after the parochial and public schools closed for the
day, the children up to twelve came to play and be read
to until six o'clock, when they were sent home, their supper appetites spoiled by a pint of milk.

One afternoon in the spring of 1926 Caroline had said
good-by to the children and had gone around, tried doors,
getting ready to close the Mission for the day. She was
putting on her hat, standing in front of the mirror in the
office, when she heard a footstep. Before she could see who
it was—she saw it was a child—two arms went around her
legs and two hands slid up under her skirt, and a red little
head was burrowing into her stomach. She slapped down
at him and tried to push him away, and finally succeeded,
but he had touched her where he wanted to with his vile
little fingers, and she went insane and struck him many

127

times, knocking him to the floor and kicking him until he crawled and ran away, out of the office, crying.

Her great fear for days after that was that his grimy hands had given her a venereal disease. He never came back to the Mission, and she resigned the next week, but for weeks she was sure she had syphilis or *something*. The incident finally sent her, dying of mortification, to Doctor Malloy, to whom she told all. He very seriously examined her—he was not the family physician—and told her to come back the day after the next for the laboratory report; and then soberly informed her that she was free to marry and have babies, that there was nothing wrong with her. When she insisted on paying him he charged her fifteen dollars. This money he gave, without Caroline's knowledge, to be sure, to the mother of the redhead, on the theory that the mother of such a child would appreciate anything in the way of a gift, without inquiring into the reason for the gift.

That was Caroline's first completely unpleasant encounter with the male sex. She thought of it constantly in the days that followed. When she asked herself, "Why did he do it?" she always came to the same answer: that that was what you could expect of men, what she had been brought up to expect of men. She had had many men run over her with their hands, and there were some with whom she permitted it. She was still a virgin at that time, but until the child made his mysterious attack she thought she had sex pretty well under control. After the attack she reorganized, or entirely disorganized, her ideas about men and the whole of sex; and the one permanent effect of "that afternoon at the Mission," as she referred to it in her frequent introspection, was that her ignorance of sex was pointed up. She knew herself for a completely inexperienced girl, and for the first time she began to remember the case histories in Havelock Ellis and Krafft-Ebing and the lesser psychologists as more than merely pornography.

Up to that summer Caroline had been deeply in love twice in her life, although from the time she put her hair up she was always in love with someone. One of the men, the first, was a distant cousin of hers, Jerome Walker. He was an Englishman by birth and education, and he came to Gibbsville in 1918. He was about twenty-five and a captain in the British army. He was through, so far as the war was concerned; they were taking more and more bone out of his left leg, and putting in more and more silver. His presence in the United States, which he never before had visited, was to teach modern warfare to the draft army. Gibbsville girls threw themselves at him when he turned up at Caroline's house on a month's leave, and he was invited everywhere, a catch. He wore slacks, which were slightly unmilitary, and the stick he carried had a leather thong which he wrapped around his wrist. His tunic was beautifully tailored, and the little blue and white ribbon of the Military Cross, which no one identified, gave a nice little touch of color to his uniform. His lack of height fitted in with the fact that he was an invalid, a "casuality," as most of the Gibbsville women—and men—

called him. He took one careful look at Caroline and then and there decided for himself that this girl in the three-cornered hat and long gray spats and nicely cut suit was going to be something worth trying for. He was quite confident he could swing it in a month's time.

He very nearly did. Caroline's father was dead, and her mother was deaf, the kind of deaf person who, not wishing to yield to her deafness, refuses to learn to read lips or to wear earphones. In the Walker mansion on South Main Street were Caroline, her mother, the cook and the maid. And Jerry.

The first time he kissed her he all but gave up his ideas of having an affair with her. It was awfully far from the war, this warm room in Gibbsville in Pennsylvania in America, and there was nothing particularly warlike about "Oui, oui, Marie, will you do ziss for me?" which was going round and round on the phonograph. Caroline, except for her horrible accent, might have been an English girl, a sister of a friend, at home. But when she got up to change the needle and the record he reached out and took her hand and drew her to him, sat her on his right knee, and kissed her. She went to him without resistance but only the thought: "Well, we can kiss, can't we?" But the kiss was not very successful, because they bumped noses in trying to get their heads at the right angles, and he let her go. She stopped the Victrola and came back and sat beside him. He took her hand and she looked at it and then looked up presently at him. They did not speak, and when she looked at him he was smiling very gently. A nervous smile came and went on her face and then she moved closer to him and really kissed him. But the moment of unscrupulousness had passed for him. She was all body and sensation and he had the terrible consciousness that while she felt this way, anything he chose to do to her, anything, would not be resisted.

This lasted a minute, two minutes, maybe five, before she squeezed back into herself and put her head on his shoulder. She was ashamed and grateful, because she never before had let herself go that way. "Let's have a cigarette," she said.

"Do you smoke?"

"I'm not allowed to, but I do. You hold it and I'll take a puff."

He got his silver case out of his trousers pocket and she smoked, not holding the cigarette very expertly, but taking appalling inhales. Cute was the word for her as she sat there, blowing smoke out of her mouth and nostrils, smoking the cigarette too fast. He took it from her to cool it off, and then they heard the quick catch of her mother's car, a Baker electric, in the driveway on the way back to the stable. Caroline got up and put Poor Butterfly on the Vic. "That's one of our old records," she said, "but I like it because it's so syncopated." Anything that had the sound of the trap-drummer's wood blocks in it was syncopated.

They often kissed after that; in the halls, the butler's pantry, and in her Scripps-Booth roadster, which had a peculiar seating arrangement; the driver sat a foot or so forward of the other seat, which made kissing an awkward act.

He went away without telling her that he loved her, and without changing her status as woman or girl. He was dead of gangrene within six months of his visit to Gibbsville, and it was another two months before his family remembered to write to them. That had something to do with lessening Caroline's grief: that he could have been lying dead in a grave while she went on thinking of him as the love of her life, while she was having a lovely time with the boys who were back from France and Pensacola and Boston Tech and the Great Lakes Naval Training Station. She was in demand, and she kissed a good many men with as much abandon as she had kissed Jerome Walker, except that now she knew how and when to stop. She was getting to be a prom trotter, too, as much as Bryn Mawr would permit, and having a perfectly wonderful time with the college boys. They were gay again now that the war was over and their universal embarrassment at not being in the fighting army was at an end, now that it was all right to be gay publicly. She was leaving for a week-end at Easton, where Ju English was in college, when her mother read the letter from England, which was mostly about how grateful the Cecil Walkers were for the hospitality their boy had received in Gibbville, as they called it. There was one reference to Caroline. It was: ". . . and if you and your dear little girl should come to England, we shall . . ." Oh, well. But not oh, well. She knew, or hoped she knew, that the reason he did not tell his mother more about her was that he didn't want his mother to think things. Still, on the ride to Easton she was depressed. When our minds run that way we date periods in our lives, and Caroline in later days and years fixed the train ride to Easton as the end of her girlhood. All her life, until she fell in love with Julian English, she was to feel that if things had been different, she would have married her cousin and lived in England, and she always thought very kindly of England. She did not, however, visit Jerome's family when she went abroad in 1925. She was only going to be gone two months altogether, and by that time she was in love with a living man.

Joe Montgomery could be classified under many headings. Drunk. Snake. Rich boy. Well-dressed man. Debbies' delight. Roué. Bond salesman. War veteran. Extra man. And so on. They all added up to the same thing. His chief claim to distinction was that he had known Scott Fitzgerald at Princeton, and that made him in Caroline's eyes an ambassador from an interesting country, full of interesting people whom she wanted to meet and to see in action. She did not know, of course, that she was a member in good standing of the community which she thought Joe Montgomery represented, which Fitzgerald wrote about. She only knew that Gibbsville was her home town, but it or the people who lived in it certainly were not worth writing about.

Joe Montgomery's home was in Reading, which is across two state lines from New York, but actually in the

133

same radius as Hartford or New London—a fact which apparently is not known to any New Yorkers or to most Reading people, but was taken for granted by Joe Montgomery. His father was so rich that he had gone down in the *Titanic,* and it was told of Henry Montgomery, as it has been told of almost every other male on that vessel's passenger list, that he had been (a) a hero, and (b) that the captain had had to shoot him dead to keep him out of the women's and children's lifeboats. Things in Joe's background included vague recollections in Caroline's mind of a Stutz Bearcat, a raccoon coat, Brooksy clothes, and some local reputation as a golfer. He knew a few people in Gibbsville, and he was a friend of Whitney Hofman's, but he seldom came to Gibbsville.

He was hardly more than a name to Caroline in 1925, when she was thrown with him for a festive week in East Orange, just before her trip abroad. She was being a bridesmaid and he an usher at a wedding there, and she was elated when he said: "Lord, God, don't introduce me to *Car*oline *Walker.* She and I are old pals. Or are we, Caroline?" He was about the best there was at the wedding, and she probably kissed him more frequently and more ardently than she did the other ushers. He must have thought so, because he stayed over in New York for her last week before sailing. The wedding fuss ended Sunday, the last day of May, and she was sailing in the *Paris* the next Saturday. He tried to monopolize her time, and all but did. He took her to see shows—"Lady Be Good," with the Astaires and Walter Catlett, which she had seen in Philadelphia; "What Price Glory?"; "Rose Marie"; Richard Bennett and Pauline Lord in "They Knew What They Wanted"; the Garrick Gaieties. It was a stifling week, although only the first week of June. The whole country seemed to want to die, and, led by a former vice president who once made a remark about what this country needed, die many of them did. Joe kept saying "*Jee*-zuzz," unable to forget the heat, and after the first act of "What Price Glory?" he had no trouble persuading her to not go back. He had his car, a red Jordan roadster, in town, and he suggested driving out to Long Island, Westchester, anywhere. "I'll swear for you and tell you some war stories," he said. "And you'll think you're still at the play."

He had enough sense or intuition not to try to talk much until they got out of the city. The heat was awful; it got up her nose, and everyone whose eyes met hers had a silly smile on his face that seemed to apologize for the weather. And she guessed she looked that way herself.

They finally came to a place on Long Island which Joe told her was called Jones's Beach. "How are you fixed for underwear?" he said.

"Oh. So that's it?"

"Yes, I guess it is. I won't go in unless you do."

Her heart was thumping and there was a shaking in her legs, but "All right," she said. She never had seen a grown man with all his clothes off at one time, and when he walked away from his side of the car and stepped toward the water she was relieved to see that he was wearing shorts, part of his underwear. "You go on in," she said. She wanted him to be in the water when she moved from the shelter of the car in her brassiere and step-ins. He got the idea and did not look until she was swimming a few yards away from him.

"What this is going to do to my hair," she said.

"Too late to worry about it now," he said. "You cold?"

"Not now," she said.

"I should have built a fire. I didn't think of it."

"God, no! And have people see it and come running down? Gosh, I'm glad you didn't."

He came out first. "Better not stay in too long," he said. "You can use my undershirt for a towel." He went back to the car and started the motor and held his undershirt, which was damp from perspiration, near the engine. "Better come out now," he said.

She came out, pulling her soaking step-ins about so as to get a maximum of modesty. Her brassiere was no good at all, and she was so angry at her swinging breasts that she wanted to cry; no matter how nice he was he couldn't fail to notice her "chest."

"Don't be embarrassed," he said. "I've seen a naked woman."

"Oh—" she mumbled. "You haven't seen me. Or hadn't."

"Please don't. You'll take the enjoyment out of the swim. Go on back and swim a little more and then come out without being self-conscious. Or anyhow, embarrassed. Go on."

136

She did as he said and felt better. She felt fourteen years old. Less. She had not overcome her embarrassment, but she no longer was afraid. She dried herself with his warm undershirt. "I don't know what I'm going to do about my hair."

"Here." He threw her a clean handkerchief. "That'll help a little." It didn't.

He gave her the coat of his dinner suit and made her put it on over her evening dress, and they had cigarettes and were only vaguely aware of the discomfort. "I guess we could have saved all this trouble by going somewhere to a regular beach, or pool."

"I'm glad now we didn't," she said.

"Are you? That's what I wanted you to say."

"Did you? I'm glad I said it then."

He put his arm around her and tried to kiss her.

"No," she said.

"All right," he said.

"Don't spoil it," she added.

"It wouldn't spoil it. Not now. At least I don't think so. I waited till you were dressed."

"Yes, and I'm glad you did. I like you for that, Joe. But even now. *You* know."

"No, frankly. I don't know what you mean."

"Yes, you do. You—oh, hell."

"Oh, you mean because I saw you without any clothes on."

"Mm-hmm," she said, although up to then she had been thinking that technically he had not seen her without *any* clothes on. Now she wished she had been completely nude. It was something you had to get over, and with Joe it had been a grand chance.

"All right," he said, and took his arm away.

They talked about her trip abroad. It was her first. He said he wished he were going with her, or could go in time to take her around Paris and so on, but he couldn't make it; he had to be a good boy at the National City, because it was time he was getting somewhere and making some money. A crooked lawyer and his mother's stupidity had reduced his father's estate. So he was working for the National City, with an office in Reading and a salary that just proved to him how worthless he was. She couldn't muster much pity for him; she had seen the Montgomery home, Mrs. Montgomery's Rolls.

"Well, this is all very nice," she said, "but I think maybe we'd better start back to town. How far is it?"

"Oh, plenty of time. It isn't far. I don't really know how far it is exactly. Let's not go back right away. You're going away so soon, and for such a long time."

"But I have so many things to do," she said. "You've no idea."

"Oh, yes, I have. Turkish towels, six. Heavy woolen underwear, six. Handkerchiefs, twelve. Two sweaters. The school will supply sheets and bed linen, but we recommend, and so on. All marked with indelible ink or Cash's woven labels."

"But I have. I have to—"

"Parents are specially urged to exercise restraint in pro-

138

viding boys with pocket money. A dollar and a half a week will be sufficient for most needs."

"Oh, Joe."

"The use of motorcycles is absolutely prohibited."

"What about cigarettes?"

"Members of the Upper Middler and higher forms are permitted to use tobacco on written permission of one or both parents."

"I could tell you some you don't know," she said.

"Such as?"

"Oh—girls' schools."

"Oh, that's easy. In cases where a girl is likely to be absent from class and other activities at frequent intervals during the school year, a letter from the family physician, addressed to the school nurse—"

"That's enough," she said. She was embarrassed and angry with herself. Here she was, talking about the most intimate part of a woman's life, with a man whom she did—not—really—know. It was the second time tonight that she had done a "first" thing with him: he was the first to see her with nothing on (she had well-founded misgivings about the protection the step-ins had given her), and he was the first to talk to her about That. She hated all the euphemisms for it, and when she thought of it she thought of it in the Bryn Mawr term: "Off the sports list."

His arm was around her again and his head was close to hers. He thought she was angry with him, and for the moment she did not care; but then she rested her face on his shoulder, and she put up her mouth for the kiss and then she let herself coast with him. He took down her dress and kissed her breasts and she patted and rubbed his head. She waited without tension for what he would do next. She thought she knew what that would be, and she did not prepare to fight against it. But she was wrong. He suddenly slipped her shoulder straps up her arms and back where they belonged. Her breath was coming as though she had stopped running a few minutes ago, slowly and deeply.

"You virgin?" he said.

"Yes," she said.

"Are you sure? Please tell me the truth."

"Mm-hmm. I am."

"Do you love me?" he said.

"Yes, I think I do, Joe."

"How old are you?" he said.

"Twenty-five. Twenty-six soon. No. I *am* twenty-six."

"Oh. Then you want to be a virgin when you get married. That's why you are now."

"I guess so," she said. "I don't know." She ran her teeth over her lower lip. "It's never been like this before." She put her arm around his neck. He kissed her.

"Will you be engaged to me?" he said. "Is there anyone else?"

"No, there's no one else important right now."

"Well?"

"Yes," she said. "You don't want to announce it now, or anything like that, do you?"

"No. I suppose we'd better be sensible and let you have your trip and two months away from me and see if you still love me."

"Do you love me?" she said. "You haven't actually said so."

"I love you," he said. "And you're the first girl I've told that to in—nineteen twenty-five—eight years. Do you believe me?"

"It's possible," she said. "Eight years. You mean since 1917. The war?"

"Yes."

"What happened?" she said.

"She was married," he said.

"Do you still see her?"

"Not for two years. She's in the Philippines. Her husband's in the Army and now they have three children. It's all over."

"Would you marry me if I weren't a virgin?"

"I don't know. I honestly don't know. That wasn't the reason I asked you if you were. I wanted to know because —do you want me to tell you the truth?"

"Of course."

"Well, I was going to ask you to spend the night with me if you weren't."

"In which case you probably wouldn't have asked me to marry you."

"Maybe. I don't know. But I do want you to marry me. You will, won't you? Don't get a yen for some Frenchman."

"I won't. I almost wish I weren't going, but I guess it's a good thing I am." Her voice was low and dramatic.

"What makes you say it like that?"

"The obvious reason. I have a theory, Joe. I've always told myself that when I loved a man enough to want to marry him, I'd have an affair with him before we announced the engagement, and then have a short engagement and get married practically right away."

"Oh. That means you haven't really been in love all your life."

"No. It doesn't mean that. Not quite. But I haven't been in love since I made that decision. Since I've found out more about sex. God! Is that clock right?"

"A few minutes fast."

"How many minutes fast?"

"Oh. I don't know."

"No, honestly. Even if it's a half hour fast look what time that means. We've got to go back. I hate to, but please, darling?"

"All right," he said.

Half way back to town she remembered something that made her want to let out a cry, to melt away, to die. The worst of it was she would have to tell him now.

"Joe, darling," she said.

"Yes, ma'am."

"I just remembered something, the worst thing I can think of. Oh, damn it all. I wish people . . ."

"What is it?"

"I'm not going to be able to see you tomorrow night."

"Why not? Can't you break it?"

"No. I should have told you before, but I didn't know we were—I was going to. All this tonight, about us. Some people are coming over from Gibbsville to see me off."

"Who? Who is the guy?"

"Well, it's not just one person. There is a man—"

"Who? Do I know him?"

"I don't know. Julian English. He's coming, and some people named Ogden. I think you know them."

"Froggy? Sure. I've met English a couple of times, too. He's a college boy, isn't he?"

"No. He's out."

"Are you in love with him? I hope not. He isn't so hot. He cheats at cards. He takes dope."

"He does not!" she exclaimed. "He doesn't do any such thing. He *drinks* too much, maybe."

"Oh, darling, don't you know when I'm fooling? I don't know anything about him. I'm not even sure I'd know him if I saw him. Yes, I would. But you're not in love with him, are you?"

"I'm in love with you. Oh, I do love you. And that's what makes it worse. I wish you could come along to-morrow night, my last night before I sail. But I don't think that'd be so good."

"Oh, no. Mr. English wouldn't like it."

"It isn't that. I'm not only thinking of him. But Jean and Froggy are coming all the way from Gibbsville just to see me off and we planned a big bender in New York tomorrow night. I'm not a bit pleased about it now, but there's nothing I can do at this late date."

"No, I guess you're right, damn it. You certainly are the will o' the wisp if I ever saw it."

"Are you going to write to me, a lot?"

"Fourteen Place Vendôme, every day."

"How did you know?"

"Oh, you're a Morgan, Harjes girl, as distinguished from an American Express girl. I'll write every day and cable every week-end. And what will I get for it? A postcard that I'd be ashamed to show to my own mother and a scarf from Liberty's and maybe a Dunhill lighter."

They stopped and bought a comb at a drug store before she would go in the Commodore, where she and Lib Mc-Creery and Is Stannard, Bryn Mawr classmates who were going abroad with her, were stopping. The breeze ended when they stopped the car, and the heat came back and everything began to get a little unsatisfactory and she wanted to go to her room and lie in the water. Their farewell was hurried and she was too conscious of looking like the wrath of God to enjoy any minute of it.

That was one of the things he commented on in his first letters. He had to stay in New York, in the heat, while she was cooling off and feeling like a human being on shipboard. Her letters were ardent and pleasant and pleased, full of new and sudden love. Nicholas Murray Butler and Anne Morgan and Eddie Cantor and Genevieve Tobin and Joseph E. Widener were on board. "I wonder if I love him" became a song the way she said it, and she would sing over and over to herself: "I won-der, I won-der."

"Who? Joe Widener?" said Lib.

"The Joe part is right."

"Joe English, the boy that came down to the boat?"

"His name is Ju, j u for Julian."

"Well, who is it, then?"

"You wouldn't know," said Caroline.

"Oh, I know. The man who brought you back to the hotel in that awful condition."

"That's the one."

But when his letters came they did not match her mood. Discontent and some petulance, and though she snatched at the love passages, she had to be honest with herself and admit that they read more like postscript material. She blamed the heat of New York and Reading and felt sorry for him and said so in her replies. He was the man all during her first trip to Europe whom she missed, with whom she wanted to share the fun of her discovery of foreign lands. And she missed him very much. Then she got a letter from him that soured her trip, or at least divided it into two phases. He wrote and wrote, for pages, but it all boiled down to one thing, which in subsequent days she recognized to be true: ". . . The truth is, darling, some kind of fate threw us together, but the same fate kept us apart the night before you sailed. Those people were fated to come and take you away from me that night. I have a feeling that if they hadn't, you would have put into practice that theory that you spoke of the night we went swimming. But they did come, didn't they? That being the case, you went away without putting your theory into practice and since then I have spoiled it as far as we're concerned with another girl. So I suppose this ought to be quits. I feel like the devil . . ."

She didn't believe the words, and then she wanted to cable him that another girl couldn't make a difference. She loved him, and she regretted as much as he did that she had not spent her last night in New York with him. If only she could have talked to him. But that was impossible, and letters or cables were no good. Late in the afternoon of the day she got the letter she groped through to an explanation for the shock of his letter (which, however, did not make her any less unhappy): he had jolted her by being, so far as she knew, the first man who had tried to be honest with her. Reason did that for her, and then for the first time in her life she made up her mind to get drunk. And that night she did get drunk, with a handsome young Harvard Jew, who turned out to be something fancy in her sex life; he took her by easy stages down the scale of Paris entertainment, ending with a "circus." She didn't remember about that until the next afternoon, when the memory, which she knew she could not have dreamt, came through her hangover. Then and there she wanted to pack and go home, but Is Stannard saved her sanity. When Lib McCreery had gone out to do some shopping Is came in and sat on Caroline's bed. "Where did Henry take you last night?"

"Oh, God. If I only knew."

"Were you that blotto?"

"Oh, Lord," said Caroline.

"Don't you remember anything?"

"Very little."

"Did he—do you remember going to a place where a man and a woman—you know?"

"I think so. I'm afraid so."

"That's where he took me, too. I thought I'd die when I went with him. I don't understand him. I wasn't nearly so drunk as you were. *I* remember. Every detail. But I can't understand Henry. He never touched me. All he did was to keep watching me. He didn't watch *them*, just me. I think he must have got pleasure out of the effect it had on me, those people. I don't think we'd better see that crowd again, that he goes around with. He wants me to go again and he wants you to come."

"God, I feel so terrible. Do you think he did anything to me?" said Caroline.

"Oh, no. I'm sure he didn't. He gets some kind of pleasure out of watching us. There are people like that. You never went the limit, did you, Callie?"

"No."

"Neither did I, and I think someone like Henry can tell that just by looking at you. I really do."

"Then why does he—oh, I wish I were home."

"Don't worry. You notice he didn't ask Lib. I've thought for years that Lib had an affair, probably more than one. So you and I are together on this. Just don't say anything about it to Lib, and if Henry becomes too insistent we can leave Paris. Can I get you some aspirin or something?"

Caroline had had her scare, and she got drunk no more. For the rest of her trip she traded nothing but her dancing ability for the attentions of the English-speaking young men who were attracted to her; and for a year after that the frightening experience with Henry What's His Name, and the disillusioning and humiliating experience with Joe Montgomery dictated her preference in men: they had to be clean, preferably blond, and not in the least glamorous or unusually attractive.

Back home, she had nothing to do in Gibbsville except to play bridge with the girls in the afternoon bridge clubs, and the mixed clubs in the evening; to take a course in shorthand and typewriting at the Gibbsville Business College, with vague notions of a winter in New York in the front of her mind; to turn out for the Tuesday women's golf tournament-and-luncheon; to wheedle contributions on the various tag days; to act as chauffeuse for her mother, who could not learn to drive a combustion-engine car; to give her share of parties. She kept her weight under 115 pounds. She bobbed her hair. She drank a little more than the sociable amount, and she grew mildly profane. She came to know herself to be the most attractive of the Lantenengo Street girls. Without getting the rush that the girls still in school would get at dances, she still was more universally popular; the boys in the school crowd danced with her and so did the males of all ages up to forty, and a few did who were more than forty. She never had to pretend that she was having a better time sitting with a highball than she did on the dance floor. The girls she knew liked her without calling her a good sport or trusting her too far with their husbands or fiancés. They really did trust her, but they did not trust their men.

At the beginning of the summer of 1926 she recapitulated, and acknowledged that she was getting a little hard. She saw most frequently Julian English, Harry Reilly, Carter Davis, and a man from Scranton named Ross Campbell. Julian English was a habit, and she suspected that he went on seeing her because she never said anything about his Polish girl, who was reputed to be beautiful, but whom no one had seen. Harry Reilly was lavish and considerate; in his way, so crazy about her that he was almost self-effacing. Carter Davis was too predictable; she was certain she could tell how many years it would be before the day came when Carter stopped drinking and trying to pick up Irish girls after church Sunday night, and settled down and married a Lantenengo Street girl. "But it won't be me," she said. "Imagine life with a man whose deepest passion was bridge. And the Philadelphia Athletics. And the Cornell football team. God!" Ross Campbell was the most likely prospect for marriage. He was older than the others except Reilly, and he was something that did not exist in Gibbsville; one of those Harvard men, tall and slim and swell, who seem to have put on a clean shirt just a minute ago—soft white shirt with button-down collar—and not to have had a new suit in at least two years. He was not rich; he "had money." He had big strong teeth and his charm had something to do with a deceptive awkwardness, a result of his height, and his St. Paul's-Harvard voice and accent. He became a non-resident member of the Lantenengo Country Club as a matter of course when he began to see Caroline, and that was when Caroline first noticed that he was, besides everything else, a snob. He told her he was going to join. "I'll ask Whitney Hofman to put me up. I think it'd be best to ask him to get someone to second me. I don't really know anyone else." He knew some others as well as he knew Whit Hofman, but Caroline saw that what he meant was that Whit Hofman, being the richest and the impeccable young man of Gibbsville, was the only man of whom he would ask a favor. And so Ross was put up by Mr. Whitney Stokes Hofman, seconded by Mrs. Whitney Stokes Hofman; initiation fee $50, annual dues $25. Then she noticed that he was a bit on the stingy side. He always added restaurant charges before signing the checks. He rolled his own cigarettes, which may have been an honest preference in tobacco, but looked like an economy; and once after winning a few dollars in a bridge game at the club he pocketed his winnings with the remark: "That covers my gas and oil expenses this trip. Not bad." This somehow did not fit in with what you would expect of a man whose life work was "keeping the estate's affairs in shape. I have to. Mother doesn't know the multiplication table higher than the six-times table." Caroline began to see that she was right about his not being a coal-region rich man. Some of the things that made him himself were things that she liked—his manners, his manner, his way of walking into any party with a smile that was pleasant enough but at the same time said, "What have you got to offer me?" She liked the simple fact of his not ever trying to kiss her; she liked it and kept postponing her inquiry as to the reason for it. But by postponing that, or any and all inquiry, she did something else; she lost interest in him. The day came when she did not have to postpone the analysis of his diffidence, and she became merely satisfied with his diffidence. There was no showdown, because she let him see what had happened: she did not care if he never came to Gibbsville. She did not condone her behavior. She knew that her friends—and not only those of her own sex—were for the first time a little in awe of her, practically rediscovering her, because Ross Campbell so obviously was interested in her. She was sorry for her friends, who already were thinking of the New York and Boston ushers; and in a not quite sincere way, she was sorry for herself. After all, there had been six or seven times when she had liked him so enormously at particular moments that she wanted to get closer to him, to put her arms around him. But she never had, and the whole thing spilled away. It wasn't long before it became very, very easy to think of him as a stick, a stuffed shirt.

At the same time she was worried and angry with herself. There was something wrong and incomplete in her relations with all the men she had liked best and loved. They were wrong, and circumstances were wrong; Jerome Walker had been too decent because she was too young;

Joe Montgomery was the man she had loved most in her life, but because of an engagement with other people, she had not seen him on the night before she sailed; Ross Campbell, who was not a great love but certainly was the right man for her to marry, had turned into nothing, right before her eyes. And there weren't any other men; led by Julian English there were a lot of men whom she had kissed or necked with, whom she disliked in retrospect with what approached a passion. Altogether she was contemptuous of the men she had known, no matter how tenderly she remembered minutes in automobiles, motorboats, trains, steamships; on divans or a few times on beds at house parties; on the porches of country clubs, in her own home. But she thought with anger that there was nothing of her that the race of men had not known—except that no one man ever had known her completely. Up to now the passion she had generated would have been enough to—she never finished that. She made up her mind to one thing: if she wasn't married by the time she was thirty, she was going to pick out some man and say, "Look here, I want to have a child," and go to France or some place and have the child. She knew she never *would* do that, but one part of her threatened another part of her with it.

Then, in the spring of 1926, she fell in love with Julian English, and she knew she never had loved anyone else. It was funny. Why, it was the funniest thing in the world. Here he was, taking her out, kissing her good night, ignoring her, seeing a lot of her and then not seeing her at

all, going together to dancing school, kindergarten, Miss
Holton's School—she'd known him all her life, had hid-
den his bicycle up a tree, wet her pants at one of his birthday parties, been bathed in the same tub with him by two
older girls who now had children of their own. He had
taken her to her first Assembly, he had put clay on her
leg when a yellowjacket stung her, he had given her a
bloody nose—and so on. For her there never had been
anyone else. No one else counted. She was a little afraid
that he still loved the Polish girl a little, but she was sure
he loved Caroline the most.

They dodged being in love at first, and because they
always had been friends, his seeing her increasingly more
frequently did not become perceptible until he asked her
to go with him to the July 3 Assembly. You asked a girl
at least a month in advance for the Assemblies, and you
asked the girl you liked best. It was the only one he ever
freely had asked her to; she knew his mother told him to
ask her to the very first one. The Assembly was not just
another dance, and in the time between her accepting and
the night of the dance they both were conscious of it. A
girl gave preference in dates to the man who was taking
her to the Assembly. "You're my girl now," he would
say. "Or at least till after the Assembly." Or she would
call him up and say: "Do you want to drive to Philadelphia with Mother and me? You're my beau now, so I
thought I'd ask you first, but don't say yes unless you
really want to." When he would kiss her she could tell
he was trying to find out how much she knew. The long

kisses in the beginning were like that; no overwhelming passion, but lazy and full of curiosity. They would halt in a long kiss and she would draw back her head and smile at him and he at her, and then without speaking he would put his mouth to hers again. He left it at kissing until one night when he brought her home from the movies and she went upstairs for a minute and saw that her mother was sound asleep. He was in the lavatory on the first floor and he heard her come down the back steps and try the kitchen door. They went to the library. "Do you want a glass of milk?" she said.

"No. Is that why you went to the kitchen?"

"I wanted to see if the maids were in."

"Are they?"

"Yes. The back door's locked." She put up her arms and he came in to them. He lay with his head on her shoulder for a few minutes and then she reached up and pulled the cord of the floor lamp, and moved in on the davenport so that he could lie beside her. He rolled up her sweater, up to her armpits, and unhooked her brassiere, and she unbuttoned his vest and he dropped it and his coat on the floor.

"Don't—don't go the limit, will you, sweetheart?" she said.

"Don't you want to?" he said.

"More than anything in the world, my darling love. But I can't. I never have. I will for you, but not here. Not—you know. I want to in bed, when everything is right for it."

"You never have?"

"Not all the way. Don't let's talk about it. I love you and I want you all the way, but I'm afraid to here."

"All right."

"Do that. Ah, Ju. Why are you so nice to me? No one else could be so darling to me. Why are you?"

"Because I love you. I always loved you."

"Oh, love! Sweetheart?"

"What, darling?"

"I can't help it. Have you got a thing? You know?"

"Yes."

"Do you think it'd be all right? I'm so afraid, but it's just as wrong to stop, isn't it? Isn't it just as wrong to stop?"

"Yes, darling."

"I'm so crazy about . . ."

6

THERE were Lute and Irma Fliegler, Willard and
Bertha Doane, Walter and Helen Schaeffer, Harvey and Emily Ziegenfuss, Dutch (Ralph) and
Frannie Snyder, Vic and Monica Smith, and Dewey and
Lois Hartenstein. From where he sat, at the side and to
the rear of the orchestra, practically in the drummer's lap,
Al Grecco could see them all. He knew all the men by
sight, and Lute Fliegler and Dutch Snyder he knew by
their first names, and the others he knew to say hello to
without his using any name on them and without their
calling him Al or Grecco or anything but Hyuh. He knew
Irma Fliegler to speak to; he called her Mrs. Fliegler.
He knew Frannie Snyder to speak to; he could have called
her Frannie or Baby or practically anything that came into
his mind, but he never said more than hello, with a distant nod, to her. What the hell; she was married, even
if that was no bargain she was married to that Dutch, and
for all Al knew she had been straight as a dye (Al sometimes wondered how straight straight as a dye was; a dye
wasn't straight) for close on to two years. So there was
no sense speaking to her. That loud-mouthed punk she
was married to, if he saw her speaking to Al Grecco there

was no telling what he would think. And do. And anyhow, you couldn't judge a baby by just one night two years ago. Maybe that had been the only time she ever cheated on that loud-mouth, and you couldn't hold that against her. She had been the easiest job of work Al ever had, or one of the easiest. He had known her in sisters' school and then as they grew up he hadn't seen much of her around town; just see her on the street now and then, and she'd say "Hello, Tony Murascho," and he'd say "Hello, Frances." And he read in the paper where she got married to Dutch Snyder and he felt sorry for her, because he knew what Dutch was: a loud-mouth Kluxer, who was always getting his face pushed in for making cracks about the Catholic church, but was always trying to get dates with Catholic girls—and getting them. When Al read about the marriage he figured Frances had got herself knocked up, but he was wrong: what had happened was that Frances's father, Big Ed Curry, the cop, had caught his daughter and Snyder in an awkward position and had given Snyder the choice of marriage or death. Al did not know this. He did know that it wasn't long after the marriage before Dutch, who was known as Ralphie to some of the girls at the Dew Drop Inn, was around the Dew Drop again, a sucker for cigarette money and one of the most unpopular customers of the institution. So one afternoon, two years before the night at the Stage Coach, Al was driving through Collieryville and he saw Frances waiting for a bus and he stopped his car. "You want a ride?" he said.

"No—oh, it's you, Tony," she said. "Are you going back to town?"

"Nothing else but," said Al. "Get in."

"Well, I don't know—"

"Okay. No skin off my ass," he said, and reached for the door to close it.

"Oh, I don't mean—I'll go with you. Only, will you leave me off somewhere—"

"Get in and do the talking on the way," he said.

She got in and he gave her a cigarette. She had been to her grandmother's in Collieryville and she wanted a cigarette and accepted a drink and was easily persuaded to go for a short ride. The short ride was short enough: half a mile off the main road between Gibbsville and Colliery-ville to a boathouse on the Colliery Dam. There was something queer about the whole thing, like going with your cousin or somebody. He had known Frances as a little girl in school, and then all of a sudden one day you discover that she is a woman that has had her experience and all that—it was queer. It was like finding money on the street; you didn't have to earn it, work for it, go on the make for it. And she must have felt the same way, because if there was ever an easy lay she was it—that day. But she said on the way home: "If you ever tell anybody this I'll kill you. I mean it." And you could see she did. And she refused to see him again and told him never to call her up or try to see her. She was a little sorry, what she had done, but he could not be sure that even that was not putting on an act. He often thought of it. He thought of it now, watching her watching Dutch dancing with Emily Ziegenfuss, with his leg rammed in between the Ziegenfuss woman's legs and trying to make out as if he was just dancing like anyone else. The son of a bitch. Frannie was all right. Al liked Frannie. But that Dutch—he'd like to paste him one. That was the trouble: women (he did not call them women, or girls, but another name which he used for all female persons except nuns) nearly always got the dirty end of the stick. Only once in a while they got a right guy, like Fliegler, for instance.

Then he began to feel a little angry at Irma Fliegler. He wondered whether she appreciated what a right guy she was married to. Probably not. She probably just took him for granted. That was the other side of it: a woman married a louse that beat her and cheated on her, and she got so she took that for granted; and another woman married a real guy, a square shooter from the word go, and she didn't see anything unusual about that. Al almost but not quite reached the opinion that all women are so used to getting the dirty end of the stick that they took it for granted when they did get it, and took for granted they were going to get it when they didn't. The hell with them. He wanted to forget about them.

But that was not possible here, at the Stage Coach. It was a woman's place. All dance places, night clubs, road houses, stores, churches, and even whorehouses—all were women's places. And probably the worst kind of woman's place was a place like this, where men put on monkey suits and cut their necks with stiff collars and got drunk without

159

the simple fun of getting drunk but with the presence of women to louse things up. Wherever there was an orchestra there were women, you could always be sure of that. Women singing the first words of songs: I got rhythm, Three little words, You're driving me crazy, Thinking of you dear, My heart is sad and lonely for you I pine for you dear only I'd gladly surrender. "Surrender my ass!" said Al Grecco, and looked across his table at Helene Holman, whom he hated now a thousand times worse than he ever had hated anyone in his whole life. All evening long he had been hating. In the early part of the evening he had hated the job Ed Charney had given him, the job of keeping tabs on Helene. She knew what he was there for all right, and she took it out on him, she took it out on him that Ed was staying home with his kid. And wife. She was the only person he could think of who had open contempt for him, and tonight it was worse than ever. "This is a swell way for you to be spending Christmas," she said. And went on from there; why didn't he get himself fixed up? What kind of a life did he lead? Was he nothing but a yes-man? Was he a unique? Did he know what a unique was? A unique, she told him, was a morphadite. . . . And he had had to take it for a couple of hours, getting no rest from her except when she would get up to sing a song. But then along about ten or eleven she began to lose her spunk. She got a little tired of panning him and she took a different attitude.

She was wearing a dress that was cut in front so he could all but see her belly-button, but the material, the satin or whatever it was, it held close to her body so that when she stood up she only showed about a third of each breast. But when she was sitting down across the table from him she leaned forward with her elbows on the table and her chin in her hands, and that loosened the dress so that whenever she made a move he could see the nipples of her breasts. She saw him looking—he couldn't help looking. And she smiled.

"You wouldn't want to get your teeth knocked down your throat, would you?" he said.

"And by who, may I ask?" she said.

"You wouldn't want them nice molars all smashed, would you?"

"Aw-haw. Big talk. Little Allie is sore because—"

"Never mind about little Allie, baby. I'm telling you something for your own good. A word to the wise is sufficient."

"I'm shaking all over," she said.

He suddenly did not desire her, but he weakened in another way. "Cut it out, will you? I'm not here because I want the job. You ought to know that by now."

Her eyes stabbed at him. "All right, then, scram. Get outa here and leave me have some fun. My God."

"Sure. Scram. Are you off your nut? Where would I go? I'd have to go plenty far if I went outa here before I get my orders. Plenty. I wouldn't even get outa here. Wuddia think that French bastard would be doing when I left? Dya think he'd leave me go? He *would* not."

"Oh, no?" said Helene.

That was interesting. It sounded as though the Fox had been making passes at Helene, which Al had suspected for a long time. But he didn't care about that now. All he cared about now was for Helene to behave herself so he wouldn't get in a jam with Ed. "I got my orders," he said, "and I'm staying here whether I like it or not or whether you like it or not."

"So I see," she said.

"And my orders is to see that you keep your knees together, baby."

"Horse feathers," she said. "Well, is it all right if I have a drink?"

"No, it ain't all right if you have a drink. You got cock-eyed once today."

"Well, then do you want to dance with me? I gotta do something besides get up there and give these butter and egg men hot pants, don't I?"

"No, I don't want to dance with you," he said. "That ain't my orders."

"Oh, you're afraid."

"All right," he said. "I'm afraid. If you want to leave it that way, I'm afraid."

She recognized the introduction to Body and Soul, which was one of the songs she sang. She walked slowly to the center of the orchestra platform.

"What does she call herself?" said Emily Ziegenfuss.

"Helene Holman," said Dewey Hartenstein.

"Holman? She has a nerve," said Emily.

"Why so?" said Vic Smith.

"Why, that's the name of a real singer. Libby Holman. Isn't that it? Libby? Or Liddy. No, Libby's right. Yes. Libby Holman. She makes records," said Emily.

"Well, she has as much right to the name as Libby Holman has," said Irma Fliegler.

"She has not," said Emily.

"She has so," said Irma. "Libby Holman isn't Libby *Holman's* real name."

"Oh," said Emily. "Well—how do you know, Irma?"

"Because I have these friends out in Cincinnati, Ohio, or at least they're friends of Lute's. Lute?"

"What?" said Lute.

"What was it those friends of yours in Cincinnati, Ohio, remember, they had that meningitis that took away their two children—"

"Spinal meningitis," said Lute, who had been talking with Willard Doane.

"I know that," said Irma. "What was their name?"

"Oh, Schultz. Harry Schultz. Why? Shall we call him up and tell him to join the party or what?"

"No, wisecracker. I wanted to know what Libby Holman's real name was. The singer."

"Oh, well, why didn't you ask me that in the first place?" said Lute.

"Well, come on, tell us what it was."

"Fred. Her right name was Fred," said Lute.

"Oh, bushwah on you," said Irma. "He never talks like

anyone else. Anyhow these friends, these people named Schultz in Cleveland—"

"You just got through telling us it was Cincinnati," said Emily. "I don't think—"

"Cincinnati, then. All right, Cincinnati. Whatever city it is this Holman comes from. Anyhow, they came from the same town as her, and they told us her real name."

"Fred, I guess," said Emily. "Oh, I don't believe it. I don't think you know anything about it, if you ask me." Emily had had her fourth highball.

"She's good. I like her singing," said Frannie Snyder.

"You *like* it?" said Emily. "You mean you actually can sit there and say you like that kind of a voice? You must be crazy, Frannie."

"I like it all right," said Harvey Ziegenfuss.

"Oh, who asked you?" said Emily Ziegenfuss.

"Nobody asked me. Can't I express my opinions?"

"No. Who asked you for your opinions? Look at her. If she's going to sing why don't she sing, and if she's going to do a hootchy-kootchy dance then why don't she do it? But at least she ought to make up her mind. She's like a burlesque show dancer."

"How do you know what a burlesque show dancer is like?" said Harvey Ziegenfuss.

"How do I know?" said his wife. "You ask me that? You, Harvey Ziegenfuss, ask me that? All right, I'll tell you. I know because you showed me. When we were first married you used to get me to get undressed one by one, one thing after another. That's how I know."

164

Everyone, except Harvey Ziegenfuss, laughed. "Aw, you're nuts," he said. But that only made them laugh a little more.

"Drinks!" shouted Lute Fliegler. "Emily, how 'bout you? Dutch, you're ready for another. Frannie, you could stand it. Vic, what's the matter with you? Not drinking?"

"I'm going easy," said Vic Smith.

"You better, too, Lute Fliegler," said Irma Fliegler.

"No worse than a bad cold, Vic," said Lute. "What was that strange noise I heard?" he held his ear in the direction of Irma.

"You heard what I said. You better go easy yourself. Vic's right."

"No worse than a bad cold," said Lute. "You're not a man till you had it once. Dewey, how about you? You know what the governor of North Carolina said to the governor of *West* Virginia."

"You mean the governor of *South* Carolina," said Emily.

"No. I meant North Dakota," said Lute. "Come on, let's get drunk, people."

"I'm cockeyed already," said Dewey Hartenstein.

"I'm getting an edge on myself," said Harvey Ziegenfuss.

"Oh, you. Who asked you?" said Emily Ziegenfuss.

"Hey, there, Ziegenfusses, quit necking right out in public," said Lute. "Wait till you get home."

"Here's to good old Yale," said Dutch Snyder, who had been All-Scholastic guard on the Gibbsville High

165

championship team back in 1914, the year Gibbsville beat both Reading *and* Allentown.

"Embrace me, my sweet embraceable you. Embrace me, my irreplaceable you, *la* la, *la* la, *la* la, *la* la, *la* dada da, um ha, um ha, um ha, um ha, *lum* dada da." Monica Smith was singing.

"Low-zee," said Emily. "Our cat sings better than that."

"Embrace me, my sweet embraceable you," Monica sang. "Embrace me la la replaceable you. Don't be a naughty baby. Come to papa, come to papa do. My sweet embraceable you."

"Everybody got their drink? Emily," said Lute, "what you need is a drink."

"Yeah," said Harvey Ziegenfuss. "What she needs is a drink. Yeah."

"Sure she does," said Lute. "I didn't say of what, did I?"

"Carbolic acid, I suggest," said Monica Smith.

"Oh, cut fighting, you two," said Helen Schaeffer, who up to this time had taken no part in the conversation.

"Another country heard from!" said Emily.

"Who wants to dance? I got rhythm, I got rhythm!" sang Dutch Snyder.

"Yeah. You got rhythm. You said it you got rhythm," said Emily.

"Well, come on, what's holding you?" said Dutch.

"Frannie," said Emily.

"I am not," said Frannie. "Go ahead and dance with

him if you want to." In a slightly lower tone she added: "You like it."

"What you say?" said Emily.

"I said you like it. Go ahead and dance with him," said Frannie.

"All right," said Emily. "I *will* dance with him. Come on, Dutch."

"Let's go," said Dutch. "I got sweet dreams in green pas-tures."

The others, except Lute and Frannie, chose or were somehow maneuvered into taking partners. Lute got up and moved to a chair beside Frannie.

"That Emily Ziegenfuss," she said. "What does she think she is? I know what *I* think she is."

"Uh-huh. Don't say it," said Lute, "don't say it. If there's one thing I don't like, I don't like to hear one woman call another a bitch."

"Well, that's what she is, all right," said Frannie. "It's partly your fault, too, Lute. You know she can't drink. Why do you keep on giving her drinks?"

"She'd be just as bad on two as she is on four or five," he said. He dropped the levity for a moment. "The only thing to do now is make her pass out. She will."

"Well, she can't pass out any too soon for me," said Frannie. "And that husband of hers, that Harvey. Trying to give me a feel under the table. Honestly! Can you imagine that? Just because she makes a fool out of him he thinks because Dutch is a sap, I guess he thinks that gives him the right to try to paw over me."

"I don't blame him," said Lute. "I'd like a little of that myself."

"Oh, you," said Frannie, but pleased. "Gee, if they were all like you, married men I mean, it wouldn't be so bad. Anyhow I burnt Mr. Ziegenfuss with a cigarette. He thought he was getting along fine and then I reached down and pushed the lighted end of the cigarette on the back of his hand."

"Oh, swell. I saw him kind of jump there for a minute."

"He jumped all right," said Frannie. She sipped her drink and she was looking around the room, over the rim of the glass. "Say, look," she said. "Isn't that your boss there, just coming in?"

"My God! Yes," said Lute. "Oh, and has he a nice package?"

"I'll say. That's his wife with him, isn't it?"

"That's her, all right," said Lute. "That's funny. They were supposed to go to the dance at the country club tonight. I know that for sure."

"Oh, that's nothing," said Frannie. "They often come here when they get tired of the club dances. I often heard them talking when I go to have my hair waved. They often leave the country club dances."

"He's nice and drunk, all right," said Lute.

"He doesn't look so drunk," said Frannie. "I've seen a lot worse."

"Yes, but that boy can drink. When he's that way you can tell he had plenty. He can drink all night without showing it. When he shows it, boy, you can be pretty sure he has damn near a quart under his belt."

"That's Carter Davis with him," said Frannie.

"I know. Carter Davis, and I can't see who the girl is."

"I can't either, but wait a minute. Oh, it's Kitty Hofman. Yeah. Kitty Hofman, and there comes Whitney Hofman. I guess he was parking the car."

"Yeah. I guess he was parking the car. I wonder if English drove," said Lute.

"Oh, I don't imagine so," said Frannie. "Not if Whitney Hofman had to park the car."

"You can't be so sure about that. English gets that way sometimes. He can always drive when he's stinko, but a big thing like parking the car—no, sir. That's asking too much."

"Well, they got a good table," said Frannie. "Look at that old Frenchman, What's His Name, moving that Taqua crowd around to make room for English."

"To make room for Hofman, you mean," said Lute.

"Oh, of course. I didn't think of that. I like that Whitney Hofman. He's so democratic."

"Well, I guess if I had fourteen million bucks I imagine I'd be democratic, too. He can afford it," said Lute.

"What are you talking about, Lute?" said Frannie. "They're the ones that you never see democratic, those with the money."

"No, you're wrong there. The ones with the dough, the big dough, they're always democratic," said Lute.

"Oh, you have everything upside down," said Frannie.

"The ones that have a lot of money, they're the ones you always think of as being the high-hat ones."

"Not me, Frannie. I always think of the ones that really have more money than I'd know what to do with, I think of them as the democratic ones. If you don't have money you're not democratic. You don't have to be democratic. You just act natural and nobody ever thinks of it as democratic or anything else. It's like a story I heard about Jim Corbett."

"Jim Corbett? Is he the one that's staying at the Y.M.C.A.? The electric engineer?"

"Hell, no. His name is Corbin. No, Jim Corbett was the fighter, heavyweight champion. They used to call him Gentleman Jim."

"Oh, Gentleman *Jim*. Oh, I heard of him. I always thought he was some kind of a crook. I heard of him all right. What's the story?"

"Well, when he was here two years ago—"

"Was he here? In Gibbsville? I never knew that," said Frannie.

"Yes, he was here for a banquet. Anyhow, one of the reporters got to talking to him about his title of Gentleman Jim, and he told the story about how he was in the subway in New York or something and somebody started pushing him around—no, that's the one about Benny Leonard. Wait a minute. Oh, yes. This is it. Somebody was asking him why he was always so polite to everybody. He is the politest man in the world, I guess, and he said,

'Well, when you've been heavyweight champion of the world, gentlemen, you can afford to be polite.' "

"What did he mean by that?" said Frannie.

"*What!*" said Lute. "Let it go, Frannie. It isn't that important."

"Well, I just don't see what that has to do with Whitney Hofman being democratic. I think he's very democratic."

"I think you better have a shot," said Lute.

"Am I dumb or something?" she said. "You act as though I said something dumb or nay-eeve."

"Not at all. You want ginger ale with yours, or straight?" said Lute.

"I'll have a straight one I guess, then you can give me another in a highball."

"That's talking," said Lute. "Oh. Don't look right away, but I think we're going to have a little company. You can look now."

"You mean English? He's coming over. Introduce me to him, will you?"

"Sure. If he ever makes it," said Lute.

Julian English had stood up and looked around the room and had recognized Lute Fliegler. Immediately he told Caroline and Kitty and Whit and Carter that he had to talk to Lute. Matter of business that couldn't wait. He excused himself and began to make his way, assisting himself by taking hold of the backs of chairs and people's shoulders, to the table where Lute and Frannie were seated.

He extended his hand to Lute. "Luther, I came all the way over here to wish you a happy birthday. All the way over here. Happy birthday, Luther."

"Thanks, boss. Will you sit down and have a drink with us? This is Mrs. Snyder. Mrs. Snyder, this is Mr. English."

"I'm pleased to meet you," said Frannie, and began to get up.

"Not leaving?" said Julian.

"Oh, no," said Frannie. "I'll stay."

"Very good. Very, very good. Very good. Luther, I came over here to talk to you on a matter of business—no, sit down, Mrs. Snyder. Please sit down. You can hear what I have to say. Luther, have you any Scotch?"

"No, I only have rye, I'm sorry to say."

"What of it?" said Julian. "Who is that man over there, Luther?"

"Where?"

"The one that's staring at us. I think he's dead. Did you ever hear the story about the dead man in the subway, Luther?"

"No, I don't think I did."

"Lucky boy. Lucky boy, Luther. I always said you were a fine fellow. Are you having a good time?"

"Pretty good."

"How about you, Mrs. Snyder? Have I the name right?"

"Yes, that's right, Mr. English. I'm having a pretty good time."

"Well, I'm not. Or at least not till I came to this table. Are you married, Mrs. Snyder?"

"Yes, I'm married."

"She's Dutch Snyder's wife," said Lute.

"Oh. Oh, of *course*. Of course. Dutch Snyder. Well, I'll be God damned. What ever became of old Dutch? I haven't seen old Dutch in years."

"He's dancing," said Frannie.

"Dancing, is he? He was always a great one for dancing, was our Dutch. So you married' Dutch. How nice. How jolly. Do you think Dutch has any Scotch, Luther?"

"No, he only has rye, too," said Lute.

"What of it? Is that any my business who has rye or who has Scotch? Wellp. I think I have to leave you now, my friends. It's been a great little visit and I want to tell you I enjoyed every minute of it. You be nice to Mrs. Snyder, Luther. She is my ideal woman. But now I have to go. I see little old Al Grecco over there and I think if I play my cards right I could get a drink of Scotch out of him. I understand he knows a fellow that can get it for you."

"So I hear," said Lute.

Julian stood up. "Mrs. Snyder—a pleasure. A pleasure indeed. Luther—I'll see you some other time. Luther and I work together, Mrs. Snyder. We're buddies. He's my buddy, and I'm his buddy. He's my buddy, I'm her Joe. Ju. If a buddy, meet a buddy, looking for the Scutch. If a buddy, meet a buddy, how's my old friend Dutch? Auf wiedersehen."

"Auf wiedersehen," said Lute.

Julian moved away, and they saw him sitting down at Al Grecco's table, in Helene Holman's chair. Helene was singing Love for Sale: "Let the poets pipe of love in their childish way; we know every type of love better far than they . . ."

"Don't get up, Al, don't get up," said Julian.

"Oh, that's all right," said Al Grecco.

"I wanted to see you on a business proposition," said Julian.

"Well," said Al, rising, "I guess we can—"

"Oh—" Julian put a hand on Al's shoulder. "Sit down, sit down. We can talk here. I wanted to know if you knew anybody that could let me have some Scotch."

"Why, sure," said Al. "What's the matter? Don't Lebrix know you? He ought to. I'll fix it right away. Waiter! Eddie!"

"No, no," said Julian. "I can get it here all right. They'll sell it to me. But I don't want to buy it. I simply don't want to buy drinks, Al. If there's anything I don't want to do it's buy a drink. I'll buy *you* a drink. I'll buy— oh, that man over there, I'll buy him a drink. But I don't want to buy a drink. See what I mean?"

"No. I don't exactly see what you mean, Mr. English."

"Just call me Mr. English, Al. You call me Mr. English and I'll call you Al. The hell with this formality. We've known each other all our lives. You know, we Gibbsville people, we have to stick together in a place like this. If we don't you know what happens? Those Hazleton people gang us. What was I talking about just before you said that?"

"What?"

"Oh, yeah. About drinks. Uh, if I don't want to do anything it's buy a drink. You know why? You want to know why I feel that way?"

"Sure."

"Well, it's like love, Al," said Julian. "You know what I mean? Or don't you see what I mean? You buy a drink, and that's all it is, just a bought drink. Whereas, on the other hand, au contraire, au contraire, Al, uh, you uh, uh, somebody gives you a drink and that's like love. Why, say, who is this?"

"You got my chair, Mister," said Helene Holman, who had finished her song.

"Not at all," said Julian. "Sit right down. Don't apologize. Just sit down. If this is your chair you needn't apologize. Just sit right down and Al will get another chair for us, won't you, Al?"

Al pulled a chair from another table.

"Shake hands with Mr. English," said Al. "He's a friend of Ed's."

"Are you a friend of Ed's?" said Julian to Helene.

"Yes, I guess you'd call it that," said Helene.

"Fine," said Julian. "Ed who?"

"Ed Charney," said Al.

"Oh-h-h. Ed *Char*ney," said Julian. "Well, my God, why didn't you say so? My God. Jesus Christ Almighty,

175

why didn't you say so? I didn't think you were a friend of Ed *Char*ney's. My God."

"What Ed did you think he meant?" said Helene.

"Oh, I don't know. Do we have to go into that?" said Julian. "What's your name?"

"Helene Holman," she said.

"Oh, yes, yes," said Julian. "What? Will you say that again, please?"

"Helene, Hol-man," she repeated.

"Oh. Helene *Hol*man. You're the one that married Dutch Snyder. How is old Dutch? Does he still dance as much as ever?"

"I never heard of him," said Helene.

"Neither—did—I," said Julian. "You're my pal. Neither did I. And I don't want to again. My goodness that's a nice gown you have on."

"I like it," she said, smiling at Al.

"Miss Holman is a very, very good friend of Ed Charney's," said Al.

"That's fine. I like that," said Julian. "And I'll tell you something else. *I'm* a very *very* good friend of Ed Charney's."

"Oh, I know," said Al. "I was just telling you, Miss Holman is, too. A very good friend. You know what I mean?"

"You don't have to draw a map, do you?" said Helene.

"You mean—Miss Holman is Ed's mistress? Is that what you mean?" said Julian.

"Yes, that's what he means," said Helene.

"Well, I don't know what to say," said Julian, and then: "Except—I do like that dress. I like that dress."

"I like it," said Helene.

"So do I," said Julian. "How about you, Al? What's your opinion on Miss Holman's dress? Come on, speak up."

"It's all right," said Al. "It's all right."

"I should say it is," said Julian. "How about dancing, Miss Holman?"

"She's tired," said Al.

"Well, in that case, she better go to bed," said Julian.

"Hey," said Al.

"What do you want?" said Julian.

"Nothing. Only remember what I told you about Miss Holman and Ed," said Al.

"My friend, I've already forgotten that little bit of gossip," said Julian. "I'm not a bit interested in Miss Holman's affairs, am I, Miss Holman?"

"Not a bit."

"Right," said Julian. "So let's dance."

"Check and double check," said Helene, and got up and went to the dance floor with Julian.

Everyone in the big room watched them. She was a good dancer, and so was Julian. And they *danced*, which was a kind of disappointment to several persons, who expected another kind of exhibition. It also was a kind of surprise to Helene, and a kind of surprise to Al Grecco. When they sat down again Al relaxed and was able to laugh at the things Julian said. Presently they were joined by Carter Davis. After he was introduced he said: "Caroline wants you."

"I happen to know she doesn't," said Julian.

"Well, she does," said Carter.

"Carter, sit down before there's an ugly scene," said Julian.

Carter hesitated, and then sat down. "All right," he said, "but only for a minute. Ju, you've got to—"

"Did you all meet my friend Mr. Davis?" said Julian.

"Yes."

"Yes."

"Yes, they met me," said Carter.

"So they did," said Julian. "Well, let's talk about something else. Books. Uh, Miss Holman, have you read *The Water Gipsies?*"

"No, I don't believe I have," said Helene. "What is it about?"

"I haven't the faintest idea," said Julian. "I got it for Christmas, or rather a member of my family did."

"A member of your family," said Carter.

"Yes, a member of my family," said Julian. "My wife, Miss Holman. Mr. Davis, this is Mr. Davis right here, he gave my wife *The Water Gipsies* for Christmas. What did you give me, pal?"

"You know what I gave you," said Carter.

"Of course I do, and I'm a bastard for not remembering it." Julian leaned forward to explain to Helene and Al: "Mr. Davis gave me a tie, from Finchley's. All the

178

way from Finchley's. Do you remember which tie you gave me, Carter?"

"Sure I do," said Carter.

"I'll bet you five dollars you don't," said Julian. "Al, you hold stakes. Here's my five. Is it a bet, Carter?"

"I don't want to take your money," said Carter.

"Oh, yes you do. Oh, yes you do. Put up your five bucks. There, Al. Now."

"How can we prove it?" said Julian. "Oh, I have an idea. You tell me what kind of tie it was, and then go over to Caroline and repeat the description of the tie, see? And if you're right she'll shake her head yes, and if you're wrong she'll—"

"She'll shake her head no," said Carter. "O.K." He got up and went over to the table.

"Do you want to dance some more?" said Julian.

"Don't you want to wait till your friend proves who won the bet?"

"The hell with him. I just did that to get rid of him," said Julian.

"But you lose five bucks," said Helene.

"Yeah, you lose five bucks," said Al.

"It's worth it," said Julian. "I got rid of him, didn't I? Come on, let's dance."

"Check and double check," said Helene. They ignored Al completely and went to the dance floor. "Is that your wife?" said Helene.

"Which one do you mean?" said Julian.

"Oh, I know Kitty Hofman," said Helene.

"Well, my wife is the other girl, yes," said Julian. "You're a swell dancer, or have I said that before?"

"No, you didn't say it before. You're not so bad yourself, Mr. English."

"Oh, call me Malcolm."

"Is that your name? Malcolm? I thought he—oh, you're giving me the razz. Okay."

"No, I'm sorry. My name is Julian. Call me Julian."

They said no more until the music stopped, and as they stood there, Julian applauding and Helene standing with her hands folded in front of her, he suddenly said: "Are you in love with any person?"

"Isn't that a personal question?" she said.

"Of *course* it is. *Are* you?"

"What makes you ask that all of a sudden?" she said.

"I wanted to know. I—" the music continued. "I wanted to ask you to go out with me. Will you?"

"When do you mean? Now?"

"Yes."

"It's awful cold out," she said.

"But you will?" he said.

"I don't know," she said. "I have a room here."

"No, I want to go outside. Out in the car."

"Well, maybe that'd be better. We can't stay long. I have to sing again in about a half an hour. Oh, I better not go. Your wife will see us, and so will Al."

"Will you go?" he said.

"Yes," she said.

They glided to the edge of the floor and broke into a

walk and disappeared. Three persons, over and above all the others in the big room, saw them go. Three persons: Caroline, Al Grecco, Foxie Lebrix.

In a little while Julian fell asleep in the car, and Helene went back to the house by herself. It was long after three when Julian felt himself being shaken and came slowly half awake. "Wha'?" he said.

"Don't wake him up," someone said.

"We have to wake him up to put his coat on. Come on, Ju. Snap to." It was Whit Hofman. "Come on."

"Here, let me," said Kitty Hofman. She started to get in the car.

"Get away," said her husband. "Come on, Ju. Carter, get in the other side. Here, take his coat. I'll hold him up and you put his coat around him and the two of us can put his arms in the sleeves."

"I know," said Kitty. "Let's put snow on his face."

"Oh, drop dead," said Whit.

"The snow might be a good idea," said Caroline.

"Who sai' pu' snow my face?" said Julian.

"Are you awake, Ju?" said Whit.

"Sure I'm 'wake," said Julian.

"Well, then, put your coat on," said Whit. "Here. Hold the other arm, Carter."

"I dowanna put my coat on. Why do I have pu' my coa' on? Hu? Who do I?"

"Because we're going home," said Whit.

"Go on, darling, put your coat on," said Kitty.

"Oh, hello, Kitty," said Julian. "How about a dance, Kitty?"

"No, we're leaving," said Kitty.

"Oh, get out of the way, Kitty, for Christ sake." said Whit.

"I think I'll go to sleep," said Julian.

"Come on, Julian. Snap out of it," said Caroline. "Everybody wants to go home and it's freezing out here. Put your coat on."

Without another word Julian put his coat on, scorning all assistance. "Where's my hat?" he said.

"We can't find it," said Whit. "The hat check girl said she must have given it to someone else by mistake. Lebrix said he'd buy you a new one."

"Turn your collar up," said Caroline.

Julian turned up the deep collar of the coat, which was a husky garment of raccoon skins. He slumped back in a corner of the car and pretended to go to sleep. Carter sat in the other corner and Kitty Hofman sat in the middle of the back seat. Caroline sat up front with Whit, who was driving Julian's car. The whooping of the wind and the biting crunch of the tire chains in the snow and the music of the motor were the only sounds that reached the five persons in the car. The married four understood that; that there was nothing to be said now.

Julian, lost in the coonskins, felt the tremendous excitement, the great thrilling lump in the chest and abdomen that comes before the administering of an unknown, well-deserved punishment. He knew he was in for it.

7

WHEN he was a boy, Julian English once ran away from home. In a town the size of Gibbsville—24,032, estimated 1930 census—the children of the rich live within two or three squares of the children of parents who are not rich, not even by Gibbsville standards. This makes for a spurious democracy, especially among boys, which may or may not be better than no democracy at all. In any case, in order to get a ball game going the sons of the Gibbsville rich had to play with the sons of the non-rich. There were not even nine, let alone eighteen, boys of Julian's age among the rich, and so the rich boys could not even have their own team. Consequently, from the time he was out of kindergarten until he was ready to go away to prep school, Julian's friends were not all from Lantenengo Street. Carter Davis would stop for him, or he would stop for Carter, when they were going to play baseball or football. They would go down the hill to Christiana Street, the next street, and join the gang. The gang's members had for fathers a butcher, a motorman, a "practical" surveyor (that is, a surveyor who had not gone to college), a freight clerk, two bookkeepers for the coal company, a Baptist minister, a neighborhood saloonkeeper, a mechanic in a garage (which he called a garridge), and a perennial convict (who was up this time for stealing 100,000 cigarettes from the Gibbsville Tobacco Company).

These boys had enough to eat. They did not have to sell papers, although the minister's son sold subscriptions to *The Saturday Evening Post* and was always talking about blue vouchers or green vouchers and the Ranger bike he was going to get when he had enough vouchers. He was not available on certain days of the week, when he had to go to meetings of the other *Post* salesmen. He was an industrious boy, and his nasal Indiana twang and the fact that he was a stranger (he had come to Gibbsville when he was five) and was bright in school all helped to make him unpopular in the gang. You could always tell his voice from the others: it was high, and his enunciation was not sing-songy like the other boys', which showed strong Pennsylvania Dutch influence. Julian liked him least of all. Best of all he liked Walt Davis, the son of the cigarette thief. Walt was no relation to Carter. Walt was cross-eyed, which somehow made him handsome, or Julian thought so. In the nights preceding Hallowe'en it was Walt who remembered the various Nights: one night was Gate Night, when you took people's gates off the fences; another night was Tick-Tack Night, when you held a button through which string had been run and wound up, against window panes, making a very effective sound until the string ran down: another night was Paint Night, when you painted sidewalks and people's houses.

On Hallowe'en you dressed up as ghosts and cowboys and Indians and women and men, and rang doorbells, and said: "Anything for Hallowe'en?" If the people gave you pennies or cakes, all right. If they didn't, you stuck a pin in the doorbell and threw the doormat out in the street and carried away the porch furniture and poured buckets of water on the porch so it would freeze in the night. Walt knew which Night was which; he got the information from his father.

The leader of the gang was Butch Doerflinger. He was fat and strong and brave. He had killed more copperheads than anyone else and was a better swimmer than anyone else and knew all about older people because he had watched his father and mother. They didn't mind, either. They thought it was funny. Julian was afraid of Butch, because Julian's mother had threatened to "report" Butch's father for beating his horse. Nothing ever came of it, and every year or two Butch's father would get a new horse.

There were things not to talk about in the gang: you did not talk about jail, because of Walt's father; nor about drunken men, because there was a saloonkeeper's son; nor about the Catholics, because the motorman's son and one bookkeeper's son were Catholic. Julian also was not allowed to mention the name of any doctor. These things did come up and were discussed pretty thoroughly, but usually in the absence of the boy whom the talk would embarrass. There was enough to talk about: girls; changes in boys which occurred at fourteen: parades; which would you rather have; if you had a million dollars what would you do; what were you going to be when you got big; is a horse better than a dog; what was the longest you'd ever been on a train; what was the best car; who had the biggest house; who was the dirtiest kid in school; could a policeman be arrested; were you going to college when you got big; what girl were you going to marry and how many children were you going to have; what was the most important instrument in the band; what position was most important on a baseball team; were all the Confederates dead; was the Reading better than the Pennsylvania rail-road; could a blacksnake kill you. . . .

There were all sorts of things to be done. There was marbles, and there was a game of marbles called Dobbers, played with marbles the size of lemons. You played it in the gutter on the way home from school, throwing your Dobber at the other fellow's and he would throw his at yours. It wasn't much of a game except it made the way home from school seem short. Some days the gang would hop a wagon—preferably a packing-house wagon or a wholesale grocery wagon; coal wagons were too slow— and ride out to the state police barracks and watch the staties drill and shoot. The gang would go out on the mountain and play "Tarzan of the Apes," jumping around from tree to tree and skinning their behinds on the bark. You had to be careful on the mountains, careful of air-holes, which were treacherous, or supposed to be treach-erous, places where the ground was undermined and liable to cave in. In the memory of the oldest citizen no life had been lost in Gibbsville as a result of a mine cave-in, but the danger was there. There was a game called Run, Sheepie, Run, and sometimes the gang would play Ku-Klux Klan, after having seen "The Birth of a Nation." Games that had their source in a movie would be played and played for days and then dropped and forgotten, to be revived months later, unsuccessfully. The gang had a Fisk Bicycle Club for a while. You were supposed to have Fisk tires on your bike, and that made you eligible to send away to the Fisk people and get pennants and caps and all the other stuff; buttons, books of instructions on wig-wag and so on. Julian's father made him buy two Fisk tires, and Carter Davis had one Fisk tire, but these were the only Fisk tires in the gang. The other members of the gang were saving up to buy Pennsylvania Vacuum Cups, and meanwhile when they had a puncture they filled the tire with Neverleak. There were cigarettes to be smoked: Ziras, Sweet Caps, Piedmonts, Hassans. Julian sometimes bought Condax cigarettes, which were more expensive. Butch and Julian were the heavy smokers of the gang, but Julian liked the smell of someone else's cigarette better than he liked smoking, and he discovered that smoking did not get him in better with Butch. He stopped after a year, using the excuse that his father had detected the nicotine stains on his fingers. Sometimes the gang would sit on the rocks on the mountain and watch the coal trains coming down the valley from the east, and they would count the cars: seventy-eight battleship cars was the highest number they ever saw and agreed upon. Sometimes

187

they would go down in the valley and when the train slowed up or stopped at Gibbsville Junction they would get on and ride four miles to Alton or the five miles to Swedish Haven. It was a cold and dangerous ride, and about once a year some boy would fall off and lose a leg or be killed under the wheels, but the practice of hopping coalies went on. It was not wise to go beyond Swedish Haven, because after that the railroad veered off too far from the highway. There was a coalie that slowed down at Gibbsville Junction every day at about three-fifteen, and it reached Swedish Haven at four o'clock, which usually gave the gang time enough to get home, either by bumming rides on the grocery wagons or stealing rides on the trolley cars, or walking. You could get home only moderately late for supper.

There was one other game that Julian did not like, because he was afraid of the consequences. That was known simply as Five-Finger Grab. There were two five-and-ten stores, Woolworth's and Kresge's, in Gibbsville, and about once a month after school the gang would wander through the stores. Sometimes they would not take a thing, usually because they were watched carefully by the clerks and the manager, whose office was placed so that he could look down on every counter. But sometimes after a tour of the store the gang would meet, and two or three of the boys would say: "Look what I got," and show what they had got in the Five-Finger Grab: pencils, magnifying glasses, screw drivers, pliers, spools of wire, nickel Rocket baseballs, hard candy, school tablets, toys, cotton gloves, friction tape—these were some of the things that would be produced by the proud five-finger grabbers. The other boys would be ashamed, and the next time they went to the store everyone would try to get something.

Julian at first would refuse to participate in the Five-Finger Grab, but when Carter Davis abandoned his side and went over to the grabbers, Julian had to do something. Once he tried to buy something—a jar of hard candy—to be able to show something after a grab, but he could not do this often; he was not given much money. A quarter a week was his allowance, and he had to have a nickel on Friday and a nickel on Saturday for two movie serials he was following, and that meant he could not buy much at the five-and-ten if he wanted to have a cinnamon bun and pickle, two cents, at recess. And so he became a five-finger grabber.

He was very successful, and when he saw how successful he was he wanted to do it all the time. Most of the other fellows in the gang stole only for the sake of stealing; that explained why some of them, emptying their pockets after a grab, would pull out white feet for women's stockings, baby rattles, cards of safety pins, wash cloths, soap, and other useless articles. But Julian became so proficient that he could tell beforehand what he was going to get, and usually he would get it. The gang would separate on entering the store, and there would be so many boys wandering around that it was hard to keep track of them.

Julian did not know that he was being watched. He had

been watched for a long time, and the manager saw that Julian was not taking things and stopped watching him. But when he began to have success as a grabber the sales-girls learned to keep on the lookout for him. They knew who he was; a Lantenengo Street kid, who did not have to steal. Several of them reported him to the manager, who thereafter forgot all about the other kids in order to keep his eye on Julian.

One day after school the gang decided to have a Five-Finger Grab, and they all trooped down to Kresge's. When they entered the store a bell rang, but they paid no attention to it; bells were always ringing in the store—signals to cash girls, signals to the assistant managers and floorwalkers and stock boys. Bells were always ringing. Julian had announced beforehand that he would get a flashlight for Butch, in return for which Butch was going to steal a large hunk of summer sausage from the Doer-flinger meat market. Not just an ordinary *slice*, that he could get for the asking, but a hunk at least a foot long.

The flashlight came as a case, battery, and lamp: ten cents for each part, thirty cents altogether. The electrical supplies counter was very near the front door, and Julian went right to it. The girl standing in front of the counter —the clerks stood in front of counters that were against the walls—asked him what he wanted, and he said he was only waiting for a friend who had gone to another part of the store. She looked at him without saying anything and kept looking at him. Well, he was not going to let her scare him, and he could outsmart her. He took out a package of Ziras, put one in his mouth, and pretended to reach in his pocket for a match, but all the cigarettes dropped to the floor, as Julian planned. The girl automatically leaned over, which was more than Julian had counted on—he merely wanted to distract her. He too leaned over, and as he did his right hand reached over the counter and he had the flashlight in his pocket before he began to pick up the cigarettes. "No smoking in here," the girl said.

"Who said so?" said Julian, and at that moment his arm was grabbed tight.

"I saw you, you little thief!" It was the manager. "I saw you take that flashlight. Miss Loftus, go get the policeman."

"Yes, sir," said the girl.

"I'll show you. I'll fix your feet for you," said the manager. Julian tried to reach in his pocket to get rid of the flashlight. "Oh, no you don't," said Mr. Jewett. "That flashlight stays right in your pocket till the policeman comes. I'll put a stop to this. Little highbrow, eh? Doctor English's son. Lantenengo Street boy. Well."

Quickly there was a crowd around, and some of the fellows were in the crowd. They were frightened, and a couple of them left, which gave Julian a sinking feeling but he did not blame them, and he was glad to see that Butch and Carter stayed.

"Go on away, you people," said Mr. Jewett. "I'll settle this." The group slowly moved away, and that was the chance Butch had been waiting for. He moved closer to Jewett and said:

"What did he do, Mister?"

"Never you mind what he did. You know damn well what he did," said Jewett.

Butch kicked Jewett square in the shin and ran, and so did Julian. They got out of the store and ran to the left, knowing that Leffler, the policeman, would be coming from the 'squire's office, at the right. They ran down one street, up another, down another, until they came to the railroad freight yards. "Jesus, I never ran so much in all my life yet," said Butch.

"Me either," said Julian.

"It's good I gave him a kick," said Butch.

"You bet. If you didn't I'd be there yet. What would they do?"

"I do' know. Send you to reformatory, I guess. I guess me too now maybe," said Butch.

"Gee," said Julian.

"What'll we do now?" said Butch.

"Gee. I do' know. What should we?"

"Well, if you go home—they know who you are at the store—so if you go home they'll have the cop, Leffler, he'll wait there for you."

"Do you think they will?" said Julian.

"Sure. He'll arrest you and the 'squire'll send you to reformatory till you're eighteen years old yet."

"Honest?" said Julian.

"That's right," said Butch.

"I won't go to any reformatory. I'll run away before I do that."

"Me too," said Butch. "I'm instigated."

"Oh," said Julian.

"I'm instigated because I kicked Jewett in the shins and that makes me instigated the same as you are."

"Well, I won't go to any reformatory. They won't catch me and send me to any reformatory. I'll run away before I get put away," said Julian.

"Well, what will we do?" said Butch.

Julian thought a minute. He watched them making up a train; the shifting engine collecting cars from all over the yard and backing them into a track near where they were sitting. "Let's hop the freight and run away?" said Julian.

"Gee," said Butch. "I don't know where they go. A coalie you know where it goes and you can get off down at the Haven, but a freight."

"We gotta do something. We don't want to get sent away to reformatory, do we?" said Julian.

"Yes, but who wants to hop a freight that they don't know where it's going. Philly, maybe, without stopping," said Butch.

"Philly without stopping! You're crazy. You know more about trains than that. It'll stop all right. They have to put water in the engine tender, don't they? They have to put on more cars and take them off, don't they? Don't they? Anyhow, what do we care where it's going? It's better than the reformatory, isn't it? Do you know what they do there?"

"No."

"Sure you do. They have priests there, Catholics, and they beat you and make you go to church every morning at five o'clock. That's what I hear."

"From who did you hear that? Who from?" said Butch.

"From—oh, lots of fellows told me that. I know it for a fact. That came from somebody that knows all about it and I'm not allowed to tell you his name. So will you go? We can sell papers in Philly. I was there often and they have fellows the same age as us selling papers there, so so can we. Younger than us. I've seen little kids I bet they weren't more than about nine and a half years old, they were selling papers right in the Bellevue-Stratford."

"Aw," said Butch.

"They were so," said Julian. "I bet you don't even know what the Bellevue-Stratford is. Where is it?"

"In Philly. Anybody knows that."

"But *what* is it?"

"Oh, I don't know. You don't know everything."

"See? You don't know. Well, it's the hotel where we always stay—" Julian was brought up then to the fact that if he was going to Philadelphia, this time he was not going to stay at the Bellevue-Stratford. "Well, are you going with me?"

"I guess so."

They waited until the train was beginning to move,

and then they got on the front platform of the caboose. They had to get off a couple of times at way stations, and finally they were caught. They were turned over to the railroad police in Reading, and were brought back to Gibbsville on the "late train." Butch Doerflinger the elder, and Dr. English were standing on the platform of the Gibbsville station when the train pulled in. The elder Doerflinger had made many, too many, remarks about his son being a chip off the old block, and he was amused and a little proud of his son. "Only twelve years old yet and hopping freights already. By Jesus, you don't know what kids are today, say, Doc?" His plans were made: a good beating for young Butch and make him work on the delivery wagon every day.

But William Dilworth English, M.D., was not thinking of the immediate punishment of his son; that was something which could be decided upon. He was not thinking of the glory of having a son who hopped freight trains. The thing that put him in the deep mood and gave him the heavy look that Julian saw on his face was that "chip off the old block" refrain of Butch Doerflinger's. William Dilworth English was thinking of his own life, the scrupulous, notebook honesty; the penny-watching, bill-paying, self-sacrificing honesty that had been his religion after his own father's suicide. And that was his reward: a son who turned out to be like his grandfather, a thief.

Julian never stole anything else, but in his father's eyes he was always a thief. In college Julian about once a year would be overdrawn at the bank, invariably because of checks he wrote while he was drunk. His father never spoke to him about it, but Julian knew from his mother what his father thought of his money habits: ". . . do try to be more careful (his mother wrote). Your father has so many worries and he is specially worried about you where money matters are concerned because he thinks it's in the blood, because of Grandfather English."

It was nine-thirty, the morning after the night at the Stage Coach. It couldn't have been more on the dot of nine-thirty by the modern little clock on Caroline's dressing-table. The little clock had no numerals but only squares of metal where the numerals were supposed to be. He lay there thinking about the pictures evoked by the sound of "nine-thirty": people still hurrying to work, coming in to Gibbsville from Swedish Haven and Collieryville and all the other little towns nearby; people with worried faces, worried because they were late to work. And the early shoppers. But there would be no early shoppers today, Friday, the day after Christmas. It was too early to start to exchange Christmas gifts. Monday would be time enough for that. But the stores had to be open, and the banks, and the coal company offices, and the business men who made a business of being conscientious about getting to work, got to work. "Me, for instance," he thought, and got out of bed.

He was wearing his underwear. His tailcoat and trousers were folded and hanging on a chair, and other things told him that Caroline had taken the studs out of his shirt, the garters from his socks, his tie, his waistcoat, and put the things in the laundry that belonged in the laundry. That meant she was up, because in the mood she must have been in when they came home last night she wouldn't have bothered to take care of his things. He shaved, bathed, dressed, and went downstairs and poured himself a drink.

"Oh, you're up," said Mrs. Grady, the cook.

"Good morning, Mrs. Grady," said Julian.

"Mrs. English come down for breakfast but she went back to bed," said Mrs. Grady.

"Any mail?"

"I don't think anything important. Christmas cards, by the look of them," she said. "Do you want eggs for breakfast or what?"

"Sure."

"Well, I didn't know," she said. "I seen you was taking a drink of liquor so I didn't know if you wanted the eggs. I'll have them ready for you. The coffee's ready. I was just having a little cup myself when I heard you in here."

"Oh, one of those little cups," said Julian.

"Hmm?"

"Nothing. Nothing at all. Three and a half minutes for the eggs, remember?"

"I ought to after four years, I ought to remember how long you want your eggs done."

"Yes, you ought to, but you don't always," said Julian. He was annoyed with her contemptuous manner.

"Now listen here, Mister English—"

"Oh, go boil the eggs, will you, and for Christ's sake shut up." There it was again: servants, cops, waiters in restaurants, ushers in theaters—he could hate them more than persons who threatened him with real harm. He hated himself for his outbursts against them, but why in the name of God, when they had so little to do, couldn't they do it right and move on out of his life?

There was no newspaper on the table, but he did not want to speak to Mrs. Grady, so he sat there without it, not knowing whether the damn paper had come, with nothing to read, no one to talk to, nothing to do but smoke a cigarette. Five minutes of ten, for God's sake; there ought to be a paper here by this time, and that old cow probably had it out in the kitchen and was just keeping it out there to annoy him. By God, she ought to be— oh, nuts. She got along all right with Caroline. That was it; the old cow, she probably knew from Caroline's manner that there was something wrong about last night, and her sympathies were, of course, all with Caroline. Well, she wasn't being paid to take sides in family quarrels, and she certainly wasn't being paid to—he got up and walked noisily to the kitchen.

"Where's the paper?" he said.

"Huh?"

"I said, where's the *paper!* Don't you understand English?"

"I understand one English," she said.

"Oh, for Christ's sake, Mrs. Grady, even you ought to know that's old stuff. Where's the paper?"

"Your wife took it upstairs with her. She wanted to read it."

"How do you know? Maybe she wanted to build a fire with it," he said, on his way out.

"There ain't no fireplace upstairs, smartie."

He had to laugh. He had to laugh, and pour himself a drink, and he was putting the top back on the bottle, which had a little chain holding a plate marked Scotch around the neck, when she brought in the large breakfast tray. He wanted to help her with it, but he would be damned if he would.

"Maybe she's asleep now and I can get the paper," said Mrs. Grady.

"No, thanks, don't bother," said Julian. He had a suspicion that Caroline not only was not asleep, but had heard every move he made from the time he got up. She was sleeping in the guest room again.

"Will you be coming home for lunch?"

"No," said Julian, although he had not given it any thought.

"Well, then, about the stuff for the party tonight."

"Oh, God. I forgot about it," said Julian.

"Well, Mrs. English says to tell you to leave a check for the liquor and champagne wine. It's to be delivered this afternoon."

"How much, did she say?"

"She said to make it out to cash and she'd fill in the amount when Grecco brings it."

Grecco. She would bring that up. And it was strange that Caroline wanted him to make out the check. She had her own money; right now she had more than he had. She had her own money, and always when they gave parties she would pay for the liquor when it was delivered, if she happened to be home, and they would settle it up later. On a party like this, which was as much hers as his, he would buy the liquor and she would pay for everything else. He wished there was going to be no party.

He finished his breakfast and drove downtown to the John Gibb Hotel, where every morning he stopped to have his shoes shined. John, the Negro who had the shine concession, was not there. "He ain't been in this morning yet," said one of the barbers. "I guess he had too much Christmas cheer, like a lot of us." Julian watched the man carefully, but he did not seem to mean anything by the remark; and Julian reflected that his conduct the night before was not something that would be talked about in barber shops. Friends meant something, and they did not talk about that sort of thing in barber shops. Still, on his way out to the car he remembered that last night was only the second of two big nights for him, and it was extremely likely that barbers and everyone else had heard about his performance with Harry Reilly. "Good God," he said, remembering. This morning he had forgot all about Harry Reilly.

He changed his mind about driving out to the garage right away. Harry Reilly had an office in the bank building and he decided to call on Harry there. It was two blocks from the hotel, and he might get a ticket for parking, but if he couldn't get the ticket fixed, it was worth the two-dollar fine to have things straightened out with Harry.

Some places the sidewalk was all clean, some places there was only a narrow path cleared away, and the snow got down in his shoes when he stepped out of the way for women. Another minor annoyance. In front of J. J. Gray's jewelry store he met Irma Fliegler. "Hello, Julian," she said.

"Hello, Irma," he said, and stopped.

She was wearing a raccoon coat and she had some packages under her arm. It was still so cold that from a short distance away women did not seem to have any distinctive features, but close up she became Irma Doane, or at least Irma Fliegler, again; still pretty, a bit on the stout side, but stout in a way that did not make her unattractive. You knew that she was not going to get stouter, or definitely fat. She had very pretty legs and hands. You remembered how pretty her hands were when you saw them with gloves on.

"Well, you certainly were a fine example of the young mother last night," said Julian. He knew it was the wrong thing to say, but some mention had to be made of last night. Better to make some mention of it than to be self-conscious about not bringing it up.

"Me? What did I do? Julian, you're nuts."

"Now, now, Irma, you don't think I don't remember. Didn't you know you stole the trombone player's hat?"

"Oh, you're kidding. You're a fine one to talk, you are. What a load you had. Did you get home all right?"

"I guess so," he said. Then he thought quickly. "I felt a little sick, haven't felt that way in years, and I was dancing, too, so I had to go out."

"Oh," she said. Maybe she believed him.

"I pulled a complete pass-out in the car. I think it was some girl from your party that I was dancing with," he said. Maybe she might believe him.

"Oh, no it wasn't. Not that they didn't want to, but you went out with the singer."

"What singer?"

"Helene Holman her name is, she sings at the Stage Coach."

"Oh, it's worse than I thought. I guess I have to send her flowers. I had some vague idea it was Frannie. I remember talking to her."

"She was there, but you didn't dance with her," said Irma. "She was having her own troubles. Well."

"See you soon," said Julian.

" 'Bye," she said.

He walked on, a little afraid that he had made a fool of himself, that Irma had not believed a word of his too-ready story that he had gone out with Helene because he was sick. But he knew that whatever he did, Irma would stick up for him. He always had liked Irma; she was the prettiest girl in high school, and a big girl, when he was a kid running around with Butch Doerflinger and Walt Davis and the rest of his kid friends. She had taught him in Sunday School, and did not report him on Sunday afternoons when he "bagged it" to go to a ball game. He wished he could tell her all his troubles, and he knew that if there was one person to whom he would tell them, it would be Irma. But she was Mrs. Lute Fliegler, the wife of one of his employees. He told himself that he must not forget that.

He went up in the elevator to Harry Reilly's office. "Hello, Betty. Your boss in?" Betty Fenstermacher was a stenographer who also ran the switchboard in Harry's office. Betty also had given her all to Julian and at least a dozen of his friends when they were all about nineteen or twenty.

"Hello, Ju," she said. "Yes, he's in all right. Can't you hear him? He's going away, and you'd think he was never away before in his life. Do I have to announce you?"

"I think you'd better. Where's he going?"

"Oh, New York," she said, and spoke into the telephone. "Mr. English is here to see Mr. Reilly. Shall I send him in?"

Just then Harry appeared, bag in hand, hat and coat on. "I'll be back by Tuesday at the latest," he was saying. "Phone Mrs. Gorman and tell her I made the train all right." He turned his face, and for the first time Julian was able to see that Harry's eye was decorated with a shiner, there was no other word for it. The ice apparently had smacked his cheekbone, and the pouch of flesh under the eye was blue and black and red and swollen. "Oh, it's you," said Harry.

"Yes, I thought I might as well come—"

"Listen, I can't wait another minute. I'm catching the ten-twenty-five and I have about four minutes. I'll be back next week." He ran through the office. Julian thought of going along with him to the station, but rejected that plan. He couldn't get anything said to a man who had four minutes to catch the train. On her own hook Betty Fenstermacher was calling the station and telling them to hold the train; Julian became conscious of this, and when she finished he said:

"What's it all about?"

"I don't know. I heard him shoot off his mouth about a lot of railroads going together. You'd think he was the one that was getting them together, the fuss and fury we been having around this office this morning. I hear you gave him the shiner, Ju. What was he, making passes at your wife or something?"

"No. Good-by, darling," he said. Ordinarily he would have stopped to kid Betty, to whom you could say anything without insulting her, but now he was still blank from Harry's breezy walk-out. It wasn't like Harry.

On the way back to the car Julian recalled that he had heard some talk about a merger of the New York Central, the Chesapeake & Ohio, Nickel Plate, Baltimore & Ohio and the Pennsylvania, and such merger certainly might have an effect on Harry Reilly's fortune. Harry had large holdings in Virginia and West Virginia, in the soft coal fields. But Harry was a teller of elaborate lies, too; and he might be using the merger as an excuse to leave Gibbsville until the black eye was less black. Julian wished he knew whether the merger really was going through. Not that he would do anything about it now, but he still had the curiosity about such things that anyone who has traded in the stock market never quite loses: inside dope is fun to have, and he might risk a hundred or so on it. No, he guessed he wouldn't. If he knew anything, there was not going to be any merger; Harry Reilly was still a four-flusher; couldn't even leave town without making it appear that he was leaving on an errand of big business.

Driving out to the garage he could think of only one thing that occurred so far this morning that wasn't especially designed to annoy him; and that was that the fact of Harry Reilly's going away, the fact that Harry was going to be away with a legitimate reason would keep people from talking when he did not show up at the party tonight. Considering the way things were going today, that was a good break. . . . Yes, there was one other good break this morning; he had not been given a ticket for parking. At that moment a cross-link on the tire chains broke, and he rode the rest of the way to the garage with the link banging, cack-thock, cack-thock, cack-thock, against the left rear fender.

He blew the horn at the garage door, and it was fully two minutes before Willie, who washed cars and was an apprentice mechanic, opened the door. Julian had left orders at least fifty times that no one was to be kept waiting at the door, and he was going to bawl Willie out, but Willie called out: "Merry Christmas, boss. How'd Santa Claus treat you?"

"Yah," said Julian.

"Well, thanks for the Christmas present," said Willie, who had received a week's pay. "That fifteen bucks come in handy." Willie was closing the door and talking above the sound of the idling motor and the sounds of the mechanics working upstairs. "I said to my girl, I said—"

"Cross link busted on the right rear chain," said Julian. "Fix it."

"Huh? When'd it break?"

"Right now, at Twelfth Street."

"Well, say, it held up pretty good. Better'n I thought. Remember, I told you Wensdee already, I said you better leave me fix them cross-links."

"Uh-huh." Julian had to admit that Willie *had* told him. He went to the office, which was in the rear of the big show room on the street floor. "Good morning, Mary," he said.

"Good morning," said Mary Klein, his secretary.

"What's doing?"

"Pretty quiet," she said, adjusting her spectacles.

"Have a nice Christmas?"

"Oh, it was all right I guess. My mother came downstairs in the afternoon, but I guess the excitement was too much for her. She had another spell around a quarter after five and we had to have Doctor Malloy out."

"Nothing serious, I hope," said Julian.

"Oh, I don't think so. Doctor Malloy said not, but those doctors, they don't always tell you the truth. I want her to go to Philadelphia to see a specialist, but we're afraid to tell Doctor Malloy. You know how he is. If we told him that he'd say all right, get another doctor, and we owe him so much already. We do the best we can, but there doesn't seem to be any sign of my brother getting a job yet, although it isn't for the lack of trying. Dear knows he isn't much of an expense and my mother, she has *some* money, but I have to keep up the building and loan and the insurance and food is so high again, my goodness."

One nice thing about Mary's morning recital of her woes was that usually you could stop her at any point and she would not be offended. "I guess we all have our troubles," he said. He had said this at least three mornings a week since Mary had come to work for him, and always Mary responded as though it were a shining new idea.

"Yes, I guess so," she said. "I was reading in the paper on the way to work about the man that used to write those comical articles in the *Inquirer*, Abe Martin, he died out west somewhere. I thought he was from Philadelphia but it said Indiana. Indianapolis, I think. Now *there* was a man—"

"Hello, Julian." It was Lute Fliegler. Mary immediately ended her talk. She disliked Lute, because he had once called her the biggest little windbag this side of Akron, Ohio, and to her face, at that.

"Hello, Lute," said Julian, who was reading a letter from a dealer in another part of the state, planning a gay party for the week of the Auto Show. "Want to go to this?" he said, throwing the letter to Lute.

Lute read it quickly. "Not me," he said. He sat down and put his feet up on Julian's desk. "Listen, we gotta make a squawk again about Mr. O'Buick."

"Is he at it again?" said Julian. O'Buick was their name for Larry O'Dowd, one of the salesmen for the Gibbsville-Buick Company.

"*Is* he?" said Lute. "I tell you what happened this morning. I went out to see Pat Quilty the undertaker this morning. I had him out a couple times in the last month and he's ready to go, or he was. He wants a seven-passenger sedan that he can use for funerals and for his family use. Or he *did*. Anyhow, I honestly figured, I said to myself, this is the one day the old man won't be expecting me to come around, so maybe I'll surprise him into signing today. And he'll pay cash on the line, too, Julian. So I took a ride out to see him and I went in his office and started kidding around—he likes that. Makes him feel young. So I noticed I wasn't getting a tumble from him, so finally I broke down and asked him, I said what was the matter, and he said to me in that brogue, he said: 'Will now Oill till you, Meesturr Fliegler, the way I hear it the coompany you do be working for, I hear they don't like people of my faith.'

208

" 'What?' I said. 'Why the Cadillac car is *named* after a Catholic,' I said. I said 'Old Duke Cadillac, he was a Catholic.'

" 'I don't mean Ginrul Mawtors, Mr. Fliegler,' he said. 'I mean Julian English, that's who I mean.'

" 'Why, Mister Quilty,' I said, 'you're all wrong about that,' I said. I told him about Reverend Creedon, what a good friend of yours he is, and how you did this and that and the other for the sisters and so on, but he wouldn't hear any of it. He said he didn't always see eye to eye with Reverend Creedon, as far as that goes, but that wasn't the point. The point was, he said, he'd been hearing some stuff about you and Harry Reilly having a fight. What the hell's he talking about?"

"I threw a highball in his face the other night," said Julian.

"Oh, that," said Lute. "I heard about that. But you weren't having a fight over religion, were you?"

"No. Certainly not. I was cockeyed and I just let go with the drink. What else? What about O'Buick?"

"Well, that's the trouble. I can't get anything on him," said Lute. "Old Quilty, he wouldn't tell me any more than what I told you, except to say he was going to take a little time to think it over before he bought anything off us. I'm afraid we're not going to move that car unless you go out and talk to him yourself, Julian."

"Do you think that would do any good?"

"To tell you the God's honest truth, I don't know. I'm up a tree. When one of these Irish bastards gets the idea you're against their church, you have your hands full bucking it. The only explanation for it in a case like this is young O'Dowd, the son of a bitch, he heard about you and Reilly having this fight or whatever it was, and he went right out and gave old Quilty this story. That's my guess. I'd like to punch him one in the nose."

"So would I."

"Well, don't *you* do it or we won't be able to *give* the product away in 1931. I might as well tell you all the bad news while I'm at it."

"You mean more bad news?" said Julian.

"That's what I mean nothing else but," said Lute. "Julian, I don't want—wait a minute. *Miss* Klein, would you mind going out on the floor a minute while I talk with Mr. English?"

"Not at all. The language you use." Mary Klein left the office.

"Listen, Julian," said Lute. "Your private affairs are your own business, and you're boss here and all that. But I'm ten years older than you and you and I always hit it off pretty damn good, so do you mind if I give it to you straight from the shoulder?"

"No. Go ahead."

"Well, I don't want you to take offense at this, and you can fire me if you get sore, but you been making a fool of yourself, and last night up at the Stage Coach—Jesus, I don't know what to say. But you oughtn't to done that, taking that dame out, that torch singer. You know whose girl she is? Ed Charney's. One of the best friends we have, in a business way. There's a guy, a lot of people don't want to have anything to do with him, and I guess a lot of your friends think you contaminate yourself by selling him an automobile. But meanwhile Ludendorf is selling plenty of Packards to the same friends, so what they think don't matter. Ed Charney is a right guy, a square shooter. He pays his bills regular, and they're pretty big bills. He likes you personally. He told me that many's the time. He says you're the only one in the whole high-hat crowd that he considers on the up and up. Well, what's the result? The result is, any time one of his boot-legger friends is on the market for a high-priced automobile, Ed sees to it that we make the sale. You don't see Ludendorf selling Packards to any of Ed Charney's pals.

"So then what? So then you turn around and pay him back by giving his girl a lay and making a monkey out of him right in his own spot, not to mention making a fool of yourself with your own wife and friends right there. You know what'd happen to any of Ed's own crowd that tried to pull a fast one like that, don't you? Why it'd be suicide, and just because your father happens to be a big shot here, Julian, don't think you're in such a good spot yourself. I don't mean Ed's going to have his gorillas turn a Tommy gun on you or anything like that. But why can't you be more careful? I happen to know Ed is plenty burned up, and, my God, I don't blame him. He's been keeping that dame for over two years now, and everybody says he's nuts about her, and then you get cockeyed and take her out for a quick jump and ruin the whole works. My God, Julian."

"You're wrong about one thing," said Julian.

"What's that?"

"I didn't lay that girl."

Lute hesitated before answering. "Well, maybe you didn't, but everybody thought you did and that amounts to the same thing. She was out in the car with you long enough, and when she came back she didn't look as if you'd been sitting there listening to Father Coughlin on the radio. What surprised me was that you'd have anything to do with her at all. Not that it's for me to say, but you always struck me as the ideal married couple, you and Caroline, Mrs. English. That's what Irma said too. I know it's the first time I ever knew of you going on the make for some dame. Honest, Julian, I don't want to talk out of turn, but if you and your wife are having family troubles, you ought to do your best to fix it up. You have the nicest, the swellest girl in the whole God damn Lantenengo Street crowd, and everybody in town thinks so, and if you take it from me—and mind, I'm ten years older'n you—you do the wise thing and patch it up. Irma and I, we have our troubles, but she knows how it is between she and I, and I think you feel the same way about Mrs. English.

"There. I've shot off my face more than I intended to, but I'm glad I got it off my chest. If you want to give me the air, that's your business, but everything I told you is the truth and down in your heart you know it, pal. I can

212

get another job, or if I can't, I'll get by somehow. If you're the kind of a guy that'd fire me for what I been telling you, then you're not the kind of a guy I always took you for, and I don't want to work for you. So that's that." Lute stood up slowly.

"Sit down, Lute." Julian was unable to say more than that. The two men sat opposite each other for a few minutes. Lute offered Julian a cigarette and Julian took it, and Julian gave Lute a light. Presently Julian said: "What do you think I ought to do, Lute?"

"Gee, I wish I knew. I guess let it ride for the time being. You were cockeyed, and that's one consolation. Maybe Charney will take that into consideration. Aw, what the hell. We'll get by. Don't take it to heart too much. I'll see you this afternoon around quitting time. I have to go to Collieryville now, but it'll work out one way or another. Shake?"

"Shake," said Julian. They shook hands and smiled, and Lute left, and Julian heard him telling Mary Klein that everything had been decided; they weren't going to handle automobiles any more; just airplanes.

"It isn't true, is it, Mr. English? What Luther Fliegler just told me?"

"What did he tell you?"

"That we were going to stop selling cars and sell airplanes instead. I don't think there's any market for airplanes around here."

"Don't let it worry you for a couple of years, Mary," said Julian. "You know Lute."

"And how!" said Mary Klein.

It was one of those mornings when he could tell himself that he was up to his ears in work or that he had nothing to do, and either with equal honesty. His hangover did not bother him inordinately; he knew he could work in spite of whatever effect the night before still maintained. He wanted to work; the difficulty was in getting started. He wanted to work to put things out of his mind, and he tried to the extent of getting out some scratch paper and pencils with the idea of working out some sort of summary or recapitulation of the year's business of the Gibbsville-Cadillac Motor Car Company. This was a good time to do that; when no salesmen would disturb him, and when there was nothing much else he could do. But the words, summary, recapitulation—they made him think of Lute and how he had recapitulated and summarized his performance of the night before, including the consequences. The Quilty business—well, he thought he knew what to expect there: O'Dowd probably hadn't said a word to old Quilty, but when O'Dowd did hear about Julian's throwing the highball at Harry Reilly, he would hotfoot out to Quilty and make the sale. O'Dowd was a good salesman, and he knew how to handle a situation like this. Julian hated to lose that sale, too, because no matter how people joke about it, when you place a car with an undertaker, you have a pretty good advertisement. Undertakers keep their cars in the best of shape, black and gleaming and polished and clean. Julian knew this from his own reaction; he often had thought that if you had to die, it

214

wouldn't be so bad to ride to the cemetery in Quilty's luxurious hearse, followed by Quilty's well-kept Studebaker sedans. Whenever he heard the tune, Saint James' Infirmary, he always thought of old Quilty. And the sale would be for cash. That wouldn't be hard to take. It certainly made it hard to lose. He wondered if Harry Reilly had gone to work already. Harry was a very rich man and handling his investments and holdings was a full-time job, but he also managed to know what was going on in other people's businesses, and it would be just like him to know that old Quilty was thinking of buying a Cadillac. It was just the kind of thing he would know. After all, why shouldn't he know it? He had lent Julian twenty thousand dollars last summer, and that was a nice piece of change no matter how much Harry might be worth. It was enough to excuse any extraordinary interest Harry might be taking in Julian's business.

Twenty thousand dollars! Why in God's name had he ever asked for that much? He knew perfectly well why he had asked for that much: at the time he needed ten thousand, but he figured he might as well get a good hunk while he was at it. Ten thousand had gone in no time: it cost, even with the cheap labor and construction costs of last summer, about eight thousand to build the inclined driveway inside the building, which he had calculated would mean eventually a great saving in electric power bills through decreased use of the elevator. So far it hadn't made much difference, if any. In fact, Julian would not have argued very long if someone suggested that the driveway was an ill-advised project. Then what else was there? Well, there were those two three-wheel motorcycles. The idea of them was a mechanic could ride the motorcycle to, say, the Davis' garage, hook some kind of gadget on the Davis' Cadillac, and drive the car, with the motorcycle trailing along behind, back to the Gibbsville-Cadillac Motor Car Company for servicing or repairs. That was another idea that was going to make a saving, but the saving, Julian was sure, had failed to make a showing on the books. And why *two* motorcycles? One was enough. More than enough. Then there were the trees, those beautiful, slender trees. Julian had conditioned himself against ever seeing them when he passed them, but now he made himself think of them. There they were out there in the little strip of grass along the curb. Seven-hundred and sixty-six dollars and forty-five cents' worth of them, including freight and planting. Julian knew to the penny what they cost, but he still was not sure of the name of them. They had been purchased while he was in a fine, naturalistic mood as an aftermath of a City Beautiful luncheon. There had been trees a long time ago where the Gibbsville-Cadillac Motor Car Company now stood, and there had been trees along the curb, but they had been chopped down. Then one day Julian went to a City Beautiful luncheon and everybody got up and said a few words about trees and what they did for a residential section—Julian's garage was in a residential section—and by the oddest coincidence there chanced to be a man from a

216

nursery at the luncheon, and Julian signed. And that about took care of the extra ten thousand dollars.

The other ten thousand had gone for expenses, real ones, like payments on notes, payroll, and so on.

Lute was right on another score: Ed Charney was a good customer. "I'm a good customer of Ed's," Julian reminded himself, "but he's a better one of mine." Something ought to be done about Ed, but he supposed the best thing to do for the present was to lay off trying to fix it up. Yes, he certainly had loused things up last night: Ed Charney sore at him, Caroline—well, he wouldn't think of that now; he was at work, and he would try to think of things only in so far as they affected his business. If Ed Charney got really sore—but he wouldn't do that; he wouldn't throw a pineapple at the garage. This was Gibbsville, not Chicago. And after all, the English name meant something around here. "No thanks to me, however," Julian said under his breath.

"Darn his buttons anyhow," said Mary Klein.

"What is it, Mary?" said Julian.

"Luther Fliegler," she said. "He makes out these slips when he gets gas, but you never can tell whether he means ten gallons or seventy gallons, the way he makes figures."

"Well, I don't think he'd be making out a slip for seventy gallons. A car doesn't hold that much gas," said Julian. "Besides, that's not your headache. Let Bruce worry about it."

Mary turned to look at him. "Sure, but you forget. You told Bruce he could go to Lebanon over the week-end."

She spoke as a woman who was carrying on in spite of all injustice. Bruce Reichelderfer was the bookkeeper, and Julian had given him the week-end.

"That's right, I did. Well, let me see it."

She handed him the slip. She was right as usual; you could not tell from the figures whether Lute had meant 10 or 70. "We ought to use the French seven," he said. "Then we'd always know. However, I guess we can take a chance that he meant ten gallons. He wouldn't be signing for seventy gallons all at once."

"Well, I just wanted to be right on it. Sixty gallons of gas, that costs money, and we can't just—"

"I know, Mary. You're right." Somehow her tone filled him with terror, the kind that he felt when he knew he was doing something bad. It was an old experience; he still thought of it in the terms of boyhood: "—when I'm doing something bad." And it wasn't her tone alone; it was her manner, and it was not a new manner. For weeks, and probably months, she had behaved like someone, a school teacher, who was meaning to speak to him about his lessons or conduct. She was Right, and he was Wrong. She could make him feel like a thief, a lecher (although God knows he never had made a pass at her), a drunkard, a no-good bum. She represented precisely what she came from: solid, respectable, Pennsylvania Dutch, Lutheran middle class; and when he thought about her, when she made her existence felt, when she actively represented what she stood for, he could feel the little office suddenly becoming overcrowded with a delegation of all the honest clerks and mechanics and housewives and Sunday School teachers and widows and orphans—all the Christiana Street kind of people who he knew secretly hated him and all Lantenengo Street people. They could have their illegitimate babies, their incest, their paresis, their marital bestiality, their cruelty to animals, their horrible treatment of their children and all the other things which you could find in individual families; but collectively they presented a solid front of sound Pennsylvania Dutch and all that that implied, or was supposed to imply. They went to church on Sunday, they saved their money, they were kind to their old people, they were physically clean, they loved music, they were peace-loving, they were good workers. And there they sat, with their back curved in at the small part, their oilcloth cuffs covering their sleeves, their fresh blouse as neat after five hours' wear as Julian's shirt after two. And they were thinking what a pity it was that this wonderful business wasn't in the hands of one of their own men, instead of being driven into the ground by a Lantenengo Street—wastrel. And yet, Julian made himself admit, Lute Fliegler is a Pennsylvania Dutchman and one of the swellest guys that ever lived. Thinking that over Julian returned to his old theory: it was possible, wasn't it? that Lute's mother had had a quick one with an Irishman or a Scotsman. A hell of a thing to think about that old Mrs. Fliegler, who still baked the best pie crust Julian had ever tasted.

Every few minutes Julian would jot down some figures as they came into his head. All the time he looked very busy, and he hoped he was making a good impression on Mary Klein. The sheets of paper that lay before him were filling up with neat, engineering style lettering and numerals. Addition, subtraction, multiplication, and division. . . .

He did. What's the use of trying to fool myself? I know he did. I know he did and no matter what excuses I make or how much I try to tell myself that he didn't, I'll only come back to the same thing: He did. I know he did. And what for? For a dirty little thrill with a woman who— oh, I thought he'd got all that out of his system. Didn't he have enough of that before he married me? Did he still think he was a college boy? Did he think I couldn't have done the same thing to him, dozens of times? Did he know—oh, of course he didn't know that of all his friends, Whit Hofman was the only one that I can truthfully say never made a pass at me. The only one. Ah, Julian, you stupid, hateful, mean, low, contemptible little son of a bitch that I hate! You do this to me, and *know* that you do this to me! *Know* it! Did it on purpose! Why? It wasn't only to get even with me. It wasn't only because I wouldn't go out in the car with you. Are you so dumb blind after four and a half years that you don't know that there are times when I just plain don't feel like having you? Does there have to be a reason for it? An excuse? Must I be ready to want you at all times except when I'm not well? If you knew anything you'd know I want you probably more then than any other time. But you get a few drinks in you and you want to be irresistible. But you're not. I hope you found that out. But you didn't. And you never will. I love you? Yes, I love you. Like saying I have cancer. I have cancer. If I did have cancer. You big charmer, you. You irresistible great big boy, turning on the charm like the water in the tub; turning on the charm like the water in the tub; turning on the charm, turning on the charr-arm, turning on the charm like the water in the tub. I hope you die.

I hope you die because you have killed something fine in me, suh. Ah hope you die. Yes-suh, Ah hope you die. You have killed something mighty fine in me, English, old boy, old kid, old boy. What Ah mean is, did you kill something fine in me or did you kill something fine. I feel sick, sick as a dog. I feel sick and I would like to shoot my lunch and I would like indeed to shoot my lunch but I will be damned if I want to move out of this bed, and if you don't stop being nasty to servants—I said r. I said a word with r in it, and that makes me stop this silly business. I wonder why? I wonder why r?

Oh, I guess I better get up. There's nothing to be gained by lying here in bed and feeling sorry for myself. It's nothing new or interesting or novel or rare or anything. I'm just a girl who just feels like dying because the man I love has done me wrong. I'm not even suffering any more. I'm not even feeling anything. At least I don't think I am. No, I'm not. I'm not feeling anything. I'm just a girl named Caroline Walker, Caroline Walker English, Caroline W. English, Mrs. Walker English. That's all I am. Thirty-one years old. White. Born. Height. Weight. Born? Yes. I always think that's funny and I always will. I'm sorry, Julian, but I just happen to think it's funny and you used to think so too, back in the old days when I knew you in an Eton collar and a Windsor tie, and I loved you then, I loved you then, I love you now, I love you now, I'll always love you to the day I die and I guess this is what they call going to pieces. I guess I've gone to pieces, because there's nothing left of me. There's nothing left for me of days that used to be I live in mem-o-ree among my souvenirs. And so what you did, what you did was take a knife and cut me open from my throat down to here, and then you opened the door and let in a blast of freezing cold air, right where you had cut me open, and till the day you die I hope you never, never know what it feels like to have someone cut you open all the way down the front of you and let the freezing blast of air inside you. I hope you never know what that means and I know you won't, my darling that I love, because nothing bad will happen to you. Oh, lovely Callie, your coat is so warm, the sheep's in the meadow, the cows in the corn. *"No, I don't think I'll get up for a while, Mrs. Grady."*

It was inevitable that every time Al Grecco went to the garage in which Ed Charney kept his private cars, he should think of a photograph one of the boys from the west had shown around. Probably a great many men—and the women of those men—in Al Grecco's line of work had

222

the same thought, inspired by the same photograph (there were thousands of copies of the photograph), whenever they looked inside an especially dismal garage. The photograph showed a group of men, all dead, but with that somehow live appearance which pictures of the disfigured dead give. The men were the victims of the St. Valentine's Day massacre in Chicago, when seven men were given the Mexican stand-off against the inside wall of a gang garage.

"It'd be a nice wall for it," Al said, as he opened the garage door.

He went upstairs and lugged a case of champagne down the steps. Then he went up again and lugged a case of Scotch down, and then he lifted them into a dull black Hudson coach, which was used for deliveries. He backed the car out into the street, Railroad Avenue, and then got out and slid the garage doors shut. He took one more look at that blank wall before he finally closed the door. "Yes. It sure would be a nice wall for it," he said.

No man could call him what Ed Charney had called him and get away with it. Not even Ed Charney. He thought of his mother, with the little gold earrings. Why, he could remember when she didn't own a hat. She would even go to Mass on Sunday with that scarf over her head. Often in the far past he had told her she was too damn lazy to learn English, but now, thinking of her, he thought of her as a good little woman who had had too much work to learn much English. She was a wonderful woman, and she was his mother, and if Ed Charney called him a son of a bitch, all right; if he called him a bastard, all right.

Those were just names that you called a guy when you wanted to make him mad, or when you were mad at him. Those names didn't mean anything anyhow, because, Al figured, if your mother was a bitch, if you were a bastard, what was the use of fighting about it? And if she wasn't, you could easily prove it. What was the use fighting about it? But this was different, what Ed Charney had said: "Listen you God damn dirty little guinny bastard, I sent you up there last night to keep an eye on Helene. You didn't have to go if you didn't want to. But what do you do? You double-cross me, you son of a bitch. I bet English gave you a sawbuck so he could take her out and give her a jump, and you sit back there collecting fifty bucks from me becuss I'm sap enough to think you're on the up-and-up with me. But no. Not you. Not you. Why, you small-time chiseling bastard, you. You dirty lousy mother —— bastard." And more like that. Automatically Al had tried to explain: all she did was dance with him; she wasn't outside long enough to do anything with English ("You're a dirty liar. Foxie told me she was out a half an hour."); English was stewed and not on the make ("Don't tell me about English. I'm not blaming him. I'm blaming you. You knew she was my girl. English didn't."), and so on. In his heart Al wanted to tell Ed the real truth; that he could have made Helene himself if he hadn't been on the up-and-up. But that wouldn't do any good now. Or it wouldn't do enough harm. Ed was crazy mad. He was so crazy mad that he said all these things to Al over the telephone from his own house, most likely in front of his wife.

224

Oh, positively in front of his wife. If she was in the same house she couldn't help hearing him, the way he was yelling into the telephone. So Al just stood there at the phone and took it without making any real comeback. At first he had been stunned by the accusation of being a double-crosser. But in Al's and Ed's line of work it is never wise to call an associate a double-crosser; if the associate is guilty, the thing to do is punish him; if he isn't guilty, it puts the idea into his head. And then when he remembered the bad thing that Ed had called him, that began to put the idea into Al's head. He hadn't made any plans about what he was going to do. Not yet. But something would have to be done. "I guess it'll be me or him," he said, thinking of that wall.

But meanwhile he had his work to do. Little jobs here and there. Odds and ends, daily routine work. Ed had been in such a rage, so burnt up, that he had forgot to fire Al, and despite everything he had said, he had not indicated that he intended to fire Al. In their line of work it was one thing to have a scrap, a mouth fight, or to be angry for a day or two at an associate. But to fire a man was something else again. You didn't just fire a guy like *that* (finger-snap). Not even in Gibbsville, which was not Chicago.

That was the trouble, in a way. In a way maybe it was a break that it wasn't Chicago, because out there they knocked each other off with less excuse than a fight over a dame. But in another way Al was sorry it wasn't Chi. In Gibbsville they never had a gang war, because Ed Charney simply didn't have any competition. Whereas on the other hand, in Chi they did. They had gang wars all the time. They were used to it. In Chi you could get away with it. In Gibbsville it would be just a murder, and they would have to make a pinch and have a court trial and all that, and the juries around here were so screwy, they might even send you to the chair. "That Rock View, I don't want any part of that," said Al.

So now he had a nice little job to do. A little odds and ends. He had to take this champagne and this Scotch out to where English lived. English, the mugg that caused all the trouble in the first place. Although as he drove along he could not stir up any very strong hatred of English, because the truth of the matter was, if you wanted to know who was responsible, it wasn't English or it wasn't even Helene with her hot pants. It was Ed Charney himself. A married man with a kid, and absolutely haywire on the subject of another woman not his wife. That was where the trouble was. He wanted everything, Ed did. Well, that remains to be seen, as the elephant said.

"I'm above this kind of work," Al said, as he lifted first one case, then the other, out of the Hudson and laid them down on the kitchen porch of the English house. He rang the bell.

"How much is it?" said the old woman.

"You don't have to pay me," said Al, who knew that English had credit with Ed.

"I said how much is it?" said the old woman, the cook, he guessed she was.

"A hundred and seventy-five. A hundred for the champagne, seventy-five for the Scotch."

The woman closed the door in his face and in a few minutes she came back and handed him a check and a five-dollar bill. "The cash is for you. A tip," said the woman.

"Stick it—" Al began.

"Don't you say that to me, you dago wop," said the old woman. "I got two boys would teach you how to talk. If you don't want the money, give it here."

"The hell I will," said Al.

"Aw, my goodness. Where you going, beautiful lady? You going somewhere?" said Foxie Lebrix.

"Can that stuff," said Helene Holman. "Will you phone down to Taqua and get me a taxi? I'll pay you for the call."

"Aw, but I hate to see you leave. I t'out you and I—"

"I know you thought, but we ain't, see? If you don't want to get me a taxi, say so and I'll walk it," said Helene.

"Wit' all dose bags?"

"You're damn right. The quicker I get out of this place the better I like it. Well, what about the taxi?"

"Wall, I would not see you walking in the snow. Maybe we see each other in New York some day, and you get me a taxi when I leave your place, eh? Sure I get you a taxi."

8

Mary klein had gone home to lunch and Julian was alone in the office, with a small array of sheets of paper on which were rows of figures, names, technical words: Number of cars sold in 1930; our cut on new cars sold; gas and oil profit 1930; tires and accessories profit 1930; profit on resale of cars taken in trade; other profit; insurance on building; ins. on equipment; ins. on rolling stock; interest on bldg.; taxes; advertising; graft; expenses; light; other elec. outlay; heat; tool replacement; licenses; office stuff, incl. stationery; workmen's compensation; protective association; telephones; bad debts; stamps; trade-in losses; lawyer & accountant fees; building repairs; losses not covered by ins.; plumber; depreciation on bldg.; deprec. on equipment; depr. on trade-in jobs; depr. on new cars not moved; contributions to charity; cash advance to self; notes due at bank; cash needed for payroll. . . . As a result of his figuring Julian announced to the empty room: "I have to have five thousand dollars."

He stood up. "I said, I have to have five thousand dollars, and I don't know where I can get it. . . . Yes, I do. Nowhere." He knew he was lying to himself; that he did not need five thousand dollars. He needed money, and he needed it soon, but not five thousand dollars. Two thousand would be enough, and with any break in the beginning of the year, after the auto shows in New York and Philadelphia (which are attended by a surprising number of Gibbsville automobile enthusiasts), he would be able to get back on his feet. But he reasoned that it was just as hard to get two thousand as five, five thousand as two. It was easier to get five, he told himself; and as he had argued less than a year ago, when he had gone to Harry Reilly for a loan, he might as well go for a neat, convenient-sounding sum. The question seemed to be: Where to get it.

Tempers are better in summer than in winter, in Gibbsville; Julian's summer life had included a good deal of Harry Reilly last summer, and it was easy enough to get away from him. If you didn't want to play golf with Harry, you said you had promised Caroline to play a match for blood with her, which did away with the necessity of asking Harry to play along. On the other hand, it was not bad to drink with Harry in a party of undershirted convivials in the locker-room, and Harry was a fair tenor and even knew songs about the roll of Delta Kappa Epsilon, Lafayette was Lafayette when Lehigh was a pup, the Lord Jeff of Amherst, and a lot of other college songs. Of course Harry got the words wrong sometimes, but Julian was no purist who would discourage the progress of a fair tenor. No, a good tenor, as locker-room tenors go.

He thought of these things. Harry must have changed

229

since then, become obnoxious or something. Julian reasoned that he could not have asked the Harry he now knew to invest so much money in the business. Well, maybe the winter had something to do with it. You went to the Gibbsville Club for lunch; Harry was there. You went to the country club to play squash on Whit Hofman's private court, and Harry was around. You went to the Saturday night drinking parties, and there was Harry; inescapable, everywhere. Carter Davis was there, too, and so was Whit; so was Froggy Ogden. But they were different. The bad new never had worn off Harry Reilly. And the late fall and winter seemed now to have been spoiled by room after room with Harry Reilly. You could walk outside in the summer, but even though you can walk outside in winter, winter isn't that way. You have to go back to the room soon, and there is no life in the winter outside of rooms. Not in Gibbsville, which was a pretty small room itself.

Well, what was the use of trying to build up Harry now as having been a swell guy last summer. Last summer Julian had needed money, and Harry Reilly had money, so he had asked Harry. And Harry had said: "Jesus, I ain't got that much cash at this present minute. Do you need it right away?" Julian had said he needed it pretty soon. "Well, I don't see how I can get it for you before tomorrow. . . . Oh, hell, sure I can." Julian had almost laughed in his face: in one minute the little worry that Harry wanted to have a month to think it over and raise the cash had come and gone. Julian had had a lot more

230

trouble in college, trying to borrow forty-four cents to go
to the movies. . . . Harry had been no different then
from the Harry he knew today. Might as well face that.
As for the Caroline angle, Julian believed in a thought
process that if you think against a thing in advance, if you
anticipate it—whether it's the fear that you're going to cut
yourself when you shave, or lose your wife to another man
—you've licked it. It can't happen, because things like that
are known only by God. Any future thing is known only
to God; and if you have a super-premonition about a
thing, it'll be wrong, because God is God, and is not giving
away one of His major powers to Julian McHenry English. So Julian thought and thought about Caroline and
Harry, and thought against them, against their being
drawn to each other sexually, which was the big thing
that mattered. "By God, no one else will have her in bed,"
he said, to the empty office. And immediately began the
worst fear he had ever known that this day, this week, this
minute, next year, sometime she would open herself to
another man and close herself around him. Oh, if she did
that it would be forever.

Julian reached in the second drawer of the desk and took
out a Colt's .25 automatic and got up and went to the wash-
room. He was breathless with excitement and he felt his
eyes get the way they got when he was being thrilled, big
but sharp. He sat down on the toilet, and he knew he was
not going to do it that way. But he wanted to sit down
and look at the pistol. He looked at it for he knew not
how long, and then snapped himself to without changing

231

his position in the slightest degree. He put the barrel in his mouth and some oil touched the inside of his lower lip. He made a "Guck" sound, and took a long breath, and then he put the pistol in his pocket and got up and washed his mouth with cold water and then he took off his upper garments, except his undershirt, and washed himself all over the head and face and arms to the elbow. He used four towels, drying himself. Then he put on his clothes again, wiped stray drops of water off his shoes, and went back to the office and lit a cigarette. He remembered a bottle of whiskey he had in the desk, and he had a long-lasting drink of one whiskey glass of it. "Oh, I couldn't," he said, and he put his arms on the desk and his head on his arms, and he wept. "You poor guy," he said. "I feel so sorry for you."

He heard the first of the mechanics' post-luncheon sounds: the thump of a baseball in a catcher's mitt. That meant the mechanics were through lunch, because one of the men pitched on a semi-pro team, and he kept himself in shape all winter. Julian held his head up and the phone rang. "Hello," he said.

"I just tried to get you at the club. Where'd you have lunch?" It was Caroline.

"I didn't," he said.

"Well, I don't suppose you felt much like it. Now listen, Julian, the reason I called is, if you talk the way you did to Mrs. Grady again, we're through. Do you hear?"

"Yes."

232

"I mean it this time. I'm not going to have you take your hangovers out on any servants. Mrs. Grady should have slapped your face."

"Say!"

"It's about time someone slapped your face. Now I want you to understand this, old boy. If you come home drunk this afternoon and start raising hell, I'll simply call up every person we've invited and call off the party."

"You'll simply, huh?"

"Oh, shut up," she said, and ended the call.

"She'll simply," he said, to the telephone, and gently replaced the handpiece in the cradle. "She'll simply." He got up and put on his hat. He stopped and debated, a very short debate, whether to leave a note for Mary Klein. "Naa, who's Mary Klein?" He struggled into his coat and drove to the Gibbsville Club.

The usual crowd was not in the club this day. "Hello, Straight," said Julian to the steward.

"Good afternoon, Mr. English. I hope you had a merry Christmas. Uh, we all want to thank you for your, uh, generous, uh, subscription to the club employes' Christmas fund. Uh." Old Straight always spoke as though he had just been sniffing ammonia.

"Well, you're very welcome, I'm sure," said Julian. "Have a nice Christmas."

"Quite nice. Of course, uh, well, of course I have no family that you'd, uh, really call a family, uh. My nevview in South Africa, he—"

"Mr. Davis in the club? Who's here? Never mind. I'll go look."

"Not many members here today. The day, uh, day after—"

"I know," said Julian. He went into the dining-room, and at first glance it appeared that it was occupied solely by Jess, the Negro waiter. But there was a small table in one corner, by common consent or eminent domain, the lawyers' table, at which sat a few lawyers, all older men and not all of them Gibbsville men, but residents of the smaller towns who came to the county seat when they had to. You did not have to speak to the men at the lawyers' table. In fact, some of the men who sat there did not speak to each other. Julian had hoped Carter Davis might still be in the club, but there was no sign of him. He sat down at a table for two, and he no sooner had given his order than he was joined by Froggy Ogden.

"Sit down and eat. I just ordered. Jess'll take your order and serve it with mine if you want to."

"I don't want to," said Froggy.

"Well, then, sit down and take the load off."

"You're feeling pretty snotty today," said Froggy, sitting down.

"Snotty isn't the word for it. Cigarette?"

"No, thanks. Listen, Julian, I didn't come here for a friendly chat."

"Oh, no?"

"No," said Froggy. You could see he was getting angry.

"Well, then, come on. I've been hearing the anvil chorus

234

all day, so you might as well join it. What kind of a fig have you got—"

"Now listen, I'm older than you—"

"Oh, it's going to be one of those. And you have my best interests at heart? That one? Jesus Christ, you're not going to give me that."

"No. I'm not. I'm older than you in more ways than one."

"What you're trying to say is you lost your arm in the war. Do you mind if I help you? You lost your arm in the war, and you've suffered, and that makes you older than me, and if you had both arms I guess you'd thrash me within an inch of my life."

Froggy stared at him until they heard the wall clock ticking. "Yes. I have a notion to bust you one right now. You God damn son of a bitch, Caroline is my cousin, and even if she wasn't my cousin she's one of the finest girls there is, Caroline is. You want to know something? When she told me she was going to marry you, I tried to stop it. I always hated you. I always hated your guts when you were a kid, and I hate you now. You never were any damn good. You were a slacker in the war—oh, I know how old you were. You could of got in if you'd tried. You were yellow when you were a kid and you grew up yellow. You chased around after that Polish girl till she had to go away or her father would have killed her. Then you put on some kind of an act with Caroline, and God help her, she fell for it. I tried to stop it, but no. She said you had changed. I—"

"You're a dirty God damn one-armed bastard, and I wish you had that other arm."

"You—don't—have to wish it," said Froggy, and he picked up the glass of water and threw the water in Julian's face. "Come on outside. I'll fight you with one arm." Trembling with rage, Julian stood up, and then he felt weak. He knew he was not afraid; he knew he could not fight Froggy. He still liked him, for one thing; and for another, he could not see himself fighting a man who had only one arm.

"Come on. Anywhere you say," said Froggy.

Julian wiped the water off his face with a napkin. "I don't want to fight you." He wondered, but did not turn his head to ascertain it, whether the men at the lawyers' table had seen the incident. He heard some children playing in the street and he thought of horrible Saturday mornings at the dentist's, when he was a kid and horses were being whipped and children were playing in the street and the car to Collieryville would be ringing its bell.

"Come on. Don't stand there because I only have one arm. I'll worry about that. Don't you."

"Go away. Beat it," said Julian. "You're showing off. You know I can't fight you."

"Come outside or by Jesus I'll sock you in here."

"No, you won't. I won't let you sock me in here, hero, and I won't fight you outside. You think I'd give people the chance to say that about me? You're crazy. Go on, beat it, General. The war's over."

"Yeah? That's what you think. You're right. I knew

you wouldn't fight. There isn't a spark of manhood in you. I knew you wouldn't fight. There isn't a spark of manhood left in you, if there ever was one."

"Run along, cousin. Go on home and count your medals."

Froggy swung on him and Julian put up his open hand and the punch made a slight smack sound on his wrist, and hurt his wrist.

"Gentlemen!"

"Don't be a God damn fool," said Julian.

"Well, then, come on outside."

"Gentlemen! You know the club rules." It was Straight. He stood in front of Froggy, with his back toward Froggy, facing Julian. He certainly made it look as though he were protecting Froggy from an attack by Julian. By this time there was no doubt about the lawyers' being in on the quarrel. They were all watching, and two of them were standing up. Julian heard one of them say something about "see what he *did* . . . one arm." He knew they were doing just what everyone else would do who heard about this: they were taking for granted that he had socked Froggy. One stout man, whom Julian knew only as a lawyer face around the court house and Gibbsville restaurants during court terms, walked over and put his hand on Froggy's shoulder. "Did he hit you, Captain Ogden?"

"Captain Ogden!" Julian laughed.

"We know all about him up the mountain," said the stout man.

237

"Are you by any chance a member of this club?" said Julian.

"A member, and what's more you never see my name posted," said the man. "Don't you worry about me being a member."

Well, that was all right. It was a slap at Julian, who had been posted two or three times, but it also was a slap at Froggy, Carter, Bobby Herrmann and just about everyone else. It was no distinction to be posted at the Gibbsville Club; it could mean that you had not paid your bill six days after the bill was presented.

"Is this man a member, Straight?" said Julian.

"Oh, yes. Mr. Luck is a member."

"Luck? Lukashinsky, if I know anything."

"What's that got to do with it. This is between me and you," said Froggy.

"Not any more, it isn't. No, Captain, it's between me on the one side, standing here alone, and you and the Polack war veterans and whoremasters on the other side. I'll stay where I am."

"Hey, you!" said the lawyer.

"Aw," said Julian, finally too tired and disgusted with himself and everyone else. He took a step backwards and got into position, and then he let the lawyer have it, full in the mouth. The man fell back and gurgled and reached fingers in his mouth to keep from choking on his bridge-work. Another lawyer came over, another Polack whose name Julian never could remember. He had a club soda bottle in his hand.

238

"Put that down!" said Froggy. "He has a bottle!" He grabbed a bottle himself, and Julian got a water carafe. All through it Straight kept saying Gentlemen, gentlemen, gentlemen, and kept out of the way.

"Come on," said Julian, to the man with the bottle. The man saw the carafe and hesitated. The other lawyers took the bottle away from him without a great struggle. The man could not keep his eyes off Froggy. He could not understand why Froggy had warned Julian.

"Go on out and get a warrant, Stiney," called the lawyer whom Julian had socked. Julian hit him again, hit him in the hands, which were covering the sore mouth. He hit him again in the ear. Froggy grabbed Julian's shoulder to pull him away, and Julian pulled up his shoulder so suddenly that it hit Froggy in the chin. The lawyer went down, not to get up for a while, and then Julian rushed Froggy and punched him in the ribs and in the belly and Froggy lost his balance and fell over a chair. Julian picked up the carafe again and hurled it at the man who had come at him with the bottle, and without waiting to see what it did, he ran out of the room, taking his coat and a hat off the hall rack. He hurried to the car.

"Hi, boy." Someone called to him. Julian had his foot on the starter and he identified the greeter as Whit Hofman. Well, Whit was a son of a bitch, too. Whit probably hated him and had hated him for years, just as Froggy had done. The car jumped out of the snow and Julian drove as fast as he could to the quickest way out of Gibbsville. The worst of that drive was that the sun glare on the snow made you smile before you were ready.

Your home is the center of many zones. The first zone is your home, the second can be the homes around you, which you know only less well than you do your home. In the second zone you know where the rainpipes have stained the shingles on the houses, you know where the doorbell button is, how much of a bedpost can be seen in an upstairs window; the length of slack taken up in the porch-swing chains; the crack in the sidewalk; the oil spots from the drip-pans in the driveway; the lump of coal, which you remember from the time it was not swept away, and its metamorphosis from day to day as it is crushed and crushed into smaller lumps and into dust and then all that is left of it is a black blot, and you are glad one day that it has been crushed and it no longer is there to accuse you of worrying about your neighbor's slovenliness. And so on.

The next zone is the homes and buildings you pass every day on your way to work. The tin signs outside little stores, the trees with the bark gnawed away by horses, the rope on the gates and the ancient weights, the places where the street ought to be repaired, the half-second view of the town clock tower between two houses. And so on.

And more zones, zones that the farther you get from the center, the longer spaces there are in the familiar things. In one zone a hundred yards of highway will be familiar, while in another zone the familiar spaces are a matter of inches. In the familiar zones remembering is effortless. An outside zone is where your brain begins to tell you where to make a turn in the road and where to keep going straight and where to blow your horn and where to slow down for a curve. Julian was in an outside zone, southwest of Gibbsville and in the Pennsylvania Dutch farming country, when he first brought himself up. He was first able to perceive that he had been driving, judging by the distance at least a half hour, when he became aware of not having a hat on. He reached over and picked up the hat beside him, but his fingers rejected the dents in the crown, and he examined the hat. The brim did not snap down in front. It was a Stetson, and Julian wore Herbert Johnson hats from Brooks Brothers. But he did not like to see men driving hatless in closed cars; it was too much like the Jews in New York who ride in their town cars with the dome lights lit. He put the hat on the back of his head, and lowered the window at his side. The first breath of air made him want a cigarette almost immediately, and he slowed down to light one from the torch on the dashboard.

The road was his. He wanted to drive on the left side and zigzag like an army transport and idle along at four miles an hour. But one time when he thought the road was his he had done all these things, finally to be arrested for drunken driving by a highway patrolman who had been following him all the while. "You'd think you owned the road," the patrolman had said; and Julian could not answer that that was exactly what he had been thinking.

So long as the engine did tricks for him he knew he was safe, but when he discovered this about the car, that it was occupying his mind and keeping it off the events of the last hour, two hours, twenty-four hours, forty-eight hours—although it was not forty-eight hours since he had doused Harry Reilly with a highball—the discovery forced his eyes to the clock. And the clock said three-eleven. It was three-eleven back at the garage, and he had to get back to see Lute Fliegler. He slowed down and stopped just beyond a country lane, he backed the car in the lane and then drove out, and the radiator now pointed in the direction of Gibbsville and not away from it. The faster he drove the less he liked the zones he was getting into. He wished he had gone on instead of turning around. To go on until he had spent his money, write a check in Harrisburg, write another in Pittsburgh, until his money was gone; then sell the car, sell it and buy a second-hand Ford, sell his coat, sell his watch, then sell the Ford, then get a job in a lumber camp or something— where he wouldn't last a minute, not a day. There was something awfully good and lucky for him in being guided out of the club and into the car and away, but something else had pulled him back. You did not really get away from whatever it was he was going back to, and whatever it was, he had to face it. His practical sense told him that the idea of going away, writing checks, selling the car and so on, eventually would catch up to him. He probably would break a law. Oh, more than that. The way things were now at the garage, he had no right to sell this car, nor even to run away. He was too tall to run away. He would be spotted.

And so he kept his foot on the accelerator, hurrying back to Gibbsville. The cigarette burned down to his glove —he could not remember putting the gloves on—and made a little stink. He threw the cigarette out and he yawned. Always when he felt sleepy while driving he would light a cigarette and it would revive him, but now he was sleepy and tired and did not want to be revived. Even the little fight in him annoyed him. He did not want to fight and he did not want to be awake.

You would look at Mrs. Waldo Wallace Walker, dressed in a brown sweater with a narrow leather belt, and a tweed skirt from Mann and Dilks, and Scotch grain shoes with fringed tongues, and a three-cornered hat. You would know her for all the things she was: a woman who served on Republican committees because her late husband had been a Republican, although she always spelt it tarriff. She would be a good bridge player and a woman who knew the first two lines of many songs, who read her way in and out of every new book without being singed, pinched, bumped, or tickled by any line or chapter. Between doing the last thing and the next she would beat her hands together in little claps, rubbing her pure, once pretty fingers together for the warmth she generated in the fingertips, and making you expect her to say something good and wise about life. But what she would say would be: "Oh, fish! I *must* have my *rings* cleaned."

A stranger, spending his first hour with her, would look at her clothes and think what trunkfuls of once stylish suits and hats and dresses she must have—and she had them. She was the prettiest woman of her age in Gibbsville, and though she did not know it and would not have accepted it, her hairdresser would have been glad to do her for nothing, she was such a good ad. She also would have made a good ad for spectacles; but she also would have made a good ad for drinking a cup of hot water in the morning, Don't Worry, take a nap every afternoon, walk a mile every day, the Golden Rule, visit your dentist twice a year, and all the other codes that she had the time and the means to live by.

Judge Walker had not left a great fortune, but there was money there. Mrs. Walker gave $250 to this, $15 to that, and never personally turned a hungry man away from her kitchen door. When Caroline was at Bryn Mawr, Mrs. Walker, according to Caroline, became president ex officio of the college, and in later years it was always with difficulty that Caroline restrained her mother from calling on Dr. Marion every time they motored through Bryn Mawr, the town. Someone once told Mrs. Walker that Caroline had great independence of spirit, and this delighted the mother and caused her to allow Caroline to develop as much as possible unassisted. Whatever independence of spirit Caroline possessed had developed unassisted before Mrs. Walker made a philosophy of it, but at least Mrs. Walker did make it much easier for Caroline, and Caroline made it as easy as possible for her mother to develop unassisted too. There had been nothing but placid love in their relationship from the time Caroline began taking her own baths. It was a comfortable relationship, only slightly disturbed, if at all, by the fact that from the time of that necessary talk when Caroline was thirteen, Caroline always thought of her mother as a person who could say "the mouth of the womb" without leaving the tiniest inference of any excitement to be had there. In the beginning of her love with Julian Caroline sometimes felt sorry for her mother as she felt sorry for all the females she liked because of what they were missing, but after a year or two she wondered if it could not be possible that her mother simply had forgot the hours of her own passion. Julian said that a lovely lady had to be passionate to get that look—and Mrs. Walker had been a lovely lady. Julian was fond of his wife's mother, a fondness that was incomplete only because he was not sure that she really liked him. But Mrs. Walker gave everyone who knew her well that feeling; and the truth was that at the moment of ordering the groceries, Mrs. Walker was as fond of Joe Machamer, the clerk at Scott's, as she was of anyone except her daughter, and the dignity in the memory of her husband, and Abraham Lincoln. (Mrs. Walker had an uncle whose home had been part of the underground railway for slaves.)

Mrs. Walker was turning the pages of a Christmas book, *Mr. Currier and Mr. Ives*, when she heard the front door open and close. "Who is it?" she sang.

"Me." Caroline took off her gloves and coat and hat,

and her mother put up her hand as though to ward off a too-affectionate kiss (it gave that impression), but when her daughter lowered her head to kiss her, Mrs. Walker cupped Caroline's chin in the palm of her hand. "Dear," she said. "Did you have a nice Christmas. Never even telephoned, did you?"

"Yes, I did, but you were out."

"Yes, I was. I did go to Uncle Sam's. You look well, dear."

"I don't feel well. I feel like the devil. Mother, what—"

"Yes, a little tired. A little strained. Why don't you make Julian take you—"

"What would you do if I got a divorce?"

"—to Pinehurst. Divorce? Oh, now, Caroline. Four years, almost five. Divorce."

"I thought so," said Caroline. She relaxed. "I'm sorry. I just came here because I had to speak to somebody and I didn't want to talk to somebody that'd blab it all over."

"Are you serious?"

"Yes, I'm serious."

"But are you? Are you serious, Caroline? That's a very serious thing, when people start talking about a divorce. We've never had a divorce in our family, and I don't think there was ever one in Julian's family either. What is it?"

"I'm just fed up. I'm sick and tired and miserable. I'm so miserable and unhappy. I'm so unhappy, Mother, I don't care if I die."

246

"Die, dear? Are you pregnant? Are you, dear? You could be wrong, you know. It might just be the strain, Christmas." She got up and sat beside Caroline. "Come here, dear. Tell me about it. Mother wants to hear all about it."

"Caroline wants to cry," said Caroline, and laughed.

"Oh, this *is* serious. Dear, don't. Have you missed the second period, dear?"

"Yes. Someone was in our seats. Oh, Mother, please. I'm not pregnant. That's not it."

"Are you sure, dear?"

"I'm positive. Mother, please don't worry about that. That's not it at all. It isn't that. I guess I don't want to talk about it," said Caroline. "I'll tell you what's the matter. I might as well. I'm through with Julian. I want to go away and get a divorce and never hear his name again for a long time. We can go to France, can't we? Can't we?"

"Well, I suppose so. This year we ought to be a little more careful, Mr. Chadwick says and Carter. Carter isn't very optimistic. But we could if we had to, go to Europe I mean. Seven. Twenty-five. Hundred and. Oh, we could go. You wouldn't want to buy many things, would you, dear?"

"I don't want to buy anything. I want a divorce. I want to stop being with Julian English and this life. All I am is tired. It's nothing more than that. I'm just tired and fed up. I'm all washed up and I want to go away. I want to sleep here tonight and all other nights. I want to

247

forget Julian and I want to talk to somebody and go away. I want to talk to somebody with an English accent or I don't know. I'm sorry."

"This is serious. Tell me all about it if you want to. Of course if you'd rather not."

"I'm not making much sense, am I?"

"Did you have a quarrel? Oh, you must have, of course."

"No. Strangely enough, we didn't. Not what you'd call a quarrel. That is, we didn't have any scene or anything. It isn't as easy as that. That could be fixed, I guess."

"Well, what then? Julian isn't in love with someone else, is he? I can't somehow I can't believe that. I don't profess to know much about Julian, or any men, for that matter, but if Julian's in love with someone else, then I'm no judge at all. If it's just another woman temporarily, dear, don't wreck your life on that account, I beg of you. Don't wreck your whole life. Men are different from us women. An unscrupulous woman can make a man—"

"Period."

"What, dear?"

"Nothing."

"Well, as I was saying, dear, please listen. A woman without any scruples—and it might be someone we know. I don't know a thing about this other woman, but there are unscrupulous women in every strata of life."

"Mother?"

"Yes, dear."

"Mother, what did you do with all the old records?"

"What old records, dear? Do you mean the Victrola records? Those?"

"Yes. What did you do with them?"

"Oh, don't you remember? I gave them to the Y.M.C.A. camp three years ago. You said at the time you didn't want them, only a few. You took *some*."

"Oh, so I did."

"If there's any special one you want we could send for it. Mr. Peters would be glad to get it I'm sure. He wants me to buy an autophonic and trade this one in, this Victrola. But I'd never use an autophonic. I never use this one."

"Orthophonic, Mother."

"Orthophonic? It sounded like autophonic. Are you sure? Mr. Peters, I was sure he said autophonic. Oh, Caroline, see?"

"What, Maman?"

"See? It's all over, isn't it? Your bad spell. Here we are, having one of our discussions about words. You and Julian. You didn't leave any foolish notes, did you, dear?"

"Oh, God no. I never thought to. Mother, do you really think I came running to you with a silly five-minute quarrel?"

"Well, after all, you're not upset any more, are you?"

"Do you really think I'm not?"

"Yes. I do. I really think the worst of it has passed, gone. Your father and I had our quarrels, too."

"When he died you said you never quarreled."

"I never said that. At least, I never tried to give the

impression that we didn't have our differences. That would be untrue. All high-strung people, people in love, they always have their differences. As a matter of fact, Caroline, I've been thinking all along, something told me there wasn't much to this. I'm nothing if not sympathetic and you know there's nothing I wouldn't do to see you happy, but I don't want you to behave like a foolish child and do things and say things you'll be sorry for later. Divorce! Why the very idea is—it's wrong, Caroline, and I don't see how you could say such things. You go on back to Julian, or stay here a while if you want to punish him, but stop this talk about divorce. Understand, I'm not defending Julian, but I should think you'd know how to handle him by this time. Flatter him, use your feminine wiles. You're a pretty girl and he loves you. Believe me, Caroline, when a wife can't hold a husband and there's no other woman, the wife had better stop and see where the lack is in herself. Oh, my. It's all so much like the time your father and I had our first quarrel."

"What was your first quarrel about—not that this is my first, but go on, dear. Tell me. Caroline wants to know."

"It wasn't anything much. It was personal. Just between your father and I, dear."

"Sex?"

"Caroline! Yes, it was, in a way. Is that—is—are you and Julian—does he want you to do something you— something . . ."

If she only knew Julian, Caroline thought; if she only

knew me! "No, dear. Julian's always been very good about that," she said.

"Oftentimes men don't understand. Many girls' lives are ruined, completely wrecked, because men don't understand how a nice girl feels. But let's not talk about that. I told you when you were married, I told you to take a firm stand on certain things."

"You never told me what things, though."

"Well, dear, a nice girl. I couldn't very well tell you some things till the matter came up. Apparently it never did, or you'd have come to me, I'm sure. You're still only a girl, though, Caroline, and if you're having trouble that way, that sort of trouble, please come to me instead of going to some friend your own age. I think things of that sort ought to be talked over between mother and daughter, not outsiders. I finally learned how to handle your father and my experience isn't worth a thing, not a snap of the fingers, unless I'm able to help you, hand it on to you. But let's not talk about it unless you want to."

"Tell me more about Father," said Caroline.

"No. No. That's sacred. Your father never worried me about another woman, not even before we were married. Julian, I think probably Julian—not that it's anything against him, because he was quite grown up when he fell in love with you. But I don't think you were the first girl in Julian's life. I've often thought so. That may be a good thing in some cases, but I don't know."

"Mother, don't talk about it if you don't want to. I'm sorry."

"Conversations like this aren't good, Caroline. I'd rather go on, living my poor useless life and loving your father for what he was, a good, decent man, than exhume chapters of our life together. Men are weak, darling. In the hands of a woman the strongest man in the world is weak, so don't think any the less of Julian or your father or any other man if he has a momentary weakness. . . . Oh, here I am, talking away about something I don't know the first thing about. But you do feel better toward Julian, don't you? If you do, that's all that's necessary."

"I'm sorry if I was inconsiderate."

"Oh, you weren't inconsiderate. You couldn't be. You were just curious. That shows you're still a little girl. Want some gum?"

"I'd love some."

"It's really very good for the digestion, and I think the muscles of the jaw need the exercise. How are your teeth, Caroline?"

"I'm going to have to have a wisdom tooth out, Dr. Patterson says."

"Well, he probably knows his business. I still like Dr. Baldwin."

"Not after lunch, though, Mother."

"What? Why?"

"He bolts his food or eats too much or something. His stomach rumbles."

"I never noticed that when I went to him," said Mrs. Walker. "Are you sure?"

"Oh, yes. I wouldn't make up a thing like that."

"Do you want to stay here tonight? Isn't there a dance tonight?"

"There's one in Reading. No, I guess I better not stay here. As a matter of fact, we're having a party."

"Oh, I didn't know that. A big party? Who are you having?"

"The usual crowd. The younger crowd, a few from the school crowd, and our own friends. Which reminds me."

"Is there anything you want?"

"No, but I must go. I was going to call it off when I first came here, but I might as well go through with it, so I must do some shopping, odds and ends. I'll see you tomorrow or next day. Give me a nice Beech-Nut kiss. Good-by."

"Good-by, darling. You're a sweet girl."

"You're the one that's sweet," said Caroline. She put on her things in the hall, knowing that her mother was standing at the window, waiting to wave to her. Well, at least she had made some kind of gesture for tradition; she had run to mother. The visit had been a fiasco, but she was glad in a way that it had been—glad that it had been a fiasco in the way that it had been, but sorry if it were to result in awakening disturbing memories, whatever they were, for her mother.

She ran down the steps and turned and waved to her mother before getting in the car. Her mother waved and then the curtains fell into place and her mother withdrew from the window. Then Caroline heard a long blast of a Cadillac horn, and she saw Julian in his car, half a block down the street, on the other side. He was waiting. She drove her car near his, staying on her side of the street, and stopped. He got out and sauntered over. He looked like hell.

"Well," she said.

"You were in there long enough. What did you have to see her for?"

"Now really, Julian. Is that reasonable?"

"Is it reasonable for you to be down here now? What's it all about? I suppose you had to take down your back hair and have a good cry and so forth."

No answer.

"Oh, that's it. Giving her a song and dance about me, I suppose. Little bride runs to mother because hubby doesn't like her biscuits. For Christ's sake. Good God, I tried to—what did you tell her? Come on, what did you say?"

"This is no place for a scene."

"It's as good a place as any. Better, in fact. It's safer for you, because I probably won't do here what I feel like doing."

"You mean punch me in the face, I suppose."

"How did you ever guess it?"

"If you take your foot off the running-board I'd like to get going."

"I suppose you heard about the club."

"I didn't. What club? What do you mean, the club? Has the club suspended you on account of the other night?"

"Now she's interested. No, the club hasn't suspended me, not as far as I know. This is a different club, this time."

"The Gibbsville Club?"

"The Gibbsville Club no less."

"What happened there? What did you do there?"

"I had a little get-together with Mr. Ogden, Captain Ogden, the war hero, the one-armed wonder and snooper extraordinaire."

"What do you mean?"

"You'll find out. You'll find out soon enough. You said something about going a minute ago. Go ahead."

"I don't want to go now till I find out what you're talking about. More trouble. God, I'm so tired of it." Her voice broke and she began to cry.

"No scenes on the street, dearie. No scenes on the street. No street scenes, if you please. It's your idea. Can't have things like this in public."

"Oh, Julian, what did you do? My God." She was now really crying. Her voice had the far-away sound of hollow pain, despairing women in removed rooms down a hospital hall, wailing women at the mouth of a blown-up mine.

"Listen, will you go away with me? Now? This minute? Will you? Will you go away with me?"

"No, no, no, no, no. What did you do? Tell me what you did? What did you do to Froggy?"

"I can't talk to you like this. Let's go home."

"Oh, no. I don't want to go home. You'll make me stay

with you. Oh, go away, Julian. Please let me alone." A horn sounded and a small coupe passed. Caroline waved. Julian waved. It was Wilhelmina Hall and the visiting Gould man, from New York. "Are they going to stop?" said Caroline.

"No. They're going on. Me too," he said.

"No. What did you do? Tell me. Come in to Mother's with me. She knows we're having a quarrel. She won't bother us."

"Like a whole lot of hell I will. I'm not going in there. I'm going."

"If you leave I'm going to call off the party and I'm going to stay here. Be reasonable, Julian. Tell me what happened."

"No. Come on home with me and I'll tell you. Otherwise no. This is a pretty good time for you to stick by me."

"I can't stick by you if you don't tell me what for."

"Blind, without knowing, you could stick by me. That's what you'd do if you were a real wife, but, what the hell."

"Where are you going? To get drunk I suppose."

"Very likely. Very likely."

"Julian, if you leave now it's for good. Forever. I won't ever come back to you, no matter what happens. I won't ever sleep with you again or see you, not even see you."

"Oh, yes, you will. You will, all right."

"You're pretty sure of yourself, but this time you're wrong. It's no go."

"I didn't mean that. I didn't mean I was sure of myself. What I meant was, you'd see me. You wouldn't be able to help it."

"Why should I want to?"

"To gloat, probably. Either you'd want to gloat, if you were absolutely out of love with me, or you'd want to see me if you still loved me."

"You're so wrong it isn't even funny."

"It isn't even funny. Lord and Taylor! Wouldn't that jar you? I'll say. You tell 'em casket, I'm coffin. I'll tell the world. Don't take any wooden nickels. . . . I'm going."

"Oh, go ahead. But remember, I'm not going to be home tonight. Not me. I'm going to call off the party, unless you want to have it. Anyway, I won't be there."

"That's all right. It only makes it a different kind of a party."

"Oh, there's no need to tell me that. But you'd better be careful with your torch singer. She knows how to handle people like you."

"You're a dear. You're a sweet girl. I knew you'd be a good sport about it. I knew all along you would be."

"Oh, go to hell, you and your cheap sarcasm."

"No wonder the chaps at the club say I'm henpecked," said Julian. He regretted it the moment he said it; club was not a word he wanted to use now. "You'll attend to the details about the party, calling people up and telling them I broke my leg and so on, will you?"

"Of course, unless you want to have it yourself and say *I* have a broken leg."

"That's better. I don't mean about you having a broken leg. But it's nicer for us to be agreeable and sort of phony about it. You know what I mean?"

"You're the authority on phony, of course, but, yes, I know what you mean. I know."

"All right, dear. Cheerio, I mean cheero. Stout fella."

"Funny boy. You're a scream."

So he left.

9

GIBBSVILLE moved up from the status of borough and became a third class city in 1911, but in 1930 the city still had less than 25,000 inhabitants (estimated 1930 population in the notebooks sent out by the Gibbsville banks to their depositors). In Gibbsville a party becomes an institution the moment the hostess tells her plans to one other person, and nothing short of a death or other act of God must postpone the party, once the invitations are given. To the persons who eventually had been invited and to those who wished they had, the English party got in the institution class a day or two after the Lafayette-Lehigh football week-end. On their way home from Easton Caroline and Julian decided to have a party "some time during the holidays." They were riding in Whit Hofman's car, with Whit and Kitty, and Kitty immediately said it would be a swell idea, and began to count off the nights when the party could not be given on account of conflicting parties. It couldn't be given the night of any of the Gibbsville dances nor the afternoon of the tea dances. Kitty Hofman finally decided upon the date. "There's the Junior League dance in Reading the night after Christmas Day," she said, "but I'm sick of going to Reading. Let them come up here for a change. We go down there and spend our money on their lousy Junior League parties, but if we ever tried to have a Junior League in Gibbsville you know what support we'd get from Reading."

No argument.

"So let them come to our parties this year," Kitty continued. "The Assembly. That money goes to charity, doesn't it, Whit?"

"In theory it does," said Whit.

"It usually ends up with Whit paying for the Assembly," said Julian.

"Don't forget, you pay your share," said Whit. "We all do. But they do come to the Assembly sometimes. Sometimes they do."

"All right. Let them come again. Let's not go to their Junior League dance. Let them help our charity. Caroline, you have your party that night. The twenty-sixth."

"How about it, Ju? That's all right, isn't it?"

"You're God damn right. I won a hundred dollars on the game. No, two hundred. But anyway, a hundred that I'll get. Bobby Herrmann will owe me his hundred."

"Well then, that's settled. The twenty-sixth we'll have our party. Our own crowd and some of the school kids, the ones that can drink. Not Johnny Dibble and kids that age, but a little older," said Caroline.

"Oh, dear me," said Julian. "My goodness sakes alive. Oh, my. We have to have Johnny. We must have Johnny

Dibble. Why, he's practically a Deke. No matter where he goes to college, he's going to be a Deke."

"Not if he goes to State," said Whit.

"Right. Not if he goes to State. No Dekes at State. How'd you know that, Whit? You know more about D. K. E. than I do. Why can't we have Johnny, Caroline? He's a nice kid. . . . Well, *kind* of nice."

"All right, we'll have him, if you insist. He drinks as well as you do, for that matter. He'll make a good Deke. Who else shall we blackball?" Caroline and Kitty worked on the list, and the next week it was in Gwen Gibbs' column on the society page of the *Standard*. Gwen Gibbs' column was a dumping ground for all society gossip on the *Standard*. There was no Miss Gibbs, of course. There was an Alice Cartwright, graduate of the University of Missouri School of Journalism, and daughter of the current Baptist minister. Miss Cartwright knew very few of the Lantenengo Street crowd and except for the Purim Ball and K. of C. Promenade she was not on any of the invitation lists. She certainly never for a second expected to be on the list of the invited guests for the English party. And she wasn't. Yet the night of the party she was the only one who arrived at the attractive home of that leading young business man and that charming leader of the younger married set; in this case, Mr. and Mrs. Julian M. English.

Julian got afraid of something the moment he walked away from Caroline and climbed in his own car. He never looked her way again after he left her. He treated his car more considerately. He moved along, approaching the business district at a moderate rate of speed, extra-careful of the rights of other motorists and of pedestrians, and resolved that since he was already a quarter of an hour late for his date with Lute Fliegler, he would break the date entirely and without explanation. He did that with a clear conscience because he effected an exchange in himself: in exchange for accepting in advance the hell and the fury of what he was going to have to face with his father and Harry Reilly and the lesser stockholders in the company, who were going to have to save him from bankruptcy—he paid himself off by keeping the rest of this day to himself. If ever there was a man in a jam, he was it, he was sure. It was no more difficult to face a fist or to enter the front-line trenches than it was going to be to meet these people, especially his father. Nobody would have the crust to tell his father about the Stage Coach episode, because his father was a kind of man who would have the Stage Coach raided for less reason than that his son had been a fool there. But someone was sure to tell him about throwing a drink in Harry Reilly's puss. It was the sort of thing Gibbsville men, their identities masked by hot towels, would be hearing often in the hotel barber shop for the next couple of weeks. And yet it was not so bad as the mess at the Gibbsville Club. The Polack lawyers would tell every— "Good Christ! Polacks are Roman Catholics!" Julian thought of that for the first time. And now he remembered seeing the emblem of the

262

Benevolent and Protective Order of Elks in the lapel of the man he had knocked down. "Is there anything I haven't done? Anyone I haven't insulted, at least indirectly?" . . . He tried to be honest and to figure out every possible bad angle to the last few days' work, in order that he could go back and find something comforting. He thought of the bad way he had treated Caroline, the many bad ways; doing something that permitted her to accept disgrace, as with the drink thrown at Harry Reilly; doing something that publicly and unequivocally and personally humiliated her, which was going out with Helene Holman. His manner toward Mrs. Grady this morning—a thing Caroline especially (and, sometimes, a little unreasonably) campaigned against. And then, a little before he was ready for it, he thought of the thing that in its way was more important than anything between himself and Caroline; that thing was the never-to-be-buried discovery that all this time Froggy Ogden had been his enemy. That was worse than anything he could do to Caroline, because it was something that did something to him. It made a change in himself, and we must not change ourselves much. We can stand only so many—so few—changes. To know that there were people who he thought were his friends, his good friends, but who were his enemies—that was going to make a change, he knew. When was the last time there had been a change in himself? He thought and thought, rejecting items that were not change but only removal or adornment. He thought and thought, and the last time there had been a change in

263

himself was when he discovered that he, Julian English, whom he had gone on thinking of as a child with a child's renewable integrity and curiosity and fears and all, suddenly had the power of his own passion; that he could control himself and use this control to give pleasure and a joyous hiatus of weakness to a woman. He could not remember which girl it had been; to forget her had been a simple manifestation of his ego; the important part of the discovery, the change, had been a thing for himself, his own moment. But he saw how deep and permanent the discovery, the change, became. It was almost as important, and no doubt precisely as permanent, as the simplest discovery of physical manhood. And there again it was the change and not the act that had been lasting and great; for he could not recall with accuracy the circumstances of that discovery.

It was easier to bear now, the discovery that it was possible that to him it might happen that there were people who bothered to hate him. Why did they bother, really? Yet they did. People also liked him. Still it was no shock to find out, for example, that a girl had been loving you for a long time before you found it out. Part of you expected people, girls especially, to like you, and there was no jolt but only a corroboratory pat on the back in the experience of hearing a girl say, "Darling, I've loved you so much longer than you have me." Girls fitted easily into their own and your own picture of someone dying of unrequited love. If they slipped out of it before you were ready, that was all right too; their slipping out frequently was the necessary reminder that an affair had run its course. It also was the necessary reminder that the realist in a woman, the good appraiser, makes her want to take a loss and get out before she is—for the purposes of the analogy—ruined.

Often Julian had faced this suspicion: the suspicion that a man who is good with women, as good as he had been, is not wholly trusted and liked by men. In the past he had thought of this many times, but he dodged the conclusion as applying to himself. Men liked to have him on poker parties, in golf foursomes, at luncheon (the Lions Club finally got him after he had squirmed away from Rotary and Kiwanis). But now he wondered if there was the slightest meaning to their including him in their gregariousness. No, there was no meaning more flattering than their habit. And as he drove the car in the garage at the side of his house he began to see things. Froggy Ogden, making a boastful confession of treachery and long hatred of him, had seemed proud of having done the job so well that Julian had not thought of him as anything but a friend. There must be others like him. Froggy had been one of his best friends. What about Carter? Whit? Bob Herrmann (who was a fool, but had a life and was leading it)? What about the wives of the men he liked? Those men, many of whom could have hated him and probably did hate him, must have told their wives. Jean Ogden, for instance. She'd known all along that Froggy hated him, but never gave any sign of warning. Did Kitty Hofman's bad manners come from

the assurance she got from knowing that Whit hated him?
. . . And if it only was hate! It would be so much better
hate than just being disliked and held in contempt. It
came back again to women; the fellows, those who knew
him best, had kidded him about his Polish friend. But all
the time they had kidded him they were being moral, and
all the time they were being moral, underneath that they
were wishing they had Mary. But Mary had been his girl.
He closed the door of the garage. Mary had been his
girl and he got again the sensation of looking at her. Just
for a second the sensation came back; the embarrassment
he had felt so many times, with wanting to look at her
beautiful body but with his eyes held by her quiet, shining
smile until then she would look at her breasts and then
look at him and the smile would be gone. And he was sure
now of what he had not quite wanted to be sure of then:
that Mary had loved him and never would love anyone
else the same way. He put her out of his mind and went
in the house and sat down and stretched out on the couch
in front of the fireplace. Oh, he went to sleep, wishing he
knew more things.

It was dark and one hand of the clock was on ten, but
Julian could not be sure that it was the big hand or the
little hand and he was too comfortable to move so he could
see his watch. Then he knew why he was awake. The
doorbell was ringing. He got up and ran his fingers
through his hair and pulled his vest and coat around and
fixed his tie. It could have been Caroline at the door. The

girl was about the same height. But when he got closer he saw she was wearing glasses. He opened the door and the air was good.

"Oh, good evening, Mr. English. I'm Miss Cartwright from the *Standard*. I'm sorry to disturb you. I thought you were having a party."

"It's been postponed. Won't you come in?"

"Well, I don't think I ought to really. But that's news." She was confused by Julian's smile. "I don't mean it's news when I don't come in."

"Well, come on in and have a drink," he said. God knows why he wanted to talk to her, but she was somebody.

"Well, for a minute. I meant to say it's news if you're not going to have the party. Is it postponed? Sickness in the family? Is Mrs. English not feeling well, or what?"

"No. I think you'd better call Mrs. English at Mrs. Walker's. She'll tell you about it."

"Oh, dear," said Miss Cartwright, lighting a Spud. "Now that means I have to get something to fill the column. I don't suppose I could run it and say the following will attend—when is the party postponed to, Mr. English, or is it indefinitely?"

"Indefinitely, I think. Do you like Scotch or rye? Or would you rather have a Benedictine or something like that?"

"Rye and ginger ale, if you have it," she said.

"Is that your car outside?" he said.

"My brother's. That is, it belongs to him and another

boy. It's just an old flivver, on its last legs, but it saves me a lot of steps and trolley fares when he comes home. He always lends it to me when he's home, but he takes it to college with him. He goes to Brown."

"Oh, Brown."

"Yes. Providence, Rhode Island."

"Yes, I've been there."

"Oh, did you go to Brown, Mr. English? There aren't many from around here go to Brown."

"No. I went to Lafayette, but I've been to Brown, just to visit."

"Aren't you going to have one?"

"Yes, I think I will."

"I hate to drink by myself. They say that's the sign of an insane person, when they drink alone."

"That's probably one of those things started by the saloonkeepers. You know, like three on a match was started by the match trust in Sweden."

"Oh, that's very interesting. I never heard that. Yes, I did. Come to think of it."

"Won't you take off your coat?"

"I really shouldn't. I can only stay a minute and get the story. Uh. Postponed. Would you care to tell me why you're postponing it, Mr. English?"

"Mrs. English would be able to tell you better. I think you ought to ask her, because it's really her party. I'd rather not talk to the press, because after all it *is* her party."

"Oh, I see," said Miss Cartwright. "Oh, don't hang it

up. Just put it on the chair or some place. This is awfully strong. I'm not used to drinking. I don't suppose I average more than a drink a week, all year round."

"I'll give you some more ginger ale."

"This is an awfully attractive house. Did Mrs. English do it herself?"

"Yes."

"She has terribly good taste. Oh! Foujita! I *love* Foujita! Is it a real Foujita or a copy? I mean—"

"It's a print. You look quite different without glasses."

"I have to wear them when I'm driving or walking. I couldn't get a license unless I wore them and if I drive without them I'm liable to be fined or have my license taken away. Why don't you try a Spud?"

"No, thanks. I can't get used to them."

"That's what *I* thought, but I did finally, and now I can't smoke any other kind. I hope I'm not keeping you from anything, Mr. English."

"Far from it. I'm glad you came."

"I shouldn't have come, but I did want to get the list of guests right. People are so touchy. Not that Mrs. English is. She's very considerate, and believe me, that's a lot. But I've made some mistakes lately about who was at whose party and so on, and some of the Gibbsville matrons have raised the devil down at the office. So I only have this list we printed in Gwen Gibbs a month ago and I wanted to be sure if there were any changes. Additions and so on, to the original list."

"It's a tough job, isn't it?"

"Oh, is *it ever tough?* It isn't really, most of the time, but once in a while we have a sort of wave of indignation or something. Women call up and just raise the devil because names were left out or parties weren't given the prominence they thought they ought to have. And of course I always get it in the end, they pass the buck to me. Some people named Bromberg, Jews, they almost got me fired last week. They took out their ad and everything, just because I didn't use a story they sent in about some imported English perambulator they bought for their baby. You should have seen the story! I couldn't possibly use it or the paper would have been a joke, but did they back me up? They did not. I finally had to run a half a stick about it, but I killed the gushy part, and so the Brombergs put their ad in again and I have to lick everybody's boots and kowtow to everybody that appears on the society page. Not Mrs. English, but I can't say as much for some of your friends. Well, thanks very much for the drink and I'm sorry you're not having the party. It's very nice to have met you. I often see you driving those beautiful Cadillacs around town. When we first came to Gibbsville I used to wonder who you were. . . . My goodness, what made me say that?"

"Have another drink before you go. Stay and tell me more."

"Oh, yes. Oh, my yes. Can't you just see me? No, I better go while the going's good. Oh, I don't mean that the way it sounds, Mr. English, but people talk so much in this town." Julian had a quick recollection of a story about the Baptist minister's daughter going without stockings. Unwillingly he looked at her legs, and she apprehended the look. "That's it," she said. "You heard it yourself. I'll never live it down, going without stockings. It's all right in front of Queen Mary, but not in Gibbsville. Well, thanks again. See you again some time."

"Don't go," he said. Unaccountably he liked her. More than that, he didn't want her to put on her glasses. She wasn't bad-looking. She wasn't pretty. But she wasn't bad-looking, and she had an interesting figure; not sensationally good, but you could have fun with it. He hated himself, but he had an enormous desire to discover this girl.

"What time is it?" she said.

"It isn't even ten o'clock. It's still in the nine class. Nine-thirty-five, nine-thirty-seven, something like that. It's very early."

"Well, one more drink, although why you want me to stay I don't know. I look a wreck. Haven't even been home from the office." She gazed around the room, just getting ready to sit down, and then she said: "Mr. English, I'd feel a thousand per cent better if you'd let me wash my hands."

"Oh, I'm terribly sorry. I'll show you."

"Just tell me where it is, I'll find it."

"I better show you. There's no light, I don't think."

"This is terribly embarrassing, or would be if you weren't so nice. I always feel more at ease with a married man. Tell you the truth, my back teeth are floating."

He was shocked and he was glad it was too dark for

her to see his face. Either that one drink had had an unusual effect, or little Miss Cartwright—who was not little, but rather reedy—could turn out to be fun. He lit the lights and then came downstairs and made himself a drink. He heard her, and then he saw her coming down the stairs, slowly now; step by step, at ease. Her steps might have meant self-confidence, in which case he did not like it and did not like her. He wanted to seduce this girl, but he wanted to do it because he was able to through experience and superior knowledge. He didn't want her to have anything to do with it except to acquiesce. Still, she was near-sighted or something. That might explain the way she walked.

"Rye and ginger ale," he said.

"Right," she said. She sat down, and now he was sure it was confidence. He almost laughed in her face. She was not a girl who would be included in anyone's list of attractive damsels, but she had as much confidence at this moment as Norma Shearer or Peggy Joyce or somebody. He knew now that she was not a virgin, no matter what he had thought ever before; and while he made a drink for her he imagined the ridiculous scene with the probably a veterinary student with two or three scholastic keys and fraternity pins on his vest—the rush of life in the direction of Miss Cartwright, and the quick rush away. He wondered how old she was, and he asked her as he handed her her drink.

"Old enough to know better," and then, "I'm twenty-three. Why do you ask that? Just curiosity or what?"

The Big Ten confidence. "What, probably. I don't know. I just wondered. I couldn't make an accurate guess myself, so I asked you."

"That's refreshing nowadays. Now how old are you?"

"Thirty."

"That's what I thought. I thought about twenty-eight, but you go around with so much older people that I thought in a town like this you—oh, I don't know what I thought. It doesn't make much difference. This drink is *much* stronger. I suppose you know that."

"Yes. I made it exactly as strong as mine. As a matter of fact I had an extra one while you were upstairs. Where'd you go to school?"

"University of Missouri."

"Oh, did you? I was thinking of going to one of the Western Conference schools one time."

"Well, you wouldn't have gone to Missouri, then. Missouri isn't in the Conference."

"Oh, I thought it was."

"No," she said. "I started at Missouri before we came to Gibbsville. I was thinking of transferring to Columbia, to save the expense of train fare and so on, but I decided to stay out there. I studied journalism."

"Oh, I see," he said. Her breasts were small. Practically non-existent while she had her dress on, but they would be neat.

"I'm sorry in a way I didn't transfer, because I'd like to have spent a year or two in New York. Soon as I get enough money I'm going to try to get a job on a New

273

York paper. The *World* is the paper I'd like to work on, but it's awfully hard to get a job there. It's awfully hard to get a job anywhere nowadays, at least on a paper. I have this friend of mine on the St. Louis *Post-Dispatch*, one of the best men they have, getting an awfully good salary. He went to New York on his vacation and he dropped in just to look around at one of the papers, and do you know what they offered him?"

"What?"

"Forty dollars a week! Good Lord, I'm getting twenty, and I don't know a thing compared to him, but forty dollars a week. That was as high as they'd go. You can imagine what *he* told *them*." She shook her head and reminisced with her eyes, not looking at Julian. So she felt more at ease with married men.

"How on earth does a man support a family on forty dollars a week? Oh, I know it's done, but on a paper I should think you'd have to dress pretty well?" Julian asked.

"That's exactly what this friend of mine said. He has a wife and child. He couldn't begin to afford to live in New York. His friends are always saying, why doesn't he go to New York. Well, that's the answer."

It certainly was, Julian reflected. It certainly was the answer. So a man with a wife and child had done it? That meant, most likely, that it had been done with more skill—and regularity—than if it had been done by a college boy. "Drink?" he said.

"Oh, all right," she said.

274

He made the drinks and went back to her with a drink in each hand. But instead of handing her hers he put both drinks down together on the small table and sat down beside her. He put his hand under her chin and she turned her face and smiled and then she closed her eyes and her mouth was open before it touched his. She brought up her knee and pushed herself full-length out on the couch, and held his head with her hands over his ears. "Just kiss me," she said, but she put her hand under his coat and opened his vest and his shirt. "No," she said. "Just kiss me." She was terribly strong. Suddenly she jerked away from him. "Whew! Come up for air," she said. He hated her more than anyone ever had hated anyone.

"Drink?" he said.

"No, I don't think so. I must go."

"Don't go," he said. He wanted to call her all kinds of bitches.

"Now is the best time," she said, but she did not get up.

"Well, it's up to you," he said.

"Listen, Joo-lian," she apologized by exaggerating the u in his name, "if I stay here you know what'll happen."

"All right," he said.

"Not all right at all. You're married to a swell girl. I don't know her at all, but I know she's swell, and you don't give a damn about me. Oh, I don't want to talk about it. I admit. I have a yen for you, but—but all the same I'm going. Good-by," she said, and she would not let him help her with her coat. He heard the wurra-wurra of the starter in her car, but he was not thinking of her.

He was thinking of the time after time he was going to hear those words in the future. "You're married to a swell girl. I don't know her at all (or, "Caroline's one of my best friends"). . . . I have a yen for you, but all the same I'm going." Miss Cartwright was already deep in the past, the musty part of the past, but now her words came out of the mouths of all the girls he wanted to see. Telephone operators, department store clerks, secretaries, wives of friends, girls in the school crowd, nurses—all the pretty girls in Gibbsville, trying to make him believe they all loved Caroline. In that moment the break with Caroline ceased to look like the beginning of a vacation. Now it looked worse than anything, for he knew that plenty of girls would do anything with a married man so long as he was married, but in Gibbsville for the rest of his life he was Caroline's husband. There could be a divorce, Caroline could marry again for that matter, but no girl in Gibbsville—worth having—would risk the loss of reputation which would be her punishment for getting herself identified with him. He recalled a slang axiom that never had any meaning in college days: "Don't buck the system; you're liable to gum the works."

He didn't want to go back and make a more definite break with Caroline. He didn't want to go back to anything, and he went from that to wondering what he wanted to go to. Thirty years old. "She's only twenty, and he's thirty. She's only twenty-two, and he's thirty. She's only eighteen, and he's thirty and been married once, you know. You wouldn't call him young. He's at least thirty.

276

No, let's not have him. He's one of the older guys. Wish Julian English would act his age. He's always cutting in. His own crowd won't have him. I should think he'd resign from the club. Listen, if you don't tell him you want him to stop dancing with you, then I will. No thanks, Julian, I'd rather walk. No thanks, Mr. English, I haven't much farther to go. Listen, English, I want you to get this straight. Julian, I've been a friend of your family's for a good many years. Julian, I wish you wouldn't call me so much. My father gets furious. You better leave me out at the corner, becuss if my old man. Listen, you, leave my sister alone. Oh, hello, sweetie, you want to wait for Ann she's busy now be down a little while. No liquor, no meat, no coffee, drink plenty of water, stay off your feet as much as possible, and we'll have you in good shape in a year's time, maybe less." He had a drink. He had another and he got up and took off his coat and vest and tie. He had another and he brought the Scotch over and stood the bottle on the floor, and he got out his favorite records, which were in three albums. He put the albums on the floor. When he got drunk enough he would want to play them, but he wanted to have them near now. He lay down and then got up and brought the seltzer and the ice bucket and stood them beside the Scotch. He examined the Scotch bottle and saw there was not much more than a pint left, so he went to the dining room and got another and opened it, then put the cork back. He drank while walking and this demonstrated the inadequacy of the glass. He had a smart idea. He took the flowers out of a vase

277

and poured the water out, and made himself the biggest highball he ever had seen. It did not last very long. He got up again and got a plate of hors d'œuvres from the kitchen. They made him thirsty. He lowered his suspenders and felt much better.

"I think, if you don't mind, I think we shall play a little tune," he said aloud. He played Paul Whiteman's record of Stairway to Paradise, and when the record came to the "patter" he was screaming with jazz. The phonograph stopped itself but he was up and changing it to a much later record, Jean Goldkette's band playing Sunny Disposish. He laid a lot of records out on the floor without looking at their titles. He spun a spoon around, and when it stopped he would play the record to which it pointed. He played only three records in this way, because he was pounding his feet, keeping time, and he broke one of his most favorites, Whiteman's Lady of the Evening, valuable because it has the fanciest trick ending ever put on a record. He wanted to cry but he could not. He wanted to pick up the pieces. He reached over to pick them up, and lost his balance and sat down on another record, crushing it unmusically. He did not want to see what it was. All he knew was that it was a Brunswick, which meant it was one of the oldest and best. He had a drink out of the glass. He used the vase for resting-drinking, and the glass for moving-drinking. That way he did not disturb the main drink while moving around, and could fill the glass while getting up and sitting down. Unintentionally he lay back. "I am now," he said, "drunk. Drunk. Dronk. Drongk."

He reached like a blind man for the fresh bottle and with eyes that he knew were sober he watched himself pour himself a drink. "No ice I get drunk kicker. Quicker," he said that aloud. To himself he said: "I bet I look like something nice now." He found he had two cigarettes burning, one in the ash tray on the floor, and the other getting stuck in the varnish on the edge of the phonograph. He half planned a lie to explain how the burn got there and then, for the first time, he knew it would not make any difference.

He got to his feet and went to the stairs. "Anybody in this house?" he called.

"Anybody in this house?

"Any, body, in, this, *house!*"

He shook his head. "Nope. Nobody in this house. You could wake the dead with that noise," he said.

He got a package of cigarettes from the table and took the new bottle of Scotch. He wished he had time to look around the room to see if everything was all right, no more cigarettes burning or anything like that, but there wasn't time. There wasn't time to put out the lights or pick up anything or straighten the rugs. Not even time to put on a coat, pull up his suspenders or anything. He went out on the porch and down the steps and opened the garage door and closed it behind him. He shivered a little from the bit of cold, and it was cold in the garage, so he hurried. He had to see about the windows. They had to be closed. The ventilator in the roof was closed for the winter.

He climbed in the front seat and started the car. It started with a merry, powerful hum, ready to go. "There, the bastards," said Julian, and smashed the clock with the bottom of the bottle, to give them an approximate time. It was 10:41.

There was nothing to do now but wait. He smoked a little, hummed for a minute or two, and had three quick drinks and was on his fourth when he lay back and slumped down in the seat. At 10:50, by the clock in the rear seat, he tried to get up. He had not the strength to help himself, and at ten minutes past eleven no one could have helped him, no one in the world.

10

OUR STORY never ends.

You pull the pin out of a hand grenade, and in a few seconds it explodes and men in a small area get killed and wounded. That makes bodies to be buried, hurt men to be treated. It makes widows and fatherless children and bereaved parents. It means pension machinery, and it makes for pacifism in some and for lasting hatred in others. Again, a man out of the danger area sees the carnage the grenade creates, and he shoots himself in the foot. Another man had been standing there just two minutes before the thing went off, and thereafter he believes in God or in a rabbit's foot. Another man sees human brains for the first time and locks up the picture until one night years later, when he finally comes out with a description of what he saw, and the horror of his description turns his wife away from him. . . .

Herbert Harley said he thought he heard a car about ten o'clock. It sounded like a Ford, starting in front of the English home, but he could have been mistaken. Or, as Deputy Coroner Moskowitz pointed out, it could have been just any car that happened to stop in front of the English home. Dr. Moskowitz wanted to have the thing all neat and no loose ends, and he wished the driver of the car would come forth and reveal himself; but he guessed he never would; that part of town was pretty secluded, you might say, and necking couples often went there. So the car probably was just some necking couple, Dr. Moskowitz said, and anyway it was an open-and-shut case of suicide by carbon monoxide gas poisoning, the first of its kind in the history of the county (and a damn nice, clean way of knocking yourself off, he added off the record). What happened, as he reconstructed it, was: Mr. English had had difficulties with Mrs. English, so he went home and got drunk and while temporarily deranged through alcohol and grief, he, being well acquainted with the effects of carbon monoxide, being in the automobile business, why he committed suicide. There was no doubt about him being insane, at least temporarily, because from the broken Victrola records in the house, and the clock that was smashed in the car, deceased manifestly had been in a drunken rage and therefore not responsible. His widow, Caroline W. English, was apparently the last one to see him alive, and that was about four o'clock in the afternoon. Mrs. English had telephoned the two servants in the house and informed them that a party scheduled for that night was postponed, and they could go home and so they went.

Fortunately deceased had seen fit to vent his rage and smash the clock in the front part of the car, which readily enabled the deputy coroner to fix the time of death at about eleven o'clock P.M., the night of December 26, year of Our Lord one thousand nine hundred thirty. Thus it

282

will be seen that seven hours elapsed between the last time Caroline W. English had seen her late husband and the time of his death. This was verified by Mrs. Judge Walker, mother of Caroline W. English, at whose home Mrs. English had been stopping from the time she last saw deceased up to the time she had been informed of his death.

This had been done by Dr. William D. English, chief of staff, Gibbsville Hospital, and also father of deceased, the first physician called after the body was discovered.

The body had been discovered by Herbert G. Harley, next-door neighbor of deceased. Mr. Harley was an electrical engineer, employed by the Midas Washeries Company, operators of the Midas, Black Run, Horse Cave, and Sadim washeries. Mr. Harley was at home reading, the night of the death of Mr. English. Mrs. Harley had gone to bed early, being exhausted as it was the day after Christmas and with children in the house, the day after Christmas you know how it is. Well, so Mr. Harley was reading a book called *N by E,* by Rockwell Kent. He happened to remember that because he had met Mr. Kent once while on a visit to New York; he had met him at the Princeton Club. And that was how he happened to remember the name of the book. He was reading it, or rather to be exact studying the pictures in it, when he heard the car start in Mr. English's garage. The time, he should judge, as nearly as he could place it, was roughly about ten-thirty. In the evening. Ten-thirty P.M. He thought nothing of it at the time, as he and Mr. English came and went and while they were always very friendly and polite in a

283

neighborly way, they never were what you would call good friends, as Mr. English traveled with, well, a different crowd from the one Mr. Harley traveled with. He had known Mr. English about four years and saw him on the average about once a day usually.

Well, so he went on reading the book and then for some reason that he couldn't explain, he got some sort of a premonition. It wasn't a premonition exactly, but more like the feeling you get when you *know* someone is in the room even before you *see* the person. That was the feeling he got, and Mr. Harley wanted to be sure to make it clear that he did not believe in spiritualism or anything like that, as he had a scientific education and he did not believe in that kind of bunk. It was all right for some people; they could believe what they liked. But Mr. Harley did not hold with that school of thought, and to prove it, he had an explanation, what might be called a scientific explanation, of why he had that feeling. The explanation was this: he had been sitting there perhaps a half an hour, and something inside him told him something was wrong. In a minute he understood what it was; it was the motor running.

All that time the motor had been running in Mr. English's car. You could feel the low vibration of it, hear the distant sound of it. Not loud, the sounds weren't; and the vibrations weren't strong. But out where they had their home you get so you know every little sound, and it was very unusual for a motor to be running that length of time. Mr. Harley debated with himself and finally decided to go take a look and see what was what. He thought perhaps Mr. English was having trouble with his car, and he was going to volunteer his assistance.

Well, the moment he stepped out on his front porch he knew there was *something* amiss. The motor was running, but the garage was dark. He got closer to the garage and he looked in a window—the one in the west wall of the garage—and all he could see was the car. The dash lights were the only lights in the whole garage that were burning. He thought it best to go tell Mr. English that he had left his motor running and to warn him against staying in the garage any length of time. Mr. Harley of course knew the danger of carbon monoxide and had known one or two cases of carbon monoxide poisoning in his engineering experience. He went up and rang the bell of the English home, then he opened the door and called out, but there was no answer from anyone. Then he ran as fast as he could back to the garage. He opened the big door and the windows so as to create a draft, and then he opened the front door of the car, and there was Mr. English.

He was lying sort of slumped down on the seat, half of his body almost off the seat. Mr. Harley had a little trouble, as Mr. English was not a small man, but finally he got him and carried him, fireman-fashion, out of the garage and laid him down on the driveway. He felt Mr. English's heart and there were no beats, and he felt his pulse, and there was no pulse. He tried giving him artificial respiration, because he knew the value of artificial respiration in such cases, and he yelled as loud as he could to his wife, and when Mrs. Harley stuck her head out the bedroom window he told her to call Dr. English.

He continued giving artificial respiration until Dr. English came, but Dr. English examined his son and pronounced him dead. They carried the body inside the house and then Dr. English thanked Mr. Harley and Mr. Harley went back to quiet Mrs. Harley, who by that time was almost out of her wits, with not knowing what it was all about.

As nearly as Mr. Harley recalled, Mr. English was attired in dark gray trousers, white shirt without a tie, black shoes. There was a strong odor of whiskey about his person. His eyes were open and his face was pinkish, or, rather, pallid with a pinkish tinge. Mr. Harley asked permission to add that in his opinion, judging by the position of the body and what he knew about such cases, Mr. English may have wanted to commit suicide when he first got in the car, but that he had changed his mind just before becoming unconscious, but had not had the strength to get out of the car.

Well, that did not alter the main fact, in the opinion of Dr. Moskowitz. All they had to go on proved pretty conclusively that deceased had taken his own life, no matter what else might have been in his mind. The jury returned a verdict to that effect.

Dr. English thought it best not to try to influence the verdict of the jury. In this case let the little kike quack Moskowitz have his revenge, which Dr. English knew Moskowitz was doing. Dr. English knew Moskowitz loved every bit of testimony that pointed toward suicide, for it gave Moskowitz a chance he had wanted ever since the time Dr. English had given a dinner to the County Medical Society and failed to invite Moskowitz. Dr. English thought he had good reason: the dinner was at the country club, and Jews were not admitted to the club, so Dr. English could not see why he should violate the spirit of the club rule by having a Jew there as his guest. Anyway he despised Moskowitz because Moskowitz once had said to him: "But, my dear Doctor, surely you know the oath of Hippocrates is a lot of crap. I'll bet your own wife uses a pessary. Or did. Mine always has, and still does." . . . Let Moskowitz have his revenge; Dr English would have something to say hereafter about the deputy coronerships. Without that Moskowitz could not live.

Dr. English thought of himself as crushed by Julian's death. He knew people would understand that; crushed. His wife, on the other hand, was a little silly, bewildered. She cried, but he did not think he heard pain in her cry. He thought he might expect a nervous breakdown when the enormity of her grief touched her, and he began immediately to plan something, say a Mediterranean cruise, which they could take together as soon as Julian's affairs were settled. Julian had been dead only twelve hours when the thought first entered the doctor's head, but it was well to have something ahead to look forward to when a sad loss crushed you. He would recommend the same thing to Mrs. Walker, and at least offer to pay Caroline's share of the trip. Not that Mrs. Walker needed it or would accept it, but he would make the offer.

Dr. English was not afraid of what he knew people were saying—people with long memories. He knew they were recalling the death of Julian's grandfather. But inevitably they would see how the suicide strain had skipped one generation to come out in the next. So long as they saw that it was all right. You had to expect things.

It was a lively, jesting grief, sprightly and pricking and laughing, to make you shudder and shiver up to the point of giving way completely. Then it would become a long black tunnel; a tunnel you had to go through, had to go through, had to go through, had to go through, had to go through. No whistle. But had to go through, had to go through, had to go through. Whistle? Had to go through, had to go through, had to go through, had to go through. No whistle? Had to go through, had to go through, had to go through.

"Caroline dear, please take this. Sleep will do you good," her mother said.

"Mother darling, I'm perfectly all right. I don't want anything to make me sleep. I'll sleep tonight."

"But Dr. English gave me this to give to you, and I think you ought to get some sleep. You haven't slept a wink since one o'clock this morning."

"Yes, I did. I slept a little."

"No, you didn't. Not a real sleep."

"But I don't want to sleep now. Specially."

"Oh, dear, what am I going to do with you?" said Mrs. Walker.

"Poor Mother," said Caroline, and she held out her arms to her mother. She was sorry for her mother, who had no great grief in this, but only sadness that was stirred by her own grief. She was just sort of on-call, ready to supply sadness which made her eligible actively to share Caroline's grief.

She tried, that first day, not to think about Julian but what on earth else was there to think about? She would think back to the early morning, when her mother came in her old room and told her Julian's father was downstairs and wanted to see her. Sometimes when she thought about it she would say, "I knew it right away. I got it immediately," but again she would be honest and accuse herself, for she had not got it right away. That there was something wrong she knew, but the truth was she was on the verge of refusing to go downstairs. She knew it concerned Julian, and she did not want to hear more of him, but her intelligence and *not* her instinct pointed out to her lying in her warm, sweet bed that Julian's father was the last man in the world to wake you up at that hour of the night—one o'clock in the morning, almost—without some good reason. He said he had terrible news for her—and it was just like prefacing a story with "this is the funniest thing you ever heard," or "this will kill you." Nothing Dr. English could say could come up to his prefatory words. But he was a considerate man; he told it all at once and did not wait to be asked questions. "Mr. Harley found Julian lying in the car, in the garage, and he was dead then, although Mr. Harley didn't know it at the time. He died of carbon monoxide, a poison gas that comes out of a car. The motor was running." Then, after a pause. "Caroline, it looks like suicide. You didn't get any note or anything like that, did you?"

"God, no! Don't you suppose I'd be up there now if I did?"

"I didn't mean to imply anything," said the doctor. "I just wanted to be sure. The coroner will ask things like that. I don't see how we can avoid a verdict of suicide, but I'll try. I'll see what I can do." He had the sound of a politician who doesn't want to admit that he can't get a new postoffice.

"Why should you want to? Of course he killed himself," said Caroline.

"Caroline, dear!" said her mother. "You ought not to say that till you're sure. That's a terrible thing to say."

"Why is it? Why the hell is it? Who said so? God damn all of you! If he wanted to kill himself whose business is it but his own?"

"She's hysterical," said her mother. "Darling—"

"Ah, go away. You did it. You, you don't like him. You did, too, you pompous old man."

"Oh, Caroline, how can you say things like that?"

"Where is he? Come on, where is he? Where'd you take him. Do *you* know he's dead? *How* do you know? I don't think you even know when a man is dead."

"He's my son, Caroline. Remember that please. My only son."

"Yaah. Your only son. Well, he never liked you. I guess you know that, don't you? So high and mighty and nasty to him when we went to your house for Christmas. Don't think he didn't notice it. You made him do it, not me."

"I think I'll go, Ella. If you want me you can get me at home."

"All right, Will," said Mrs. Walker.

"Why did you call Mother first? Why didn't you tell me first?"

"Now, dear. Good night, Will. I won't go to the door."

"Aren't you going to take me to him? What's the matter? Is he burnt up or mangled or what?"

"Oh, please, darling," said Mrs. Walker. "Will, do you think—for a minute?"

"Yes, I guess so. I just thought it'd be bad for her while the news is fresh."

"Well, then, if you really want to see him tonight, dear," said Mrs. Walker.

"Oh, God. I just remembered. I can't. I promised him I wouldn't," said Caroline.

"You *promised* him! What is this? What are you talking about? You knew he was going to kill himself!" Now the doctor was angry.

"No, no, no. Don't get excited. Keep your shirt on, you old—" in her mouth was one of Julian's favorite words, but she had shocked her mother enough. She turned to her mother. "We both made a promise when we were married, we promised each other we'd never look if one of us died before the other. If he died first I—oh, you know." She began to weep. "Go away, Doctor. I don't want to see you. Mother."

They stayed there a long time, Caroline and her mother. "It's all right, it's all right," Mrs. Walker kept saying, and she kept herself from weeping by thinking of the sounds that Caroline made. It was strange and almost new to hear Caroline crying—the same shudders and catches of breath, but in a firmer voice. That made it new, the firmer voice, the woman part. The little girl in woman's clothes, who never could put on girl's clothes again. What was it Pope said? Was it Pope? This dear, fine girl. A thing like this to happen to her. It was as though Julian had not existed. Only Caroline existed now, in pain and anguish. Poor girl. Her feet must be cold. They went upstairs together after a while, the mother prepared for a long vigil; but she was not used to vigils any more, and sleep won.

All night Caroline did not sleep, until long after daylight she lay awake, hearing the heartless sounds of people going to work and going on with their lives regardless. The funny thing was, it was a nice day. Quite a nice day. That was what made her tired, and in the morning she did sleep, until near noon. She got awake and had a bath and some tea and toast and a cigarette. She felt a little better before she remembered that there was a day ahead of her —no matter how much of it had been slept through. She wanted to go to Julian, but that was just it. Julian was more in this room, more in the street where he had walked so angrily from her car yesterday, much much more in the room downstairs where once upon a time she had become his girl—than what was lying wherever he was lying was Julian. She looked out the window, down at the street, not one bit expecting to see that he had left footprints in the street. But if the footprints had been there she would not have been surprised. The street sounded as though it would send up the sound of his heels. He always had little metal v's put in his heels, and she never would hear that sound again, that collegiate sound, without—well, she would hear it without crying, but she would always want to cry. For the rest of her life, which seemed a long time no matter if she died in an hour, she would always be ready to cry for Julian. Not for him. He was all right now; but because of him, because he had left her, and she would not hear the sound of the little metal v's on a hard-wood floor again, nor smell him, the smell of clean white shirts and cigarettes and sometimes whiskey. They would say he was drunk, but he wasn't drunk. Yes he was. He was drunk, but he was Julian, drunk or not, and that was more than anyone else was. That was what everyone else was not. He was like someone who had died in the war, some young officer in an overseas cap and a Sam Browne belt and one of those tunics that button up to the neck but you can't see the buttons, and an aviator's wings on the breast where the pocket ought to be, and polished high lace boots with a little mud on the soles, and a cigarette in one hand and his arm around an American in a French uniform. For her Julian had that gallantry that had nothing to do with fighting but was attitude and manner; a gesture with a cigarette in his hand, his whistling, his humming while he played solitaire or swung a golf club back and forth and back and forth; slapping her behind a little too hard and saying, "Why, Mrs. English, it *is* you," but all the same knowing he had hit too hard and a little afraid she would be angry. Oh, that was it. She never could be angry with him again. That took it out of her, that made him dead. Already she had begun the habit of reasoning with him: "But why did you do it? Why did you leave me? Everything would have been all right if you'd waited. I'd have come back this afternoon." But this time she knew she would not have come back this afternoon, and he had known it, and God help us all but he was right. It was *time* for him to die. There was nothing for him to do today, there was nothing for him to do today. . . . There, that was settled. Now let the whole thing begin again.

"Kitty Hofman's downstairs," said her mother. "Do you want to see her?"

"No, but I will," said Caroline.

It was the news room of the Gibbsville *Standard*. "Don't forget, everybody, it's Saturday. We have early closing. First edition goes over at one-ten, so don't go to lunch." Sam Dougherty, the city editor of the *Standard*, had been saying that every Saturday for more than twenty years. It was as much a part of him as his eyeshade and his corncob pipe and his hemorrhoids. As city editor he also had to read copy and write the Page One headlines.

"Say, Alice," he said, putting down his pencil and interrupting his reading of a story.

"What?" she said.

"What do you hear on this English suicide? Any of your people have anything to say on it?"

"No," she said.

"Did you *ask* anybody about it?" he said.

"No," she said. Then: "I heard the boss tell you to play down the story."

He shook his head. "See?" he said. "That's your trouble, Alice. A good reporter knows ten times as much as he ever prints. That's the kind of stuff you ought to know. Off the record stuff. The angles, girl. The angles. You oughta always get the angles of every big story, even when you can't print it. You never know when it's going to come in handy, see what I mean?"

Harry Reilly went to his hotel to wash up a bit before meeting a man for lunch. There was a message for him, and when he got upstairs he put in a call for Mrs. Gorman at Gibbsville one one one eight, Gibbsville, Pennsylvania.

"Hello."

"Hello."

"Hello. Hello, is that you, Harry?"

"Yes. What can I do for you?"

"Listen, Harry. Julian English killed himself last night."

"He what?"

"Killed himself. He took some kind of a poison in his garage. Carbon oxide."

"You don't mean carbon *mono*xide?"

"That's it. It's a poison."

"I'll say it's a poison, but he didn't take it. It comes out of the motor."

"Is that it? Well, I didn't know that. I just knew it was some kind of a poison and he took it in his garage."

"When? Who told you?"

"Last night. Everybody in town knows it by now. I heard it from four or five different people and I didn't leave the front porch all morning. I went to seven o'clock Mass, but otherwise I haven't been—"

"How do they know it's suicide? Who said so? It could happen to anybody. Was he drunk?"

"Yes."

"Well, then, he might of fell asleep or something."

"Not at all. He went in the garage and closed the door. He had a bottle of liquor with him, I heard. The way I heard, Caroline was going to leave him. She was at her mother's."

"Oh."

"That's why I called you, Harry. You didn't have anything to do with it, did you?"

"Christ, no!"

"Well, you know how people are—"

"I know how *you* are."

"Never mind the insults. I'm trying to do a favor for you. You know what people are apt to say. They'll say you had something to do with it, because English threw that drink in your face the other night. They'll put two and two together and get five."

"What are you talking about?"

"Are you dumb or what? They'll say he was sore at you because you have a crush on Caroline."

"Aw, where's it eatin' you, for God's sake, woman. English was in my office yesterday. He came to see me. He was in my office twenty-four hours ago and I talked to him."

"What did you talk about?"

"I didn't have time to talk much. I was hurrying to catch the train to New York. You're trying to make trouble where none is. Is that all you wanted to talk about?"

"Isn't it enough? You wanted to know about English, didn't you?"

"Only so I could go right out and send some flowers right away, that's all. I liked English and he liked me, or otherwise he wouldn't have borrowed money from me. I know that type. He wouldn't borrow a nickel from me if he didn't like me. Calm yourself, honey, don't get excited about nothing. That's your trouble. You have nothing to do any more so you sit home and worry. What will I bring you from New York?"

"I don't want anything, unless you want to go down town to Barclay Street. I notice this morning Monsignor needs a new biretta and it might make a nice little surprise for him, but remember. Purple. He's a monsignor."

"Don't you think I know that? All right, I'll buy him

one and have it sent in your name. Anything else? Because I have a lunch appointment any minute now."

"No, I guess that's all."

"Everything all right otherwise?" he said.

"Yes, everything all right. So I guess I'll hang up. Good-by, Harry."

"Good-by." He hung up slowly. "He was a real gentleman. I wonder what in God's name would make him do a thing like that?" Then he picked up the telephone again. "I want to order some flowers," he said.

The girl stood waiting while the man checked his hat and coat. She was tall and fair and had been told so many times she looked like a Benda mask that she finally found out what it was. The man was tall and stoop-shouldered and expensively comfortable about his clothes. He took her elbow and guided her to a tiny table across the room from the bar. They sat down.

A young man who had something to do with the place stopped and said hello, and the other man said, "Hello, Mac, nice to see you. Mary, this is Mac, Mac, Miss Manners." They smiled, and then Mac went away, and the man turned to Mary and told her Mac was the brother of one of the men that owned the place and what would she like or a Martini?

"A Martini, rather dry," she said.

"Two," said the man, and the waiter left them.

They lit cigarettes. "Well," said the man, "how do you feel?"

"Hmm," she said, with a smile.

"Ah, you're darling," he said. "Where do you come from?"

"Originally I came from Pennsylvania," she said.

"Why, so do I. Where are you from? I'm from Scranton."

"Scranton? I'm not from there," she said. "I live in a little town you never heard of."

"But what part of the State? What's it near?"

"Well, did you ever hear of Gibbsville?"

"Sure I heard of Gibbsville. I've visited there often. Are you from Gibbsville?"

"No, but near there. A place called Ridgeville."

"I've been there. Just driven through, though. Who do you know in Gibbsville? Do you know Caroline Walker? That's right, she's married. She married Julian English. Do you know them?"

"I know him," she said.

"Do you know Caroline at all?"

"No. I never met her. I just knew Julian."

"Well, I didn't know him very well. I haven't seen either of them in years. So you're from Pennsylvania."

"Uh-huh."

"Mary Manners," he said, "you're the prettiest girl I ever saw."

"Thank you, kind sir, she said," she said. "You're all right yourself, Ross Campbell."

"I am now. I will be if you go away with me this afternoon."

"Not this week-end."

"But next week-end I won't have Ed's car."

"You can hire one. No, I have to watch my step. We shouldn't of come here, Ross. Rifkin comes here sometimes and his friends, a lot of movie people, they all come here."

"Come on, while I have the car."

"No, positively not. Not this week."

"Lute, give me five dollars. I want to pay the garbage man."

Lute Fliegler was lying on the davenport, his hands in back of his head, his coat and vest on the chair beside him. He reached in his trousers pocket and took a five dollar bill from a small roll. His eyes met his wife's as the money appeared, and she was grateful to him for not saying what they both were thinking: that maybe they had better be more careful about money till they saw how things were. She went out to the kitchen and paid the garbage man and then came back to the living-room. "Can't I make you a sandwich, Lute? You ought to have something."

"No, that's all right. I don't feel like eating."

"Don't worry. Please don't worry. They'll make you the head of it. You know more about the business than anybody else, and you've always been reliable. Dr. English knows that."

"Yeah, but does he? What I'm afraid of is he'll think we were all a bunch of drunks. I don't mean that against Julian, but you know."

"I know," she said. If only daytime were a time for

kissing she would kiss him now. All this, the furniture, the house, the kids, herself—all this was what Lute was worrying about. She was almost crying, so she smiled.

"Come here," he said.

"Oh, Lute," she said. She knelt down beside him and cried a little and then kissed him. "I feel so sorry for Caroline. You, I—"

"Don't worry," he said. "I still get my check from the government, and I can get lots of jobs—" he cleared his throat "—in fact, that's my trouble. I was saying to Alfred P. Sloan the other day. He called me up. I meant to tell you, but it didn't seem important. So I said to Al—"

"Who's Alfred P. Sloan?"

"My God. Here I been selling—he's president of General Motors."

"Oh. So what did you say to him?" said Irma.

THE END